Secrets of Gwenla

BY LAURIE PENNER

COVER DESIGN
BY RACHEL ROSSANO

Dedication

Secrets of Gwenla is dedicated to my husband David, whose remarkable singing voice and guitar playing has drifted into my spirit countless times, carrying my heart away to wonderful places.

Contents

Dedication iii

Map vii

Acknowledgements ix

Pronunciation Guide..xi

Prologue 1

Part One..3

Chapter One: The Rescue..5

Chapter Two: The Secrets...12

Chapter Three: The Fortress...19

Chapter Four: Places 27

Chapter Five: Music Cells..33

Chapter Six: The Pit...38

Chapter Seven: The Valley 42

Chapter Eight: The Window 49

Chapter Nine: Doors 55

Chapter Ten: The Problem 62

Chapter Eleven: Safety...70

Chapter Twelve: The Books..76

Chapter Thirteen: Conflict 82

Chapter Fourteen: Riddles 89

Chapter Fifteen: The Truth 96

Chapter Sixteen: Pain...105

Chapter Seventeen: Friends...113

Chapter Eighteen: The Plan 121

Part Two...129

Chapter Nineteen: The Underground 131

Chapter Twenty: The Storm...138

Chapter Twenty-One: The Under Hall......................................146

Chapter Twenty-Two: The Poor 155

Chapter Twenty-Three: The Pain...165

Chapter Twenty-Four: The Move 174

Chapter Twenty-Five: The Death...183

Chapter Twenty-Six: Light...188

Chapter Twenty-Seven: The Tyrea 193

Chapter Twenty-Eight: Cracks.......................................199

Chapter Twenty-Nine: The Breakthrough........................203

Chapter Thirty: The Stand..209

Chapter Thirty-One: The Council 215

Chapter Thirty-Two: The Trial.......................................221

Chapter Thirty-Three: Separation 228

Chapter Thirty-Four: Silence 235

Chapter Thirty-Five: The Cabin 240

Chapter Thirty-Six: The Refuge.....................................246

Chapter Thirty-Seven: Desolation..................................253

Chapter Thirty-Eight: Jonar 258

Chapter Thirty-Nine: The North 266

Chapter Forty: The Revelation.......................................273

The Sequel..278

About the Book 279

About the Author..280

What's Next?.......................... **Error! Bookmark not defined.**

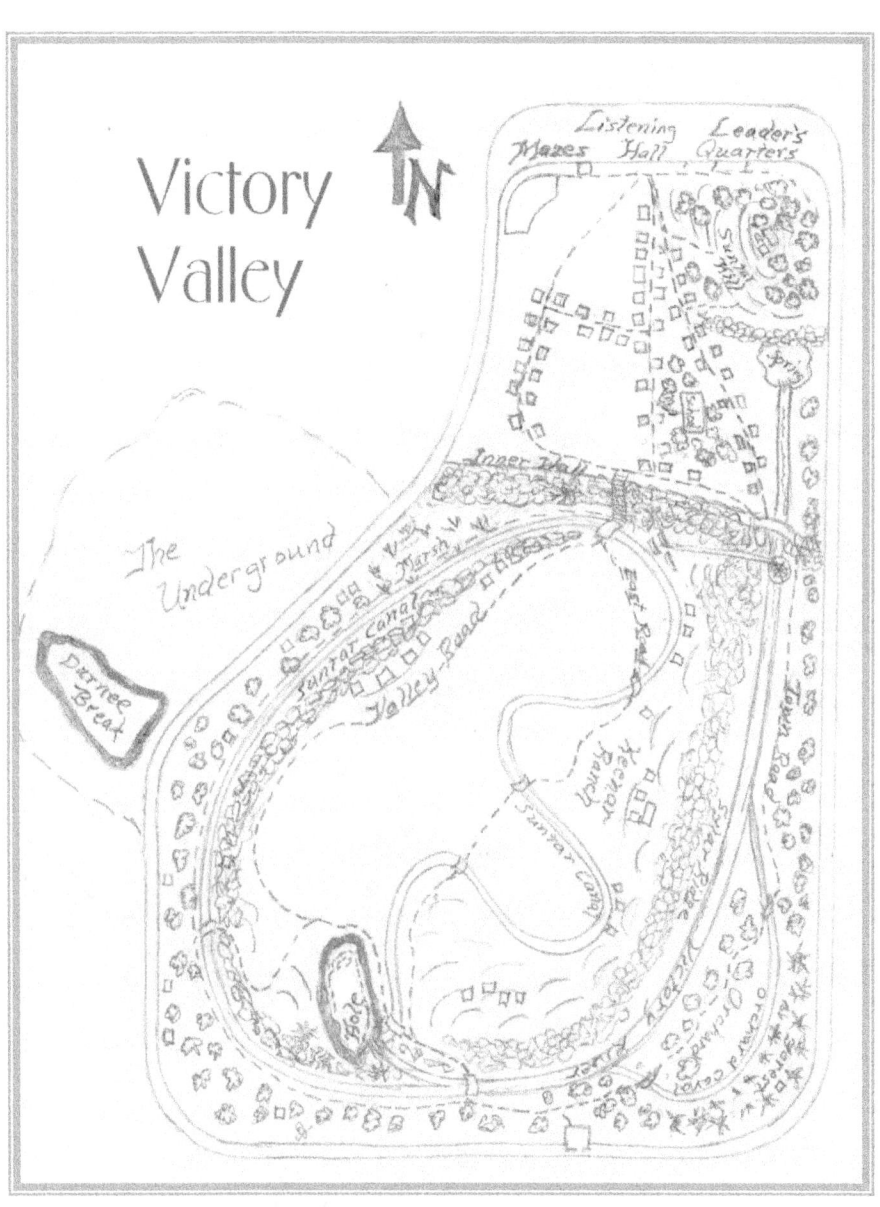

Map

Acknowledgements

Many thanks to my sister Judy and her husband Dan, who did extensive editing of *Gwenla* for me in an effort to keep it alive. Sorry I took so long to finish, Judy and Dan. Thanks to you both for the time and effort you put into the editing that gave me the confidence to work on my sentence structure (whether you remember it or not!) Judy, you have continued to be an amazing encouragement for all of my writing.

Thanks to daughter Jodi for help with content and continuity editing and your encouragement.

Thanks to Vicki Lucas, my social networking friend, talented fantasy author, and experienced editor. You helped so much with editing, grammar, and punctuation, as well as many other suggestions that I greatly appreciate.

Thanks to my wonderful husband David, who encouraged me throughout the writing of *Gwenla* for thirty-five years. David came up with the descriptive scenes which portray Gwenla and Captain Suntar. *David, you have been my best (and worst) critic for the characters and symbolism in the book, and I appreciate your honesty.*

Most of all, I thank the Lord for bringing me to the point of publication, which many times appeared to be much more of a dream in my heart, than it was a reality.

Pronunciation Guide

Bothleil: Both-LEEL
Cisco: SIS-koh
Daleil: Daw-LEEL
Dawnli: DAWN-lee
dekat: Deh-KAT
Delegar: DEL-uh-gar
Delwyn: DEL-win
Gwenla: GWEN-luh
Harol: HAIR-ul
Jadleil: Jad-LEEL
Jesero: JEH-su-roh
Jonar: JOE-nar
Jonaris: joe-NAR-iss
Julyiah: Jool-EYE-uh
Keenar: KEEN-ur
Libreani: Lib-ree-AW-nee
Lisyiah: Lis-EYE-uh
Livi: LIV-ee
Marni: MAR-nee
Rikial: RI-ki-ul
Ruti: ROO-tee
Suntar: SUN-tar
Sylar: SIE-lar
talia: ta-LEE-uh
Teka: TEE-kuh
Tomli: TOM-lee
tyrea: tie-REE-uh
Zuriel: zoor-EYE-ul

Prologue

Where are they?

Julyiah's tiny fingers searched the grass shimmering in the sunlight. Dragging her hand through the growth, she allowed the cool, silky blades to run through her fingers. Scrutinizing the spots of ground that showed up, she found a pointy rock to dig a little path in the dirt where the grass grew thinly.

Where could they be?

Shaking her head, Julyiah's four-year-old brain worked with increasing frustration. They had to be in the valley, because her teacher told them that morning that Gwenla brought them with her to the fortress, and since no one had ever left, they must still be here … somewhere. She flopped down on the green blanket and gazed up at the sky.

Could they be in the clouds?

Pink and gray colors formed among the white puffs overhead as the sun lowered in the west. Julyiah's eyes filled with the beauty, distracting her from her mission.

"Jul!" her mother called from the nearby trees. "It is getting dark soon—time to go."

"Yes, Mama," Julyiah said, her eyes darting around the area in one final effort before her mother made her leave.

Maybe they are in the water!

Julyiah scurried back to the stream and stared into it, the edge of her *talia* trailing in the wet current. She grabbed some pebbles out of the water, and studied the dripping handful before looking back into the sparkling depths. The creek reflected the vibrant clouds, her blonde hair, and her clothing—a yellow talia, which ran over the top of her muddy blue leggings.

Someone was approaching.

"Time to go home," her mother said again as she walked up beside the child. "What are you looking for?"

"Secrets," Julyiah said, unwilling to move her gaze from the water.

"What secrets?"

"The Secrets of Gwenla."

"What?" Laughing, Livi took her imaginative daughter's hand and helped her up to a standing position. "Come, we must go," she said, still chuckling to herself.

Julyiah stood in compliance, but she did not plan to give up. She would come back and keep searching—the entire valley if she had to. The leaders said no one had ever found the Secrets of Gwenla.

She would do it herself.

Part One

May the eyes of your heart be enlightened.
Ephesians 1:18a

Chapter One: The Rescue

♪

It was fuzzy.

Multiple bands of red, black, and white ran around its body, which hunched itself in half before plunging forward the distance of an eyelash. It worked its way around what it might consider a huge boulder before launching over to a green leaf several times its own size.

Some kind of caterpillar, fourteen-year-old Julyiah decided, picking up the leaf. *I have never seen one this tiny.* She set the leaf and insect inside her leather bag with care, cinched it, and stood. The Agricultural Authority would know whether it was a good or bad bug, and she wanted all the contact she could get with the people at work there.

Any living thing fascinated Julyiah as far back as she could remember. She had studied most of the creatures and plants in the area and hoped to join the Agricultural Authority when she finished school. The AGA spent every day of the week investigating animals, birds, plants, and insects, and Julyiah could think of nothing more wonderful to do in life.

The mammals in her world were limited to sheep, goats, and horses, plus a few working dogs to guard and herd them. The leaders had considered horses a luxury in the small area at first—eating more than they were worth; but the Keenar Clan kept their horses when the walls were sealed, sharing their own portion of grain with the creatures. The clan grew wealthy in local trade as a result.

Plants and insects thrived in the area due to ample moisture, but the AGA tried to eliminate the ones not wanted or needed. Although Julyiah regretted they could not keep many flowers, she understood the reasons. Almost all of the available dirt had to be kept for farming or there would not be enough food to go around.

Farmers and ranchers traded fenced-in patches of ground on a regular basis to maximize grain, vegetable, and meat production.

Unusual birds flew in from outside the massive wall that surrounded their little world, but normally flew right back out again. The avian population consisted of a few wild birds that lived in the trees, plus the ducks and chickens on the farms. Unless they could be caught, birds were shooed away from gardens and farmlands. The resources within the fortress walls were inadequate to share with any uninvited creatures.

Julyiah squinted at the bright sun glaring off the spring water rising from the ground, pooling before it flowed down the hill to the rest of the valley. In a quiet part of the pool, she saw her reflection, indicating light brown curls flowing down her arms to replace the blonde hair of childhood. A light blue talia hung to her knees, with brown leggings underneath. Her mother had resorted to dark leggings on her long ago because she always got them dirty, kneeling in the mud or crawling over a rock.

Blinking at the reflection of her wide blue eyes, Julyiah wondered whether she was getting pretty. Uninterested in boys much, Julyiah preferred other living things. She also had not yet passed through the *Understanding*, so her world remained simple and full of childlike play. In her case, play meant doing something outside.

Parents informed their children about the Understanding early, because a child could pass through it at a very young age. No one could predict whether the passage would be a good or bad experience, and children needed some kind of preparation.

Adding another world to one's existence was intriguing, and being an adventurous type, Julyiah tried to visualize how it would happen to her. Would it come naturally, or in a crisis? Or while she encountered some great pleasure? Almost anything could trigger the Understanding, or so she had been told. It was frustrating for her transition to take so long when all other young people her age already understood. Yet she would just have to wait. Adult terrors and intense joys would remain a mystery until her time came.

The strong scent of warm pine needles from two nearby trees invaded her senses, transporting Julyiah back in time to the day she went picnicking with her mother at the south end of the valley—the day she was searching for the Secrets of Gwenla.

Smiling to herself, Julyiah shook her head. What a foolish idea that was! Not knowing what a secret was, she expected to find one? Amused, she followed the rest of her childhood goal to the present. She still wanted to know what the mysterious secrets were, and where, but had learned over the years that *finding* them was unlikely. Gwenla's successor, Jon, must have put them in a safe place before Gwenla died, because they had never been recovered.

Julyiah walked from the east side of the valley toward the west side along the cliff trail, guided by the well-trodden dirt path that wandered between fruit trees and *Teka* bushes. Named after the farmer who discovered them, the pliant leaves of the Teka bush served as paper and utility cloths. Flourishing without water or care, Teka bushes grew to hip height wherever they were not cut down. The rocky cliff and the hard school grounds just north of the cliff held the greatest crops of the prolific bush.

Spotting the school buildings through the orchard trees as she passed Town Road, Julyiah glanced north towards the small town. The light green Teka bushes alongside the road waved in the breeze, which appeared to be picking up as Julyiah continued. The bushes had been a great part of the playing area for the schoolchildren, providing shade, leaves for schoolwork, and places to hide behind or sit under for lunch. Plus they were nearly indestructible.

Wait—what is that?

A bit of red flashed high up on the West Wall. Julyiah headed straight for the color. Climbing the wall was forbidden, but a bright flower would be yet another discovery she could report to the AGA. The Authority had ongoing permission to use a ladder in investigating anything unusual growing in dirt crevices higher up along the wall as long as they did not go over the top. Of course, no ladder invented was *that* tall.

As she crossed the intersecting path that led to the top of the cliff staircase on the Inner Wall, Julyiah heard happy voices from the area far below. Smiling, she realized the school picnic that included parents was in process. Too bad it was windy. Not that the children would mind, but the adults were always nervous in the wind.

Continuing on her mission toward the red spot on the West Wall, Julyiah hoped she would be able to see from the ground what was growing in the crevice. As she passed the top of the tallest tree in the area—the huge pine tree that grew in the marsh near the West Wall—Julyiah wondered how much taller it was this year. She remembered as a child looking down upon the apex of the tree from the rock face where she now stood, and here she was, looking up to it as it waved in the increasing breeze. If she became a part of the AGA, Julyiah would work to protect all the inedible trees that were left in the valley—all twelve of them.

A scream penetrated the air from the bottom of the staircase. Several moments of eerie silence followed as anxiety skittered through Julyiah. Rushing to the edge of the precipice, she stopped at the metal rail and peered over it. Gasping, she spotted four-year-old Marni hanging in a precarious position over empty space—one small hand gripping the rail post partway down from the top and the other hand slipping sideways on a smooth rock. A fall from that height would mean certain death.

"Marni!" A young woman holding a baby hurried across the grass below and started running up the stone stairs.

Julyiah was just a few steps away from Marni, and she was the closest person to the endangered child. Without thinking, Julyiah flung her right leg over the rail, a firm grip on the metal with both hands as she stepped onto the outer edge of the stairway. One foot slipped, causing her hands to grasp the rail tighter. She searched with her feet for a stable spot along the dangerous rim, trying not to think about how far it was to the bottom.

The breezes grew stronger, and for a moment Julyiah's heart jolted with the reality of how hazardous the wind could be. Was this why adults were so afraid of it? It appeared to have a mind of its own and bent against her, whipping her this way and that as though trying to push her off the cliff.

It is just a storm. Julyiah tried to calm her heart as she eyed the dark clouds drifting in overhead. She had better hurry before it rained, making the rocks and railing slick.

Marni's mother Nety arrived, breathless from ascending 120 stairs in the close weather, frantically searching for someone to hold her newborn baby. Shoving the bundle toward an eight-year-old girl who had followed her, Nety kneeled and grabbed her daughter's flailing arm with one hand, holding onto the rail post with the other.

"Mama!" cried the girl. The child had no ledge to stand on. Her sandaled feet were propped against the vertical wall, held in place by friction. One shoe fell from her foot and cascaded off several rocks before hitting the ground below. "My shoe!"

Trusting in her mother's hold on her one arm, Marni let go of the rail post and reached below her in an attempt to grab the other shoe before it followed the lost one, but her sweaty arm began to slip through her mother's grasp.

"Marni—No!" Nety screeched, letting go of the rail post and flinging herself flat on the stones, reaching out to grab hold of her daughter with both hands. Nety held on fiercely, but lying on her stomach with Marni's body weight hanging over the ledge, Nety had no leverage to pull the girl toward her.

With the situation worsening, Julyiah gave up the search for a secure footing. She looped both of her legs around the base of the abandoned rail post, crossing her feet to lock herself into place. Leaning back and away from the railing, she hung onto it with her long arms extended like she did from a tree limb when she was a child. For a moment, the world spun as she let go of the railing and lowered her upper body until it was parallel with the cliff face.

Inching sideways with her hands pressed against the rock behind her and twisting her body, Julyiah was able to station her chest under Marni's scrambling feet. The child whimpered as she viewed the young woman in such a strange position below her.

"Just put your feet right here," Julyiah patted her chest, raising her head and shoulders a little, to present an easier target. She hoped her stomach muscles would hold up.

"I am ... scared," the girl stammered before her wistful eyes veered up to her mother's face.

"It is going to be all right," Nety said. "Do what Julyiah says."

Whimpering again, Marni let her feet settle on Julyiah's chest. The weight of the child was a little more than Julyiah expected. She would have to hurry.

Pushing her hands against the rock face, Julyiah pulled her head up toward the waiting mother. The action lifted the child up as well. As soon as some of Marni's weight shifted from herself to Julyiah, Nety was able to pull the child toward her. Little by little Nety scooted back, dragging her daughter over the smooth stone surface until Marni could again grab the rail post. When Nety was able to free one hand from Marni's arm, she drew her other hand behind the child's head and hastily pulled her to safety, sobbing with relief.

Her mission accomplished, Julyiah lay back, weak and shaking so much that she feared she would not have the strength to pull herself upright again. Resting a moment, she listened to the group of people above laughing and crying over the rescued child.

A raindrop struck her face. Another fell on her knee as her hair whipped into her eyes. The clouds above had turned black, and the wind buffeted her body as though trying to dislodge her last hold on life. Panic flooded Julyiah, but her energy was spent. She attempted to lift her head and shoulders again and failed. The raindrops fell with increasing regularity.

"Help!" Julyiah cried weakly, terrified. She had saved the child from falling, but who would save her?

Nety reluctantly let go of her wayward daughter and with a sharp "Stay here!" she turned to assist Julyiah. A young man and a teenage boy who had just come up the stairs also stepped up to the rail post. Positioning themselves on each side of the post, they gripped the railing with one hand and reached over the precipice with the other. Leaning forward, they each grabbed one of Julyiah's arms.

Pulling her up, the man held her fast and waited for the boy to get into a better position for rescue. "Thank you, Zuriel," Julyiah whispered to the young man, trying to regain her breath.

At last, Zuriel let go so the tall teenager could pull Julyiah away from Zuriel, under the railing and to the stairway, where the boy grabbed her close and warmed her trembling body.

The rain came down harder, wetting the stones all around them, but Julyiah did not care. Feeling safe at last, she turned her head and looked into the eyes of the strong boy who held her in his lap. "Thank you, Delwyn."

Chapter Two: The Secrets

♪

For months after the rescue of Marni, Julyiah dreamed she was falling off a cliff. The nightmares seeped into her waking hours with visions of tumbling into endless darkness. Her mother tried to help her through the experience.

"You are passing through the Understanding, as all children of our race must do. The places you see in your heart are reflections of your mood. Your rescue of Marni in the storm probably triggered this change. Do not worry. When you get over the fear, you will no longer continue seeing these visions."

Julyiah did not get over the fear. Even after the nightmares went away, she was still afraid of heights. Her goal could no longer be the AGA because the members had to climb ladders and trees, and she panicked at the thought. Pursuing her other great interest— children—Julyiah hoped to teach them about the animals and plants she loved.

When she was not at school or outside, Julyiah devoted her time to reading educational books. The AGA loaned books to the school that they had written over the years about the flora and fauna in the valley, and these were some of Julyiah's favorites. She frequently remained after school to look through them, fascinated with every creature and plant.

One day as she was reading a book about insects at a stone table just outside the classroom, Julyiah set the book down for a moment. Determined to find a *chesian* beetle for herself, she figured the best place to look would be deep under a rock. A large rock right next to the table was so low and flat on top that the original excavators for the school had left it there as a bench for the children. It was also a light rock, so it glowed at night and provided safety for any who visited the school after dark.

Dragging a garden spade and shovel out from a nearby shed, Julyiah began to dig right next to the rock. The book described the chesian beetle as residing an arm's length below the surface of the ground, close to a single rock, so Julyiah figured she could dig a hole and scoop the dirt back in when she was done. The fact that the insect lived in beetle communities surrounding large rocks increased her chances of finding one.

It was a nice, sunny day—perhaps too nice to be digging. The hard ground would not budge, and Julyiah wondered whether anything could possibly live underneath. Yet the book noted in particular that the chesian beetle, once underground, rarely came out again. There could be hundreds of them living below! She longed to add the tiny, multi-colored insects to her collection at home. Having seen a pickaxe in the shed, she walked back to get it.

Standing by the rock, Julyiah stopped to gaze out over the valley floor, hoping to see a horse or baby goat running around on someone's farm. School had let out just before she decided to read, so some children ran about laughing and playing at a farm below, a working dog barking at them as they ran behind a barn.

A shadow moved across the ground toward her location. Looking up, Julyiah's eyes widened in astonishment. A huge dark cloud paused directly overhead, with a bright white cloud underneath it. The white cloud had rainbow colors in it, but there was no moisture or rain to cause this, and the colors were confined to the width of the cloud. Julyiah's eyes went from large to small as she squinted to see the colors better. Before long, they dissipated, and she wondered if she had truly seen them at all.

Gathering a deep breath, Julyiah prepared to dig. Swinging the pick at the base of the rock, she broke out a fist-sized portion of the ground. Another few flings of the pick produced more dirt clods until a dark porous earth appeared.

Whew! Using the shovel again, Julyiah dug out the crumbly stuff until her hole was bigger and the dirt below loose enough to work at with the hand spade.

Kneeling in the lumpy pile of soil she had made, Julyiah scooped out more earth until she calculated she had gone the depth required. Still no beetles. Stabbing the dirt pile with the spade, she paused in her labor, huffing out a grunt. The book said the beetles were abundant in the area, and she could see no reason why they would not be in this spot. She decided to go a little deeper before she gave up.

Julyiah stood up with the big shovel in hand and placed the blade of the tool inside the hole. One last, big shovel full, and if that did not get any results, she would assume she had picked the wrong location. She placed one sandal on the footrest and stood on it. The ground gave way so fast that Julyiah nearly toppled over sideways.

A slit in the ground opened below her, a handbreadth wide. Julyiah dropped the shovel and fell to her knees near it, leaning over to scoop out the dirt and widen the hole. Something must be buried there, she was certain. *Perhaps… perhaps?*

At first, Julyiah was disappointed because her digging only uncovered more rocks under the ground. It might be nothing except a space in between rocks that caused the hole. But as she continued her handwork, a different kind of substance was seen under the rocks—*leather!*

After more removal of dirt, Julyiah revealed a cavern-like area that ran underneath the big rock, with a piece of leather protruding from the hole. With pounding heart, Julyiah dug out more stones and pulled on the satchel until it gave way. She brushed off the dirt, marveling that the leather bag in her hands might be 400 years old.

Undoing the latch, Julyiah held the bag at arm's length before opening the top, unsure of what might emerge. The large satchel was filled with writings, and as Julyiah unfolded the old but intact Teka leaves with care, she saw Gwenla's name at the top. *Gwenla's Secrets!*

Julyiah jumped up and, after putting the book about insects back inside the schoolroom, she took off toward the Listening Hall. The leaders needed to see what she had found.

♬

Delwyn spotted Julyiah hurrying toward the North Wall, carrying an old leather satchel. "Jul!" he called out, hoping to find out what she was doing. At age sixteen, he had been close to Julyiah's level in school, and he had maintained warm feelings for her ever since the day he helped to rescue her.

His heart leaped when she turned Delwyn's direction with a brilliant smile.

"Delwyn!" Out of breath, she rushed over to his side, looking at him in wide-eyed excitement. "Y-you will never g-guess what I found!"

"The Secrets of Gwenla?" he asked, laughing. He had heard for years about her desire to find the hidden writings.

Julyiah pressed her lips together and pouted. "Well… yes," she replied, looking irritated, "as a matter of fact, I did."

Delwyn's mind staggered as his heart filled with confusion. If this was true, there was no wonder at the way she reacted. He had stolen her happy announcement. Yet how could it be true? She had to be teasing him.

"What? Are you joking?" he asked her.

"I do not know if I want to show you now…" Julyiah's peevish smile warned Delwyn that he had made a severe misjudgment in his response just now.

"Sorry, I was only teasing you," Delwyn explained. "I did not think it possible…."

"Of course you did not. You do not know me that well."

But I certainly want to…

Julyiah swished one arm from front to back, causing her talia to twist and ruffle from side to side. She gazed at him with lifted chin, wide eyes, and uplifted brows, as though holding something valuable back until he was worthy to receive it.

"May I see what you found?" Delwyn asked with what he hoped was ample humility. He trusted she had found something, but whether it was Gwenla's long lost writing was yet to be seen.

Julyiah opened the satchel and pulled out the ancient leaves full of text.

Delwyn gasped, awestruck. Taking a step closer to Julyiah, he gazed into her eyes with new admiration. "You are an amazing person, Julyiah."

"I know," she said, biting at her lower lip as though not certain about this but excited to be told so.

"I cannot wait to read the writings," Delwyn said. "Perhaps we can study them together sometime?"

Julyiah turned to go, but looking back she gave Delwyn a shy smile. "Perhaps."

Delwyn had to continue on his path to the south, or he would be late for work. Yet he thought Julyiah was agreeable about seeing more of him. The idea made him smile.

♪

At the Listening Hall, Julyiah told the Keeper of the Hall for that day that she had an urgent need to see one of the leaders. The guard whistled for a messenger to assist him, since he could not leave his post. A keeper in a blue uniform hurried to the spot.

"Please take this young lady to Jonar's office, and inform him that Julyiah Hartbrook has an urgent request."

"Yes, sir," the younger man replied and waved Julyiah to follow him.

Jonar's personal keeper Menila sat outside Jonar's office door dressed in the red uniform of the Valley Law. When the young man explained the situation, Menila reached out his hand toward the leather satchel, causing Julyiah to pull back instantly.

"I… I am sorry," she said. "But this should not be seen by anyone but a leader." Twinges of guilt reminded her that she had just shown the contents to Delwyn, but she chose to ignore them.

Menila nodded, went inside the office, and shut the door. He emerged a few minutes later to escort Julyiah inside.

"Julyiah, come in," Jonar greeted her as he rose from his desk. "What brings you to see me?"

"I found Gwenla's writings," Julyiah burst out, unable to hold back the news another minute.

Jonar's face paled, and Julyiah was surprised at first. What had caused his reaction? *He must be awestruck!*

Jonar dropped to his desk chair and reached out a hand. "Please... may I see?" he asked in a low voice. "Have you read any of this yet, my dear? Has anyone else seen them?"

"I only read enough to know it is Gwenla's," Julyiah beamed. "I did not understand any of it... not yet." *I will go down in history as the person who found Gwenla's secrets.... Wait until Mother hears about this!*

Jonar smiled, looking relieved. "Wonderful job! You have done us all a great service. I will read this myself right away." Jonar leafed through the Teka leaf pages, shaking his head. "After all these years! Where did you find this satchel?"

"Under the ground—under the light rock at the school," Julyiah said. "I had better return and clean up the mess. I was looking for a chesian beetle, and...."

"Oh yes, you should go back and clean up—fill the hole in so that it does not stumble someone."

Julyiah blinked. "I will, but may I ask a question? Will... I mean, may I also be allowed to read the writings?"

"Certainly, child, but we leaders like to verify certain things." Jonar's keen gaze caught Julyiah's eyes. "I hope you understand, Julyiah. I will make sure you have a chance to read them. Have you told anyone about this yet?"

"Y-yes," Julyiah stammered.

Jonar shook his head, but he did not look angry. "Please tell people you *may* have found Gwenla's writings—just until we can confirm it. No sense in getting everyone excited."

"I will!" Julyiah grinned.

Julyiah hurried out the door, wanting to proclaim her find to the world. Back at the school site, two boys had gathered around her big hole next to the rock.

"I found the Secrets of Gwenla," she announced to them. "I mean, I may have found them. The leaders are checking."

The boys blinked and shrugged. "The what?" one boy asked.

"The Secrets of Gwenla," the other boy said. "Can you not hear?"

The two little boys ran off, a little young to know the importance of her discovery. Of course, she was a mere four years old when she started her own search. The one boy's question about the other boy's ability to hear caused Julyiah to chuckle as she picked up her shovel to scoop dirt back into the hole.

As it turned out, it was a child's question that introduced Julyiah to her greatest adventure.

Chapter Three: The Fortress

♪♪♫♪

Five hundred travelers made their grim descent down the side of the hateful mountain. Their faces, images of determination and fear, were set against the mighty presence of the wind.

The wind sought to pluck them from where they stood and fling them into the abyss but was strangely impotent in carrying out its purpose. Rather, it was left to ravage the land all around, dislodging huge boulders and trees but restrained from touching the little group of helpless people.

"Keep them close together, Captain. I do not want to lose any more," a stern female voice called out above the cacophony of sound. Taller than most of the men, Gwenla strode ahead of the others, her waist-length red braid standing out on the back of her blue robe. Her powerful, long limbs, typical of female Libreans, were feared by man and beast alike. Her skin bore a remnant of green from her ancestors. She was the Keeper of the Sacred Books. In her arms, she gripped the weathered leather satchel containing the precious tomes, including her mysterious book of riddles. Gwenla had collected important secrets over her long life and recorded them by command of the One. No one understood them yet; they were reserved for a future time.

Captain Suntar raised his muscular arm in salute and strode to carry out the order, his sandy-colored hair blowing wildly about his face as his horse wound through the rows of people. The crowd pressed toward the rocky wall to make room, avoiding the edges of the road that dropped off in a direct plunge to the canyon below.

"Stay close!" Suntar bellowed at intervals as he passed row after row astride his tall gray mount. Several looked up, encouraged by their leader's commanding voice. They nodded in agreement, knowing that to stay close was the key to their survival. That very morning they had lost a reckless young man who *ventured a short way up a different path. The wind had blown him off the ledge before anyone could get to him. Many had resorted to tying a rope lead to their children in an attempt to prevent another catastrophe.*

Within two days, they arrived at the fortress, the one that Suntar's ancestors had built. The sight of their new home was disheartening, for it was in need of extensive repair.

Captain Suntar supervised the construction that followed, bravely carrying on day after day, though he was ready to drop from exhaustion. The wind never stopped, and the construction wore on for many weeks. Suntar observed the group's weakened condition one night, listening to the coughing and the discouraged conversation around the campfires. Provisions ran low. Knowing the persistent wind would soon turn the area into a scorched wasteland, he wondered if there would be enough time left to save the inner valley. He peered up into the blackness, trying to see his workers overhead. For an instant, the entire scene was lit by lightning from the north, and the massive walls of the fortress towered above him. It looked evil in the night, but it was their salvation from the onslaught. It rained north of the fortress, mysteriously ignoring the area to the south. But a river ran through the valley, and both crops and people would be safe once they had mended every breach.

Many more had perished. We must get done, *he thought,* or we will all die.

♪

Julyiah looked up from the old book she was reading, and shaded her eyes from the afternoon sun. "That is all for today." With an understanding nod, she listened to the moans in her class from the seven to eight-year-olds who had been listening. "We will read more tomorrow."

Two large napcot trees covered with white blossoms shaded the tiny area, but the students crowded onto various sunny patches on the cold stone benches at the table, attempting to keep a little warmer in the chilly spring air. They talked among themselves, when the story was over. Some wiggled their toes in the grass, while others played with napcot blossoms.

Setting the book on the stone table, Julyiah blinked at the memory of setting the book about insects on the same table four years ago, just before she dug under the rock and found Gwenla's secrets. Congratulated over and over by the community's leaders and her friends in the following weeks, Julyiah had to wait a long time before she got to read the writings.

After months of study and discussion, the leaders confessed they did not understand the writings and released the book to have its own music cell so that everyone could read it for themselves. They ordered the Teka leaves nicely bound together and a leather cover made for the book. Lines were long the day the book was available. Many people flocked to see the precious writings, but just as many came out of the music cell shaking their heads in confusion.

Julyiah felt the heat rush to her cheeks as she recalled how many hours she and Delwyn had spent alone together in that music cell to study the book. Assuming from the start that he was more interested in her than the *Book of Secrets*, she had been correct. It was too bad they had not understood the riddles any better than the others, but it had brought them closer together as they talked about the book and other subjects.

The metal engraving on the cover of *Captain Suntar* flashed in the sunlight, bringing Julyiah back to the present. "Would anyone like to comment on the portion I have read?" Julyiah asked her class.

"Captain Suntar was one of our family," Lisiya Suntar said, the golden curls in her perfectly arranged hair bobbing in agreement. "If it were not for him, none of us would be here, safe inside this fortress. He was so brave! Our family has always been brave..."

"And YOU are SO special," Jonli Driscoll returned in mock admiration, dropping his jaw. He pretended to look into a mirror and primp, checking his dark hair for tangles. Lisiya's lower lip pushed into her upper one. She appraised the plainly dressed boy, before dismissing him with a contemptuous turn of her head and lift of her chin.

"Miss Hartbrook..." another child interrupted as he made his way over toward Julyiah, with a puzzled twist of his mouth. "That was so long ago. What does it look like outside the wall now?"

The question slammed into Julyiah's mind, almost like a rock hitting the side of her head. Pictures of the Devastation disrupted her heart, with boulders flying and cliffs crumbling below her feet. The image presented a terrific contrast to the peaceful afternoon and her serene state of mind. *What is happening?* Julyiah stared at Tomli Tarni, unable to speak for a moment.

The children looked back and forth with curiosity between the wall and their teacher. Tomli watched Julyiah with wide, innocent eyes. His question hung in the air, awaiting an answer. While Julyiah worked on her reply, her nervous fingers combed the ends of the soft curls in her hair.

"After the Devastation?" Julyiah asked, stalling while she worked to remain calm. Preferring to keep to the historical aspects of the Outside, Julyiah did not want to know what was out there. They were taught that the Winds of Devastation still lurked on the Outside, waiting to come in if given the chance. What it was like outside long ago was history. What it was like now was ... disturbing. Was it any different? The community had been isolated for over 400 years and she wanted to keep it that way.

"I want to know what it is like out there now."

Julyiah nodded, glancing at the West Wall nearby as though it might assist her. "I see," she delayed again, standing and holding her finger to her chin to indicate she was in thought. As a teacher, she had anticipated answering this question *some day*, just not *today*.

All the children grew quiet, eyes riveted on Teacher in obvious hopes of hearing everything possible about the mysterious Outside. She could see their imaginations running wild and some holding their breath. Most parents refused to tell their children anything about the Outside, saying, "Maybe when you are older." *No doubt hoping their teacher would explain it.*

Children did not understand the fear that adults showed over the Outside, or during windy conditions, because they did not see inside their hearts until they were older. It was not until the Understanding came upon them that their hearts opened to reveal the good or bad places inside that could affect them as much as the reality around them.

Answering a child's questions about what seemed obvious to an adult was difficult, especially when the adult did not want to think about it. Julyiah moistened her lips and took a breath. "The Outside is a vast wasteland." Julyiah plunged forward with her rehearsed explanation. Averting her eyes from the children, she was unable to think of anything original to say and knew what their reaction would be. "There are no trees, no plants, not even grass. It is all dirt and rocks."

A collective sigh of disappointment escaped the listening children. They had heard all of this basic description before. Julyiah knew they were wondering how a barren, desert region could terrify adults.

Adults like me.

"But... is it bigger than Victory Valley?" Tomli asked, looking around.

Now there is an original question.

Julyiah heard a couple of children from the wealthier families snickering, and she turned to give them reproving glances. "Oh yes, thousands of times bigger than this valley," Julyiah told Tomli.

"I knew that," Lisiya Suntar said. "We learned that in Victory Class last week."

"Okay, Lisiya," Julyiah said, observing the conceited grin on the elaborately dressed, much pampered daughter of the well-known Suntar Clan. Julyiah looked at the others. "I am sure many of you knew that." The children nodded, and some glared at Lisiya, indignant with her remark.

Before Julyiah continued, she recalled her Teacher's Training the summer before on the sensitive subject of the Outside. Every new teacher knew they must learn what to say and how to say it.

"The children get curious about the Outside as they grow older," Leader Jonar had instructed. "We must discourage any desire they have to seek what is out there, especially until they go through the Understanding, after which they will see for themselves. When they ask about the Outside, get a permission pass to look out of the South Window. They will be awed by the size of the world around us but will also no doubt observe its unpleasantness. Even though they will not take on the necessary fear until their adult transition into Understanding, they will remember there is nothing on the Outside to attract them.

"The South Window viewing should be the end of a child's curiosity. Some who have decided to depart our safe haven have been lost. You do not want this to happen to any child in your class."

Julyiah avoided even thinking about the Outside, so talking about it was abhorrent. Whenever the subject came up her heart always flashed back to the day she hung over empty space in order to rescue Marni. Since that day she had fought the nightmare sensation of being on the edge of a cliff, the windy depths pulling at her soul as though it could persuade her to step off the edge.

"The Voice sang with the Music on the Breeze to Gwenla in M1700 to warn our people of the Devastation," she recited from Teacher's Training. "Of course, we no longer hear Music in this way. Music was recorded on sound rocks back in Gwenla's time and put in the music boxes by our leaders. If we tried to hear the Voice somewhere else, we might hear the Lying Wind, which as you know, brought the Devastation." Julyiah shivered. "The deadly Wind claimed many lives in ancient times and is still alive on the Outside, prowling the wasteland like a savage beast looking for a stray victim."

Young eyes darted toward Teacher again. Adults also did not talk about the Lying Wind.

"All were protected inside the fortress when the Devastation came," Julyiah went on, concentrating on the concept of *protection*. "There is a window in the wall—"

"A window in the wall?" Samli Wester exclaimed with an incredulous expression, looking around as though he might find where this was located. Some of the other children were surprised as well.

"Yes," Julyiah responded, feeling the edge of her personal cliff returning. "The Libreans knew that the Lying Wind was crafty and could sneak in through windows and over the top of walls that were too low." She pointed to the top of the tall structure nearby. "So they reinforced the wall, building it higher than the tallest trees and blocking off all the windows except one—the South Window. This window is blocked, but we can get permission to have it opened."

Julyiah shuddered in fear at the thought of a South Window viewing with the children. The window was high off the ground, and just thinking about it caused her to take a step backward in an effort to feel safer. She noticed the children watching her with eyes full of curiosity. Her eyelashes fluttered as she focused on getting through her answer to Tomli's question. Longing to steer the conversation elsewhere, her mind searched for the haven of a different topic. Tension made her voice higher than usual.

"After two months, the Devastation died down, and some looked out the South Window. Everything was blown into a wasteland. A hot, dry wind still blew on the Outside, but the safe valley became quiet, peaceful, and green. If it had not been for the Music that came to Gwenla, all would have died outside the wall, and none of us would be here."

The children were silent a moment as they pondered this sobering tale. Julyiah let out a sigh of relief. She had told all the necessary facts, and the children seemed subdued. The subject was closed.

"But, you said we should not try to listen to the Music on the Breeze," Tomli said, frowning, "or we might hear the Lying Wind. So, why was it a good thing that Gwenla listened to the Music on the Breeze? And how could we hear the Lying Wind if the wall blocks it out?"

Julyiah stared at Tomli in dismay, and trembled as the spring breeze picked up momentum, sending white blossoms cascading all around her. She eyed the breezy scene in alarm, and the precarious cliff edge came rushing back to mind. She could sense a rocky wall behind her, and it seemed to be pushing on her, attempting to shove her off into nothingness. The wind raged against the cliff. Inside her heart, she grabbed for holds in the rocks, which all seemed to be loose and threatening to go down with her. The narrow ledge she stood on was getting thinner....

"Some things... cannot be answered, Tomli," Julyiah stammered. She pulled on her hair and grimaced, before forcing her hands to stay at her sides. Trying to stay calm, she smiled, but her left eyelid twitched in rebellion. "We must trust our leaders and the sacred books. I do not think you should ask those questions."

Julyiah turned around to signal the end of the discussion, but she tripped over a hidden stone and let out a little yelp, bringing giggles out of the children. Julyiah wished they would be fidgety and noisy as they so often were at the end of class, but their focus remained on her.

Feeling their eyes asking more questions, Julyiah took hold of the tree branch. "Tomorrow we will study these napcot buds," she said, trying to look more confident than she felt. "Soon the golden napcot fruit will start to grow inside each blossom...."

Where is that school bell?

A short, thin-haired man emerged from the school building at last, and he pulled on the rope that was attached to the school bell. Julyiah jumped at the sound but glanced at the man in relief.

"That is all for today," she announced, her voice sounding weak. The din of cheering voices and running children shattered the tense quiet of the afternoon.

Chapter Four: Places

♪

Julyiah went to the table and picked up the book, one of the few written works in the community aside from the sacred books. The Suntar family often loaned out volumes from their personal library for teaching. Julyiah noticed with fascination that her hands shook as she walked back to the school buildings, finding her way down an outside corridor to her classroom, and yet she felt calmer now that the questions were over. Opening the metal door to the stone building, she drew back as the air heated by the metal roof rushed out to greet her.

"I should have left this door open," she said out loud to no one in particular. Grimacing, she considered the insects that would invade the room and looked with envy at some of the other buildings which had been converted to stone vaulted ceilings to make them cooler in the summer.

Inside the room, Julyiah gathered a pile of Teka leaves together to correct and headed back outside. Surprised and delighted, she saw her fiancé Delwyn Sarroll coming up Valley Road to meet her. His deep blue eyes locked on hers in warm recognition. The plain brown wool dekat wrapped around his chest and waist did not hide his muscular physique. Julyiah's heart leaped at the sight of him, but relaxed as Delwyn's presence brought a sense of security into her troubled day.

"Hello, Del! Where are you today?" Her heart thumped as she watched a grin spread across his rugged features and a sparkle in his eye. Running a hand through his dark, neck-length hair in a failed attempt at neatness, he moved closer to her.

"I am in a meadow full of flowers," he said, moving his hand upwards through the air as though the sky was full of the graceful buds. His eyes pierced the depths of hers, and his husky voice told her his happy place was because she was near. Joy swept through her when he reached out and took her hand.

"Where are you?" Delwyn asked Julyiah.

Julyiah paused, looking at the ground. A few minutes earlier, she felt like she was in the middle of screaming babies with a headache. But a negative response when asked about one's heart place was not socially acceptable, and Delwyn's presence was already changing her mood. Imagining a better place to be in she looked up into his welcome gaze, putting her arms up around his neck. "By a bubbling brook," she answered.

Delwyn leaned down to plant a warm kiss on her lips, and he traced his fingers across her cheek to sweep her hair aside. At his touch, Julyiah took in a deep breath to relax and laid her head on his chest a few moments before stepping back.

"Lessons to correct?" he asked, pointing to the Teka leaves she held in one arm. The childish charcoal markings on the large, pale leaves were spelling words. After correcting the Teka leaves, Julyiah could wipe them off and use them again, until they became too limp to write on.

The unimportant chatter was comforting, and Julyiah's gaze drifted to Delwyn's eyes with a grateful smile. "Yes," she replied, glancing down at the lessons. She folded the flexible leaves in half and stuffed them inside a pocket in her talia. "Shall we go?"

The two began walking toward Julyiah's house, not far away. "How did you get away from your work today?" she asked. Delwyn worked each weekday from morning to evening driving a transport wagon up and down the lower end of Valley Road or assisting at the Keenar Ranch. He was paid by Rikial Keenar, who owned all of the horses in the community.

"I did not get off." Delwyn's eyes crinkled in a wry smile. "I am taking a message to Jadleil Suntar from Rikial—the answer is still *No*." The wealthy Suntar Clan had a standing offer to buy one horse from the Keenar Clan, but their offers were never accepted. "Like the rest of the Keenars," Delwyn chuckled, "Rikial still feels that the Suntars gave up their rights to any horses when they planned to leave them on the Outside. He does not mind at all that he has a monopoly on the animal."

Julyiah knew about the ongoing rivalry between the Suntar Clan farmers and the Keenar Clan ranchers. According to fortress history, the Keenars were the clan willing to keep horses in the area and share their meager supply of grain with them until the crops and other food supplies became plentiful. Delwyn was one of the privileged few who were allowed to work with the delightful animals.

The conversation ebbed, and Julyiah's thoughts took the opportunity to wander back through her recent troubles. Her mind replayed the conversation with the children that day. Deciding to get the pass to the South Window right away, she thought to get the field trip over with by tomorrow.

"I was just stopping by on my way to Suntar Hill," Delwyn said. "Your house is on the way."

Julyiah's fingers pulled the ends of her hair and Delwyn noticed. He took hold of the nervous hand and frowned, gazing with intent into her eyes. "Where did you say you were?"

Julyiah halted her steps also. She faked a smile again, looking up at him with loving eyes.

"I am in a small forest clearing," she said, waving her arm overhead in a graceful gesture, "where the sun warms a spot of ground, and tall trees, many trees, grow all around."

"Sounds wonderful," Delwyn said with care, raising his eyebrows. He dropped her hand and pulled off one of the leaves on a nearby Teka bush, smoothing it with his hands. "I wonder what it is like with so many trees," he said with a smirk. "But Jul, I do not believe you were in that place a moment ago."

Julyiah pursed her lips and kicked at a tiny rock in the road with her brown leather sandal. He could read her so well! Yet was that not one of the reasons she loved him?

"You are right," Julyiah admitted. "I did not want to bother you with a ridiculous school problem."

"Where has it put you?"

"In several strange places, mostly confusing. A few minutes ago I was sliding into a gloomy pit, barely able to scramble out. I do not know what was in the pit, maybe nothing."

"That could be serious."

They continued on in silence, and turned on another road. Several stone houses lined the sides. Julyiah tried to focus on the stones and blank out the images in her heart, but the images were too strong.

"It is upsetting," Julyiah shrugged, patting his arm to show her appreciation while trying to hide her insecurity. She rubbed her eyelids to hide the twitching. "The children asked me about the Outside today. Everyone in Teacher's Training last summer seemed on edge about the subject, but I thought it would not be hard—that I would tell the children what I have been told to tell them. Alas, it was not that easy. The children asked different questions than what the leaders taught us. Even to think about the questions put me on the edge of a cliff again."

"Do you want to tell me the questions?"

"I do not think so." When Julyiah's thoughts drifted back to Tomli's question, the ground beneath her feet dissolved away, leaving her hanging over nothingness. The wind thrashed around her, and the silent call from unimaginable depths grabbed at her soul.

"No!" she cried out, talking to herself more than to Delwyn. Reaching out instinctively, she clutched his arm, looking at the dirt road under her feet, concentrating on the fine puffs of dust each step threw up into the air as she tried to pull her heart back from the abyss.

"It will be all right," Delwyn replied, moving his hand to her arm but keeping his eyes on the ground.

The vision left, and Julyiah let out a shaky sigh. "You see? Even the thought of this subject puts me in a terrible place. You know, it is so important that these children learn the truth. Maybe the Wind is trying to interfere."

"You need to listen to the Music," Delwyn suggested, studying her face. "Go through a music cell and read a passage from Silia. Are you going through the music cells each week?"

"Of course," Julyiah snapped in a loud voice, amazing herself with the sharpness of her response. She looked at Delwyn's eyes, her brows drawn together. "I am sorry—it is not your fault. A good place has eluded me today, so I will go through a music cell right now."

Delwyn became quiet, and Julyiah saw the tension in his jaw. She should not have talked about this to him. Not understanding it herself, she was drawing him into her confusion.

They walked by her house on the corner of the next road, and Julyiah turned to stare at the magnificent North Wall that towered above them, allowing her eyes to travel over the beautiful light stones that shone brighter as the daylight waned.

"My mother is almost finished with my wedding talia," Julyiah said, hoping to sound happy while changing the subject, yet she spoke in a stiff tone, willing her emotions to catch up with the words. Turning back toward him, she wanted to discern whether Delwyn had been able to move on after her outburst.

♫

Delwyn was willing to avoid the touchy subject and think about their upcoming marriage. "Hm... good!" he said, pulling out of the pit he was thrown into as a result of Julyiah's reactions. "Are we almost ready then?"

As he awaited her response, Delwyn allowed his eyes to take in the beautiful young woman standing by his side. Her light brown curls glistened in the early evening light while her large, expressive eyes looked into his with complete trust. How could he not love her?

"Yes. My father has arranged for the carriage," Julyiah said. "I chose the forest hideaway because I thought you would like that too."

Delwyn pictured the thick gathering of trees at the southeastern corner of the valley. A small cabin for the newly married had been built there, away from the community traffic. Two other cabins set up elsewhere in the area had beautiful views, but Julyiah and Delwyn both loved trees, and the forest remained their dream place. Owned by the leaders, it would never be sold because wood was rare.

"Just two weeks away," Julyiah announced, looking up at Delwyn with a shy grin.

"I will wait impatiently," he whispered in her ear, delighted when she shivered at his closeness. Before long, Julyiah would be his bride, and everything would be wonderful.

Chapter Five: Music Cells

♪...♪♫♫

Two invisible beings hovered over the walking couple, observing them closely, listening to everything they said. In this undercover world, the beings manifested merely as sounds and flashes of color or non-color, which streaked the air in their own environment as they debated.

"The girl is right within my clutches," one hissed to the other. A black cloud, chokingly thick, followed the threatening statement as the being attempted to settle over Julyiah's head but failed.

Julyiah stopped and looked with concern at the dark mist moving across the sky high above before she turned forward again, hurrying her steps. Delwyn observed her actions, frowning, but he said nothing.

"You will never persuade her. See how afraid she is," the cloud said in triumph.

"She will come to me," the other replied. Pastel shades arced over him, breaking into dancing sparkles that leaped about, each producing a different tune but coming together again, blending into a rainbow. The voice sung in rhythm with the colors.

The two ethereal observers watched as the young couple headed farther up the road.

"They are headed for the music cells."

"That could be good... or bad."

Julyiah and Delwyn were followed to another fork in the road.

"She was coming in my direction," said a ferocious howl, blurry swirls of gray and black sweeping around it, "until you interfered."

"I could say the same."

"You will never get anywhere with these people," the dark one predicted with a low growl. The threatening currents continued with intermittent moaning sounds. "They believe I only exist as

Wind, and they can hide from me inside their walls, but I will influence them a great deal as long as they think that."

"We shall see," said the colorful One. "It is not what they do right now that matters or even what they think. It is what is in their hearts." The hues around him changed to brilliant yellows and arced higher, becoming white at the top and forming a star.

The sinister blob cowered. "Do you always have to be so bright?" He curled into a smaller ball. "I will tell you what is in their hearts—fear. I shall follow her to the music cell."

"All right, but do not interfere."

"Me? Interfere? You are the one that is always interfering. Why do you not let them go down the path they choose?"

"I do."

"And they call you the truthful one and me the liar. If only they knew..."

"Yes, indeed. But they will."

♪

Julyiah stopped walking as Delwyn turned to head toward Keenar's town house. "Nice walking with you," he told Julyiah, giving her a short, publicly acceptable kiss. "I will see you tomorrow night for dinner?"

"Yes," Julyiah responded with a smile. "And... thank you for being so understanding. I am sure I will be all right soon."

"I hope so. Have a nice place."

"Have a nice place."

Julyiah continued a short distance to where the road ended at the North Wall. The Listening Hall lay directly ahead, in the center at the base of the wall. The leaders' homes rose above the Hall and to the right, just over the leaders' offices. Julyiah paused to view the beautiful balconies and windows in the side of the wall, overlooking the valley. Everything sacred was here. Julyiah hoped to find comfort from the upheaval she had experienced that day by going through a ground-level music cell, where she could read one of the books in peace. She turned left on Victory Road, walked up to the music cell station, and opened the door.

"A music cell today?" asked the keeper, a wrinkled man with thin hair and no expression.

"Yes, please," Julyiah replied.

"What kind of music cell do you need?" the keeper asked in a cordial tone, looking at her without apparent interest.

"One of comfort."

"The *Book of Silia*."

"Yes."

The attendant led her to several rooms built within another, larger room. He continued down the hallway past some of the doors, and Julyiah enjoyed the coolness of the thick walls and vaulted ceilings. Warming stones, replaced on a regular basis, regulated the temperature. Light rocks lit the way along the passage and gave off a friendly glow.

With a heavy sigh, the keeper opened a wooden door at the end of the hallway. Julyiah admired the elaborate carving in the oak door as she passed through. Just inside on the left, a box awaited her coins, which supported those who cared for the music cells. The keeper followed her with little sound, and she wondered if he was bored or anxious to go home for the day.

The windowless room seemed oddly refreshing to her. She knew she would find peace in here as she always had. *This was a good thing to do today.* Noticing the musty smells within the cool rock walls, Julyiah looked around. A gold-covered plaque on the wall read, "Welcome to the safety of a music cell." The leaders often told them it was safer to read the books deep inside the walls, where no wind could get through.

A book and box lay on top of a wooden pedestal. The keeper opened the box and a melody emerged, inspiring Julyiah to sing with it. A little self-conscious until the keeper left the room, Julyiah sang with more abandon when she felt he was no longer listening.

Julyiah's heart pounded as she finished singing and approached the sacred *Book of Silia*. Opening the book, she turned to a place she had never read—passages 232 and 233:

Music brings man to where he should be—whether it is in an open field or a closed-in fortress. Man is in a good place when Music is his companion.

Julyiah felt peace flow through her heart. "The words are true," she breathed. "So true." The Voice whispered truth in her heart as she read, and she saw a tremendous waterfall with colors spurting from the rocks below, causing her to gasp in awe. Having never experienced such a good place before, she wanted to stay there.

The keeper had opened a curtain, behind which was a painting of a green vale, location unknown. Julyiah had seen all of the paintings before. The picture showed trees lining a blue river with a pretty, trickling waterfall, but the scene barely resembled what she saw in her heart, so she looked away.

Julyiah turned a page to read more:

"The Breeze brings Music to man. He lifts up his head; his ears open wide; his heart expands in great joy."

The Breeze! Conflict rose within her again as she realized what bothered her: Tomli's question seemed valid. Why was it wrong to listen to Music on the Breeze? How could it be wrong when the sacred *Book of Silia* said how wonderful it was? All the books spoke of hearing Music on the Breeze. She could not remember Gwenla ever saying it was a bad thing, and a Keeper of the Books would know.

The questions in Julyiah's mind disrupted her peaceful place. Struggling with images of open places where the Breeze brought the Music, she imagined what she had seen earlier happening in the scene before her—a huge waterfall with singing colors darting about. Such pictures were incredibly beautiful. How could they produce such turmoil within her?

But it is not done anymore. We no longer listen to Music on the Breeze. It is obvious that the Music in this box revived me. No one hears the Music on the Breeze now. No one. The leaders changed our ways.

But why?

Julyiah frowned, trying to dislodge her wayward thoughts as she turned the pages again. Determined to redirect her mind to more acceptable thinking, she stopped at the 83rd passage: "The One sends Music, and the Voice sings the truth on the Breeze."

A lot had been taught about Music coming from the One, but she had never thought much about the second part of the passage. The Voice sings the truth on the Breeze? Was this wrong too? She read on to another passage before she could get confused again, looking for something soothing that would settle her mind and heart. Finding one of her favorite passages about peace, Julyiah tried to soak it well into her heart.

When she was done, the keeper led her back out of the music cell. The sun had gone lower, and the West Wall was casting its long shadow over the town. Julyiah gazed at the giant stone structure a moment.

"Did you find what you needed, Miss Hartbrook?" the keeper asked, showing the only discernible interest in her thus far.

"Yes... I believe I did," Julyiah said, knowing her real feelings would not be acceptable.

"Have a nice place."

"Have a nice place," Julyiah returned.

♪ ... ♪ ♫ ♫

The unseen beings conversed again as Julyiah left the music cell.

"She is coming my way again," one said.

"No, she is coming to me," the other replied.

But, as yet, there was no way to tell for sure.

Chapter Six: The Pit

♪

Julyiah did not sleep well that night. Many dreams took her to places alternating between beauty and evil. There was a recurring dream, too. Little Tomli was in a pit, an evil one. She tried to reach out to him but was afraid she would fall in also. Slimy creatures in the pit were pulling Tomli down, and though Julyiah grabbed hold of his hand and tugged to pull him out, she was slipping through deep mud, sliding toward the edge.

She woke late, and the sun was up. The angle of the morning light shining through her misty glass window told her she had a short time left to get to the school. Leaving the *soofa* mattress unmade and her clothes strewn about, Julyiah grabbed bread from her tiny kitchen, retrieved milk out of the cold box, and sped outside.

A few steps later, Julyiah turned back to pick up two dimming light rocks that were sitting on a table by the front door. Hurrying back out the door and up a ladder, she put the rocks on her roof to regenerate in the sun before rushing back up the road. Puffing, she brushed her wavy hair in careless movements, regretting that she had not brought her mirror.

The test—she had forgotten the school papers. Oh well, the children would not want to hear how they did, not in this case.

The permission pass— *Oh yes*, she sighed in relief. It was in the pocket of the rosy talia she wore. Having picked out the clothing to wear the night before, she had put the pass in a pocket so she would not forget it. Thoughts of the pass brought back memories of her conversation with Leader Jonar the day before, a conversation she did not want to think about.

"This is bad," Jonar had said, frowning after Julyiah told him of the questions Tomli had asked. "The Lying Wind has gotten to this poor boy. Perhaps his parents have allowed it by discussing things they should not have."

As the white-robed leader paced the full length of his office, Julyiah's eyes took in each wooden item in the room that he passed. The beauty of the precious material fascinated her: carved bookends, an oak pencil holder with a wooden pencil inside (even the pencil had carving because it was not used), the elaborate pedestal with the *Book of Zemar* atop it. This was Jonar's favorite book to use in his messages, his captivating voice holding the listeners' ears well.

"But," Julyiah protested when Jonar paused, "I believe his father has told him not to listen to Music on the Breeze."

"Yes," Jonar said, pausing in his pacing to look at her. His piercing blue eyes shone out of his aging face with wisdom. "That is a good observation, Julyiah."

Julyiah smiled and felt her face turning red. One always appreciated a compliment from the leaders, even more so from Jonar, the most respected leader. His blond hair was turning white around his ears. Julyiah's heart stirred as she realized he was growing older. What would they do when Jonar was gone? None of the other leaders had the authority or wisdom that he did.

"Perhaps his grandfather then," Jonar suggested, his eyes darkening as he looked out the window toward the town. "He has not come to the Listening Hall for some time. He does not seek Music. As the 337th and 338th passages of Zemar tell us:

Be not Music deaf,
For Music is your life—
Coming to you and playing upon
The very strings of your heart.
All who are Music deaf
Will go to the Pit of Silence,
For Silence is what they love.
But all who love Music
Will find life.

Julyiah's heart jumped as she recalled the words Jonar quoted from Zemar. The *Pit of Silence* stuck in her mind like an insect buzzing around one's sweaty face. Her recurring dream hit her with full force. Was Tomli already in the Pit? Was that what she kept sliding into? Maybe she could have saved him, but not now because she had questions too. She did not mean to doubt what she had been taught, but she had.

The thought continued to plague her when she arrived at the school. Julyiah determined to put these strange ideas out of her mind and help Tomli. Yes, that must be what the bad dream was for—it was a warning that any questioning of the traditional way would steer the young boy in the wrong direction.

Julyiah barged into the classroom just as the school bell rang, the metal door hitting the side of the stone building with a loud *clap!*

The children inside were quiet within seconds, staring at her in astonishment. Their teacher was never late or rushed.

"Good day," Julyiah said with an uncomfortable effort to catch her breath, wondering whether she had some hair sticking up in strange places where the hurried brush had not reached it. Her hands smoothed her hair, while she attempted a nonchalant stroll over to her desk. She smiled, knowing that it probably looked more like a grimace. "And where are we today?"

"In a nice place," they all chorused. "And you, Miss Hartbrook?"

"In a nice place," she lied, using the polite response as taught to the children. In reality, she was in a dimly-lit tunnel, feeling her way along because she could not see. *Funny*, she thought, *how we teach the children to lie about social graces but are so strict about the Lying Wind.* She shoved this unorthodox thought from her jumbled mind and headed for her desk.

"Miss Hartbrook?"

She spun back around at the sound of Tomli Tarni's voice. *No, Tomli! Do not ask those questions!* They were sliding together into a pit again....

"Did you correct our papers?"

Julyiah choked out a sigh of relief as the pit in her heart faded away.

"I... forgot them, I am sorry. But we have a field trip today!"

The children cheered and discussed among themselves where they might be going. Julyiah used the noise to take a deep breath and settle in at her desk. She saw Lisiya Suntar's hand raised.

"Yes, Lisiya?"

"Are we going to the South Window?" the girl asked with some excitement in her voice.

"Oh... yes!" Julyiah said, wishing again it was all over. "We are leaving right after reading and will have our mid-day meal in the forest—how does that sound?"

Excited voices began to chatter while Julyiah stared at them numbly. Reading. She must get on with the reading. Maybe when the South Window trip was over. Maybe then everything would be normal again.

Chapter Seven: The Valley

♪

The anticipated time for the trip arrived. Julyiah and her enthusiastic class headed out on Valley Road, noontime meals in hand. Occupied with the children, Julyiah herded them together, stopping fights and rowdy play, keeping them from hitting each other with their metal food containers. She was too busy to think about the moment when the South Window was unveiled—the moment when she might have to answer questions. The evil places were gone for now, and she did not care to experience them again. She had a more pressing problem directly in front of her.

About 500 paces from the school buildings, the little group approached the top of the Inner Wall. The stone structure dropped to the lower elevation ranches and farms, accessible at this location by the stairs—the same place where Julyiah had rescued Marni. The children scampered to the stairs, shouting about who would get to the bottom first. A waist-high railing ran the full length of the switchback stairs, but being responsible for twenty rowdy children kept Julyiah alert. "No running!" Julyiah called in a watchful voice, fearful of children falling off the stone edge, as Marni almost had that fateful day four years before.

As I almost did.

The cliff overlooking the valley loomed ahead of her, but she did not look, trying not to think about the distance to the bottom. Shivering as she approached the staircase, Julyiah closed her eyes briefly. *Do not think about it. Do not look down. Just get there, one stair at a time.* Marni always assisted her.

"Miss Hartbrook, can I hold your hand?" Marni asked in a sweet voice.

Julyiah looked at the girl gratefully. Marni was not afraid—not yet. But the girl knew Julyiah's fears. "I think that is a good idea," Julyiah said, trying to hang onto some semblance of dignity.

At the bottom of the stairs, the rest of the group waited with fidgety feet for Julyiah and Marni. However, they knew better than to heckle the pair, for their teacher had been admired as a hero for her bravery—Marni would have died without Julyiah's rescue.

The group walked on, crossing the bridge that arced over the Suntar Canal. The Suntar Clan had built the canal a few years after the original settlement. Captain Suntar, along with his wife and three sons, had staked an immediate claim to the highest elevation of land in the northern end of the community. Suntar Hill rose the height of six men above the town, and a large spring made a pool at the base of the hill, where a river flowed south along the top of Sylar Ridge. Suntar Hill was filled with trees, so the ambitious family constructed wooden boats to carry passengers down the river from the north to the south end, along Victory River. Yet the boats had to be hauled back in wagons to the beginning of the river each time, causing a lot of work.

One day the inventive Suntars discovered that they could divert the river to form a canal at the south end and cause the water to run gradually north again along the ridge next to the West Wall. The differing elevations allowed the running water to make a wide circle, like a great basin, dropping a little in elevation until it arrived back at the Inner Wall.

To facilitate boat hauling up to the river, the Suntar Clan also built a boat-lifting device that used water-wheel power. Hooked to a pulley and cables, the boats were pulled up from the valley floor to the top of Sylar Ridge, where they could be launched again in the river. Thus one could travel from north to south and back again, using the river going south and the canal going north.

To drain the canal, they continued to divert the water at the Inner Wall to wind south again through the valley, to water the crops and animals before it traveled all the way back to meet the river. At this point, both bodies of water dropped off through the huge opening in the ground known as "The Hole."

They would not be taking the canal boat today but the Transport Wagon. The eager children ran to climb into the painted wagon, which was made from one of the old wooden boats. They chatted in excited voices about the huge black draft horses in front and discussed who had ridden a horse before and who had not. Lisiya Suntar dominated the conversation since her father, Jadleil, had been able to buy her horseback rides several times from Rikial Keenar.

"I do not think you have ridden that many times," Lisiya insisted, as the wagon lurched forward and began to travel down Valley Road. "These horses are busy working day and night. How could you have the chance to ride?"

"Well, how could you have the chance then?" Rikial Keenar's grandson Jefen returned. "How could you have ridden more than me when I live on the same property with them?"

Julyiah listened to the banter awhile, hoping it would play itself out. She tried to ignore the spat by enjoying the budding of spring all around her. Birds sang in every tree they passed by, and wildflowers could be seen here and there where the spring plows had not yet turned them under. They also grew in several spots right on the sides of the wall, where jutting rocks had formed ledges and gathered dirt over the years. Passing birds dropped stray seeds, and on occasion a new variety of flower or herb would show itself. Julyiah sighed, remembering how she had wanted to join the Agricultural Authority and be part of the examination process of new plants and insects.

What was that? Julyiah whipped around, looking behind her. A high-pitched sound like a scream had rent the air far to the north. It sounded like something outside the wall. A couple of the children heard it and turned as well. Julyiah watched for a large bird to appear, but saw nothing. *Perhaps it was one of Keenar's horses in town.*

"Ow!" The children's bickering had gone too far. Lisiya was unable to tolerate being outdone, so she had called Jefen a liar. Growing tired of the abuse, Jefen pulled Lisiya's hair. Lisiya reacted with a terrific flood of tears. As usual, Julyiah had to deal with the girl's behavior.

"There now, Lisiya, it cannot be that bad," Julyiah soothed, wishing she could discipline her instead. "You two calm down. You will ruin the day for the others."

Lisiya gasped. "You... you had better do something!" she insisted in an ominous tone. "He pulled my hair, and my mother will not like that, if you know what I mean." Lisiya pulled her chin toward her chest in defiance and glared at the scenery.

This threat to tell her mother was one Lisiya often used, but it was not taken lightly. Julyiah had been confronted by Ruti Suntar before, and she did not wish to face another scathing lecture from the patronizing woman. The spoiled Lisiya was the "princess" of Suntar "castle." Julyiah dreaded her first year of teaching with Lisiya Suntar in her class but had told herself it was for just one year.

"Lisiya," Julyiah began in an assertive manner, but not so stern as to threaten the child's inflated ego, "you were calling Jefen a liar and would not stop. No one likes to be called a liar, and I am not sure your mother would like to find out you said that to Rikial Keenar's grandson."

The Suntar Clan's ongoing desire to own horses was well known to everyone in the community, including Lisiya. Julyiah knew the girl would have trouble continuing her complaint. Lisiya stared at Julyiah a moment, her inner struggle apparent as she pursed her lips. Throwing threatening glances toward some of the children who giggled at her frustration, she folded her arms, lifted her chin, and turned away.

The wagon veered to the west, turning off of Valley Road to go around the Hole. A waterfall the height of twenty men spilled off the edge of the Hole and landed below, inside a vast underground chamber unseen by most valley dwellers. Hundreds of people lived there in semi-darkness, carrying on their daily lives in a world where the sun shown briefly each day.

The horses strained in their collars as they pulled the wagonload up and over a canal bridge and turned south. This was an unusual treat for the children, who scrambled to one side of the wagon to gape at the huge hole in the ground below them as they traveled around the southwestern corner of the community. The huge oval opening was over 100 paces from one end to the other. The children peered to see through the spray of the falls where the river and canal water dumped in, and they spotted a few people traveling on Access Road, which disappeared into the darkness below.

As usual, the children's imaginations speculated as to what might lurk in the depths of the Underground, since none had ever been allowed down there. One could walk to the edge and look over the stone railing at the top, if one was not afraid of heights. From there, a few structures could be seen at the base of the waterfall but not much else. A terrific mist rose up as a result of the water hitting rocks at the bottom, blurring what little could be seen.

The children knew of the metal mines below, and the hundreds of tunnels like honeycomb in the surrounding walls. Adults discussed the wicked city of Durnee when children were not around, but they still knew about it. Durnee had no laws, and the people did not listen to the sacred books or leaders. Jonar taught that the Lying Wind came down through the other hole—the one outside the wall—and influenced those in the Underground. "We stay away from such people and follow the better way as the books command."

The children liked to make up stories about people turning into monsters and coming out of the caves at night to terrorize everyone. Julyiah noticed the fascination with the Hole and its dark reaches. So many people had turned away from the bright valley, seeking pleasure in the foul, dark city under the ground.

The landscape above was beautiful and safe, yet such people chose the evil.

"Is it true the people starve and die down there?" Marni asked, breaking in on Julyiah's thoughts.

"Yes." Julyiah nodded as she gave Marni a solemn glance. "They listen to the Lying Wind, who tells them it is more fun down there. But when they live there, they become trapped and are unable to see the truth anymore. They grow dissatisfied, quit working, and look for recreation, running out of food and supplies. That is how the Lying Wind works—it deceives the people."

"But my father says there is not enough food for us all anymore," Jonli Driscoll said, "because the farms cannot grow that much. He says there are too many people. He has been down there, and he says that some of the people do not have enough food, even if they work all day."

Julyiah was confused. How strange, she thought, that she was unable to connect these thoughts. The people of Durnee arose in her heart and stood, dirty and in ragged clothing. Their drawn and tired faces disturbed the idea of their plight being their own fault. Their hands tried to reach out to her, kept reaching....

The vision slipped away as abruptly as it had come, but it left Julyiah shaken. Never giving much thought to the people in the Underground before, she wondered if some were indeed suffering through no fault of their own.

"I... do not know, Jonli," Julyiah stammered out. She smoothed her talia and looked with feigned interest at the scenery.

"Are you all right, Miss Hartbrook?" Jonli asked.

Julyiah smiled, trying to regain her composure.

"Were you in a bad place?" Marni asked, her concern evident.

"Yes," Julyiah answered, but she pondered her own answer. "I think so," she added, staring at the Hole and realizing she did not understand what had happened to her at all.

The wagonload of children passed the fork of the canal head and now traveled alongside the South Wall next to the river. The forest lay to the east, straight ahead of them.

"We are almost there!" Tomli seemed excited.

Julyiah swallowed her fears.

Chapter Eight: The Window

♪

The Transport Wagon stopped in front of the South Wall, which towered above them, its plain, flat gray surface glistening in the bright sunlight. The group disembarked, walking towards a small entry building, which jutted out from the thick wall. Out of breath, Julyiah knocked on the metal door, jumping at the loud, hollow sound. Two men answered, dressed in the red uniforms of the Valley Law and armed with swords. They did not smile.

"No one is allowed in here," they barked, drawing their swords. The children's previous chatter stopped. Julyiah's pulse raced. When she had come to see out of the Window as a child, these guards had been just as stern and intimidating. Even now she could remember nothing of that day except the terrifying sentries.

"Uh—" Julyiah began as she fidgeted in her pocket for the permission pass, "we have come to look out the window, and I have—"

"No one looks out the window!" One guard bellowed, frightening the already subdued children, who huddled together behind their shaking teacher.

Julyiah's fumbling fingers latched onto the elusive pass, which stuck inside her pocket as though not wishing to be seen. Yanking on the clay tablet, she whipped it out and gripped it with both hands, holding it up with both hands like a trophy, with Jonar's golden seal of approval flashing in the sun.

One of the guards took the pass and examined it. "Just a moment," he said and disappeared. Meanwhile, the other stood guard, staring at an imaginary spot over the heads of the waiting group.

"This is fun," whispered one of the boys.

"Was that not your father?" Julyiah asked Jonli. "I did not know he was a guard here."

"Yes," Jonli answered with a lift of his eyebrows. "He is a good one too."

"Yes, I can see that," Julyiah agreed, willing herself to stop trembling. *There is nothing to fear. We have permission.*

Jeris Driscoll returned with the pass, smiling. "Welcome!" he said, his personality changed. "I hope I did not frighten you, Miss Hartbrook."

"Oh... well, you were merely doing your job," she said with a sigh of relief.

Driscoll entered the doorway and motioned for the visitors to follow him. Escorted down a long hallway lit with some dimming light stones, they walked into the blackness, which loomed before them. The other guard brought in more light rocks for better visibility, but the shadows prevailed in many corners, causing the children to speculate about what might lurk therein.

Holding a light so they could see, Driscoll went ahead of the group until they arrived in front of an ancient, heavy wooden door that was locked. Pulling out a set of keys, he inserted one into the lock until it clicked. The old door screeched in ominous protest as he tugged it open and pushed it to one side.

They started up some dilapidated stairs, and Julyiah shivered as she attempted to maintain order and a reasonable noise level among the children. Driscoll placed small, newly sun-charged light rocks in special crevices as they ascended. The other guard remained at the rear, so Julyiah knew no children had been left behind.

Upon reaching the top of the stairs, they went into a small, dark room that was empty except for a stone pedestal next to the outermost wall. The guard motioned everyone back from the outer wall, as they drew out their knives and cut away the wax seals from the edges of a large stone in the wall. About an arm's length in both width and height, the stone was set into the wall, but removable. Clasping their hands onto some holds which had been carved into the rock, the guards tugged on the stone, easing it out of place until its weight rested on the sturdy pedestal next to the wall. Light began to leak into the room from the Outside and excitement grew amongst the children.

Before pulling the stone all the way out, the guards stopped a moment, catching their breath. Driscoll pulled out a clay plaque from his pocket. Holding a light rock over it, he began to read: "Long ago our ancestors, the Libreans, came to this fortress..."

The children squirmed and picked at each other's hair and clothes. They had heard the story many times, and fidgeted with impatience as they waited for the adventure to continue.

"And now," Driscoll said, "witness the Devastation of the Lying Wind!"

The guards pulled the stone block all the way out onto the pedestal, leaving a gap all around it. The children crowded around the block to see out, fighting over who would be in front. A crevice the width of a man's hand seemed too small a space for twenty pairs of eyes to peer out at the great unknown, but the taller children moved their bodies aside after a time, allowing the shorter ones to see out of the lower viewing area. A few took one look and turned away. Others fought to keep their spot.

"Take turns, Children," Julyiah ordered. "Do not crowd."

"It is big!" Tomli exclaimed.

"I can see most of that from my house," Lisiya bragged. "We live on a tall hill. We can see what the leaders see."

"Then perhaps you should let someone else have a turn now," Julyiah suggested with a sly smile, knowing Lisiya was as interested in viewing out the window as anyone else. The others ignored Lisiya, knowing she could not have seen that much from anywhere inside the community. Lisiya lingered a while longer before she gave up her spot.

"It is a bunch of dirt," Jonli commented in disappointment. "Is that all there is?"

"Look at those distant mountains," Julyiah suggested, wondering whether they were dry and barren also. She had no desire to look out the window again, but she pictured wide-open meadows and thick forests with wild animals—animals they had never seen but only read about. Perhaps on those distant mountains the children now gazed upon. Yes, was that not green she could see on them in her mind? Or was it gray?

The next moment she was there, wandering among grassy slopes full of wildflowers and surrounded by tall trees—hundreds of trees. And she heard something— Music! It sped through her heart like a running stream. Before Julyiah could think of what was happening, she relished the peaceful symphony within her.

Julyiah's mind jolted her back to what she was doing and the rules she must live by. *What have I done?* A cliff edge appeared in her heart, causing a rush of adrenalin—why, she could fall off any moment! The Lying Wind had gotten to her again—deceived her with pictures of pleasant places.

It must be the open window. Certainly there is air coming through from the Outside....

"How ... long should ... we look?" Julyiah stammered with a questioning glance toward Driscoll. "What about the... Wind?"

"Miss Hartbrook, if people can be tricked by the Lying Wind from inside the wall, why do you worry about hearing it from the Outside?"

Tomli, no! Julyiah tried not to panic since she had anticipated this particular question and had also been counseled by Jonar on exactly what to say.

"We do not ask such questions, Tomli," Julyiah recited the reply she had practiced, "or we ask one of the leaders. They may be able to help you understand. I cannot."

Tomli nodded with a downcast expression and took another turn at the open crevice. Julyiah forced herself not to think about the question or the mountains, and the cliff receded in her heart. She sighed in relief. Would it be that easy after all?

"I think we should close the window now," Driscoll said, looking at Julyiah with a strange quirk to his mouth and one raised eyebrow. She smiled with a question in her eyes, wondering what his look meant.

The children seemed agreeable about leaving. There was nothing much to look at and, other than the size, nothing impressive. It was a windy, dusty desert.

Back outdoors, Julyiah directed the children to the forest, 500 paces farther down Town Road, which ran across the south end of the fortress, curving around the southeastern corner where the forest resided. The children talked more about the mysterious walk through the hall and up the staircase than they did the view out of the window, which must have been a disappointment after what they had imagined. Jonar's wisdom was evident in suggesting they look through it to relieve their curiosity.

Just outside the stone-fenced sheep pasture they walked through, a small clearing opened up that was too rocky for crops. After trying to move the rocks out, the farmers had given up. Grass and flowers grew among the rocks, surrounded by a few tall trees. An irrigation ditch diverted from the river ran through the area like a tiny stream, providing a rare park-like setting in the restricted community.

After eating the meals they brought, the children scampered about, looking at each bright flower and examining pinecones and ferns with glee. They climbed on the larger rocks and pretended to be the heroes they had heard about in Victory Class. Most of the stories were ancient ones from the sacred history books, written by the Libreans in the Pre-Silence time thousands of years before.

"I will kill you," one child pretended, waving an arm in sword-like fashion while posing as an evil Tusknot Knight from the p500's.

"You will not," another child replied. "I have heard the Music on the Breeze, and I will have victory over you!"

The two children staged a mock battle, using arms as swords in lieu of sticks which, being wood, were always confiscated from the grounds.

Julyiah looked on in silent approval. *How nice,* she thought, as she gazed at the forest scene. Thinking how secure it felt to keep the Music on the Breeze in the past where it belonged, she took in a deep breath of the fresh air, glad to be out of the musty confines of the South Wall.

It is like a nightmare is over. Maybe I can finally relax.

♪♪ ♫♫

Two beings stood nearby, watching the scene.

"This is indeed lovely," said one, smiling.

The other was silent.

"She is stabilizing."

"It is temporary."

"I am sure you wish it was," the other returned.

Silence again.

One of them hissed, a black cottony mass billowing out from it in a rush of anger. "She will come my way. There is nothing you can do. They always come."

"This one is different. She will fight to reveal the Secrets and who I really am."

"Fight?" A derisive howl of laughter split the darkness with a hollow sound. "Fight? That one? She cringes in terror whenever she thinks of me or anything frightening."

"She will fight," the other repeated, bright colors skipping around the melodic voice. Each color made an individual sound like a butterfly that could sing. Periodically, the flutters would all stop moving at the same moment to burst forth with a harmonious chord.

The voice that flowed with them was vibrant with life, color, and dynamic Music.

Chapter Nine: Doors

♪

Julyiah was in a festive place later in the day. She had worked past her anxiety, having gotten through the South Window viewing, and now eagerly focused her attention on her upcoming wedding. All afternoon she hummed a familiar music box tune and worked out her invitation list on a wet clay tablet. She saw herself dressed in the beautiful talia her mother had made, with Delwyn by her side... forever. *Sigh.* In a couple of days, her parents would hire a messenger to go around the valley and invite everyone on the list as tradition dictated, though all friends knew of the approaching event.

When Delwyn arrived for dinner, Julyiah rushed to hug and kiss him warmly. "I am so happy Del," she whispered.

"Me too," he replied.

As Julyiah puttered about, checking the chakia stew on the stove and washing a few tinit berries from her window box garden, she chatted about her day with the children, and how her fears all seemed to be for nothing. As she talked, the wide spaces and thick forests she had seen kept returning to mind as though in response to her bright mood.

Had she been in a good place all along? Why had she considered it wrong? Oh yes, she had also heard Music on the Breeze... or perhaps she only thought she did. Whether it was bad or not, she did not want to think about it. The window viewing was over and Tomli's questions laid to rest. Time to get on with her life and enjoy it.

Julyiah paused in her one-sided conversation and turned toward Delwyn. In her delightful mood, she had missed the distraction that was now so apparent on his face. Worry lines scrunched his forehead as he gazed out the window.

"Where are you?" she asked pointedly, hands on hips and a voice that indicated only the truth was acceptable.

Delwyn gave her a weak smile and examined his hands, picking at a blister on his thumb before looking outside again. "I was working at Keenar's today," he said, "and got into trouble."

"Trouble?" Julyiah's eyes grew wide.

"Not with Keenar or the Law or anything like that," he laughed, rising to face her. "I mean, I was dreaming of something I should not have been. Do you want me to lift that pot?" he asked, interrupting himself when he saw her about to move the chakasia onto the table.

"Yes, please," she replied, fetching the butter for her bread from the cold box. She noticed the box was not cold enough and made a mental note to chill the warming stone. Focusing on the table, she pursed her lips to think about what she might have forgotten. Bowls… Utensils… *Napkins!*

Julyiah rushed to retrieve some soft, folded Teka leaves from the cupboard. The tough but pliant leaves grew frayed and absorbent after many other uses and became good for wiping one's hands. She gave one to Delwyn, keeping another for herself.

"I should not talk about what I saw today." Delwyn's facial lines deepened. He looked around as though someone else might hear and focused on the thumb blister again. "I dreamed of horses and wide open spaces."

Julyiah's pulse raced at his words. She put the final touches on the table and sat down. *Delwyn saw open places today too?*

In her heart, Julyiah saw something odd—a closed door in front of her. *What is this door?*

"We should be thankful," Delwyn said, and they both sang a thankful music box tune while holding hands and smiling at each other across the table.

"I suggest we eat before it gets cold," Julyiah said when the song was over. She wondered what was behind the door. Reaching out in her heart to open it, she pulled back, afraid.

After they began eating Julyiah asked in as casual a tone as she could, "What did it look like?"

Delwyn's eyes rose from his buttered bread to focus on Julyiah. "Did what look like?" His gaze turned back to his food. "This is good. What kind is it?"

Flattered at the compliment, Julyiah allowed herself to be diverted from her mission. "It is an herb bread," she grinned. "The herbs are my secret."

"I am glad you learned to cook, and did not spend all your growing up years outside," he chuckled. Delwyn's countenance brightened as he ate. Continuing to discuss the food with enthusiasm, he pressed her concerning her secret herbs.

Julyiah wanted to go back to the previous topic but wondered how she could do that without dampening his spirits again. Finding no way to change the subject, she feared too obvious an approach. After they finished eating, the closed door loomed before her again.

"Was that petkin in the chakasia?" Delwyn asked as he helped to clean up the blue clay dishes and put away the leftovers. "I like that extra spiciness." Delwyn folded the bread inside a greased Teka leaf, tied it shut with a waxed string, and headed for the cold box. He opened the door on the box and felt the smooth, thigh-sized rock that lay at the bottom of the stone structure. "You need to cool your warming stone," he commented.

"I know," Julyiah said. "Del?" Somehow, she had to talk about what he had seen. "What were you dreaming of today?"

Delwyn looked at her strangely and frowned as he poured water into a metal washing tub. "I told you... I should not talk about it. The subject puts me in a bad place." He stared at the blue bowl in his hand, and scrubbed at a tough spot with a leaf-wrapped stone.

"I am sorry," Julyiah said, reaching to turn his shoulder towards her. "It is just that I was dreaming of open spaces today too, and I wanted to know if... if somehow we were in the same place." She was in front of the door in her heart again and it was still shut, but her hand rested on the knob.

Delwyn searched her face as though he might read there what she had seen. Then he looked back to the dish he was washing. "I see," he muttered.

After two more dishes passed through his hands, Julyiah could wait no longer. "Do you not... I mean… are you not curious about why we were in similar places?" She dried dishes with new vigor, wishing she could force him to speak. Her hand wanted to turn the doorknob she kept seeing, but she resisted.

Silence followed except for the clank of dishes. "Yes, I am curious," Delwyn said. "I am also sorry to be a cause of frustration to you, but do you think we should talk about this? Thinking about open places has caused you problems—why do you want to pursue the subject? And how many times has Zuriel warned us about such things? He is not merely a friend, you know."

Julyiah bit her lower lip. "Yes, I know. He is a wise leader." She tilted her head to the side and wandered back to the table, trying to understand why she wanted to share her experience with him.

Delwyn dumped out the water into the stone sink where it drained noisily down through a metal pipe to the outside of the house. Julyiah watched him stare at the sink a moment before nodding his head. "All right."

Taking her hand, Delwyn led her over to some reed chairs near the fireplace built out of rocks. The warming stones inside had captured the heat of the few pieces of coal Julyiah had been cooking with, and the warmth felt good as the approaching darkness brought a spring chill into the air. Sunset came early each day, as the sun slipped behind the wall.

Delwyn studied his blister while Julyiah waited, and he looked up at her with a thoughtful purse of his lips. "I was in the pasture on Keenar Hill, exercising the boss's new colt Rally, while the other horses were out working. As Rally ran around me on the line, I became aware of beauty all around me—like the birds in

Keenar's two oak trees." Delwyn's eyes glittered with interest. "It was as though this entire area opened up. There was... well, I know this sounds terrible, but there were no walls! And the fields were covered with beautiful flowers instead of crops.

"There were horses—" Delwyn's face lit up as he moved his calloused hands through the air to illustrate. "Hundreds of horses were running through huge pastures and meadows. There was no horse limit like we have now because of all the space and grasses.

"You would have loved it, Julyiah." Delwyn gazed at her tenderly. "There were all kinds and colors of horses and so many baby ones, running... so much room...." Delwyn's voice drifted off, and Julyiah saw with no little shock that he was on the verge of weeping.

The two sat in silence while Delwyn regained his composure. Afraid to speak as she sorted her own thoughts, Julyiah stared at the warming stones, finding colorful marks and fine lines on which to concentrate.

"What open place did you see?" Delwyn asked.

Julyiah bit her lip as she realized it was her turn. She told him of her open meadows and forests full of trees and streams. She explained how she somehow saw these things in the mountains when looking out the South Window. Delwyn did not comment, but his eyes told her of his intense interest.

"What does it mean?" Julyiah asked. *And what is this door in my heart?* She tried to bore a hole in it with her heart's eyes.

Delwyn stared at a painting done by Julyiah's father years ago of the community, and she was not certain he had even heard her. Her father had painted flowers in the fields instead of vegetables.

"Julyiah, was there anything else in what you saw?" Delwyn asked, still gazing at the painting. "Was there anything rather... significant?"

She knew there was. Music had come on the Breeze, but she had not been willing to mention that part—not yet.

"Well... yes..."

"What was it?" Delwyn prompted again. "Go ahead. You can tell me."

"You... will not tell anyone, will you?" Julyiah hesitated, biting her lip, while already knowing she could trust him. Yesterday's pit yawned below her, the air in it wafting upward with a foul stench.

"Of course not, darling girl." Delwyn took her hand in an encouraging grasp, and the vision of the pit faded out of her sight. The door resurfaced instead, and she started to turn the knob.

"I heard Music—I mean, in my heart," Julyiah said, not daring to look at his face lest she see disapproval. She concentrated on the plant in the kitchen window of her tiny house to steady her nerves.

He did not say anything right away, and with her secret out she feared his lack of response. Was it a bad idea discussing such things, even though they had such a strong mutual trust? She ventured to look at him, but his face was unreadable.

"You will not think I am terrible, will you?" she pleaded. "I could not help it. The Music just... happened, and I tried not to feel happy in the openness, but it was so beautiful! At first, I thought I was merely in a good place, because I was not trying to hear Music on the Breeze. And it was only in my heart—not something I heard with my ears." Julyiah frowned at that thought. "At least I do not think I heard it with my ears."

"You are not terrible," Delwyn said, pulling her hair back and gazing into her face. "How could anyone think such an honest heart terrible?"

Delwyn's reassuring smile helped Julyiah to relax. "I felt drawn to enjoy the beautiful scenes, colors, and sounds, but I was concerned about the Lying Wind coming through the window. Tomli asked another one of those strange questions. What do you think, Del? Do I need to ignore all of this and purge my heart of these pictures?"

He frowned and looked away. "The leaders would say you should."

Julyiah ignored the pit that came back to mind. "But Tomli's questions seem so valid," she said, "and I could not help wondering—how could hearing the Music on the Breeze be wrong? Our ancestors considered the experience to be most sacred. Why do we not want to hear the Music in this way? That is how the Voice sang the truth in the old days."

Julyiah's hand reached out to turn the knob on the door in her heart. She noticed there was a tiny dent in the metal and could feel it with her fingers when she touched it.

A loud pounding on the door startled her, and Julyiah jumped as she struggled with which door was vibrating with someone's fist. Gasping, she realized there was someone knocking on the front door of her house. *The leaders! What if they found out what we were discussing?*

Julyiah shuddered with dread.

Chapter Ten: The Problem

♪

"It is probably my mother," Julyiah said, trying to sound encouraging as she got up to open the door. Her parents lived near her and often stopped by. However, her legs shook as she stood in the entry a moment, wishing she did not have to respond to the knock.

Julyiah opened her front door, her heart squeezing with panic when she recognized the red uniform and expressionless face of Menila, Jonar's personal messenger. The gold insignia on the shoulder of the man's dekat indicated his authority. Julyiah had heard stories about the Valley Law storming people's houses when they were a threat to the community.

Was she dreaming? *They could not know what we were discussing*, she assured herself, swallowing her fears. Collecting her thoughts back in order with difficulty, she stared at the man, trembling.

"Julyiah Hartbrook?" he questioned in a business-like tone.

Why was Menila here, and why did he speak to her in this official manner?

"Y-yes?"

"Jonar the Most Respected requests your presence. Immediately."

Julyiah's heart dropped like a lead ball to the floor, and she felt unable to breathe. The pit was below her, and her heart rolled toward it.

"Why?" Delwyn asked. He had jumped up at the sight of Menila and hurried to her side, putting his arm around her protectively.

Menila eyed Delwyn coldly. Julyiah knew the man had never liked Delwyn, but she had the right to ask why she was being summoned. It should not be considered improper.

"They did not say," Menila responded, looking at Julyiah alone, as though he need not concern himself with her companion.

"They?" Julyiah asked, trying not to gasp it out. "Can... can I bring Delwyn along?" Her eyes turned toward Delwyn's and his concerned gaze told her he was there for her.

"It is permitted," the man replied, still not looking at Delwyn. "But you are the only one that is requested."

"I am coming," Julyiah blurted out, interrupting him. Julyiah grabbed her woolen cape, took Delwyn's hand, and followed the messenger as he turned to head toward the North Wall. Jonar's office was not far away.

Main Street was bustling with early evening activity and all the horses in town were in use, pulling small carriages full of people or products up and down the thoroughfare. The food market, household goods store, and farming shop were lit up with light rocks—some bright yellow and others the dimmer green shade or faint blue. The colorful hues together with the friendly chatter of shoppers and the busy clop of horses' hooves wove a festive picture.

The North Wall itself added to the gaiety, displaying light rocks of its own—huge stones, as big as a carriage. They had soaked in the lengthening daylight of spring and shone brighter as the sky darkened. Glimmering throughout the entire valley—both in the wall and in the houses—light rocks shone with a cheerful glow. The boathouse to the east and the Hole to the southwest radiated greater brightness due to large light rocks. In a little while, the yellow would dim to the *green fade* stage for the night. During the long summer days, the sun-charged rocks took too long to fade to green so they were covered with screens to help the outdoor animals and plants go through their proper cycles.

Menila led Julyiah and Delwyn toward the brightest part of the wall. The leaders could afford the best in light rocks—the clear ones with none of the gray smokiness of the lower grades. These shone bright white for hours and were inset into the sides of the North Wall to the keep the sacred area well lit. The biggest one was just outside the Listening Hall itself so that one could visit at any time and feel the welcome glow of light.

The three walked down the noisy street in a silence justified by the activity around them. Julyiah and Delwyn followed the red uniform inside the Listening Hall and walked past the many chairs and other wooden objects that Julyiah always admired. For once, however, she did not give them a glance but stared ahead at the door to Jonar's office.

They, the man had said. Her heart ached to know who *they* were. Time froze as Menila knocked on the door. Julyiah stared at the doorknob. Was this the one she had seen in her heart? She watched in anticipation as the metal knob was turned and the door was opened, revealing the contents of the room.

Julyiah gripped Delwyn's hand tighter as they stepped into Jonar's office, feeling as though they were entering a dream. She surveyed the room's occupants in astonishment. Leaders Jonar and Cisco were often in Jonar's office, but the presence of Jeris Driscoll and Tomis Tarni sent prickles of anxiety skittering through her. The conversation in the room died out as the couple came in, and the men stared at Julyiah and Delwyn with polite smiles.

"Hello, Julyiah," Jonar said with a stiff, enigmatic expression. He offered her a chair next to his own. Delwyn remained standing, close to Julyiah's chair.

"Hello, Delwyn," Jonar greeted. "Where are you folks today?"

"Nice place," they both mumbled in polite reply. Julyiah thought how nothing could be further from the truth. With a wry twist to her mouth, she considered her true heart position—hanging over a dark, smelly pit, clinging to the edge for her very life. The stuffy air rose in a smothering blanket of gloom. She could not tell what she was hanging on to, but it felt thin and flimsy. The widespread tension in the room told her the upcoming conversation would not be pleasant.

"You went to the South Window today," Jonar said, his tone inscrutable. "Tomli asked another question."

Is that what they are worried about? Julyiah's eyes darted around the room at the men, her pulse rising until she thought her heart would bounce right out of her chest. "I told him exactly what you said to tell him," Julyiah responded with as much dignity as she could muster, "that we should not ask such questions." Julyiah gulped down the anxiety that rose in her throat as she spoke. She could not think of anything that Jonar or the others could be upset about. She had responded to Tomli the way Jonar had told her to.

"Yes, you told him correctly." Jonar nodded with a fatherly smile. "Please remain calm."

Julyiah did not think she had shown any signs of agitation, but she swallowed a few times and attempted to show more confidence than she felt. Cisco smiled at her, but Tarni and Driscoll did not. They would not look at her and studied the floor. Adrenaline shot through her as Julyiah realized she was considered the cause of some unknown blunder.

"Then what..." Julyiah coughed as she choked out her words. Delwyn patted her shoulder and squeezed. "I am ... sorry." Julyiah stammered. "I do not know why I am so nervous."

But I do know why....

Jonar chuckled. "We shall have some tea." He rang a little bell on his desk and a blue-uniformed keeper appeared in the side doorway. "Herbal tea all around," Jonar ordered, without looking up. "Something calming."

Is he saying the others are also nervous? Julyiah wondered as she smiled with some hesitance at Jonar. Maybe the issue was not regarding something she had done. Maybe it was someone else's error.

Having something hot to drink did have a tranquilizing effect on her, and Julyiah exchanged smiles with Jeris Driscoll. Tomis Tarni still looked aloof and sullen. He ran his hand over his balding head and gaunt face over and over, as though trying to wipe away an undesirable substance.

"Is that better?" Jonar continued in a soothing voice after the tea had been distributed. Julyiah felt like Jonar was her closest friend in the room other than Delwyn. *Thank goodness Jonar is in such a place of authority!* She sipped the tea, grateful to have something to occupy herself.

Jonar focused on Julyiah again. "Tomli asked a question, Julyiah. What was it?"

"The question..." Julyiah's mind raced as she tried to remember. "Um... he asked why the Lying Wind... no... why we worried about the, uh, why we worried about the open window..." Julyiah's voice rose as she frantically sought a better response to the question. "Oh... it was something about the Lying Wind, and I told him he should not ask such questions." Her hands shook as she tried to steady her tea.

"All right, Julyiah," Jonar said, soothing her with his handsome smile. "We understand that you responded well. Jeris here can testify to that, I believe."

Testify? What did I do? Julyiah glanced at Jeris Driscoll, who whispered something to Cisco. Cisco nodded to Driscoll in reply.

"Why did Tomli ask the question, Julyiah?" Jonar interrupted her desperate attempt to understand what she might have done. The leader set his hand-painted cup on his desk, watching her as though expecting an immediate response. Yet, how would she know why the boy asked the question? Was it not Tomli's imagination?

"Julyiah?" Jonar's looked at her with an intensity she did not like. He was no longer smiling. "Can you tell us why Tomli asked the question?"

"No," Julyiah answered.

The silence that followed was filled with tension, until a loud voice exploded from the other end of the room. "It was because of what she said!" An enraged Tarni vaulted out of his seat, sending the chair sliding in screeching protest. He stepped forward and pointed straight at Julyiah. Delwyn instinctively moved in front of her as her cup rattled on the saucer in her shaking hand. She cowered, feeling helpless under Tarni's glare.

"Stop!" Jonar roared, spinning around and pointing to Tarni's chair. Tarni showed some reluctance as he went back, righted the chair and sat, mumbling. He again wiped his face and head with nervous hands. Julyiah had the feeling that this was not the first time Jonar had dealt with his outbursts. Tremendous apprehension surged back upon the group while Julyiah set her cup and saucer on a table, quite sure she could no longer hold it without spilling the contents.

A weighty silence engulfed the room as Jonar dropped back into thought. He smiled at Julyiah, but she continued to tremble, unable to control her quivering lips.

Jonar walked around the room with two fingers on his chin, as though indicating careful thought. "You have always been an honest person, Julyiah, and I believe from your reactions tonight, you know nothing of what you have done. It was simply an oversight, a blunder."

Jonar's soothing voice helped Julyiah relax. Whatever the "error" might be, Jonar realized it was done in ignorance. How thankful she was that Jonar was in charge!

"I was wondering..." Delwyn broke in at a pause in Jonar's dissertation with no little irritation in his tone. "What exactly is Julyiah accused of?"

"Accused?" Cisco asked, leaning forward in his chair with a sudden frown. "There is no accusation here. Unless there should be?"

"Well, it sounds like an accusation to me," Delwyn insisted. "Does it to anyone else?"

Tarni's fierce-looking face turned red with anger. "If no one else will accuse her, I will!" He stood again. The whole room followed suit except for Julyiah. Voices rose in argument, but she felt weakness washing over her, begging for an outlet. Brushing a tear from her eye, she took Delwyn's hand when he offered it.

"Men, please sit down, and let me explain everything to Julyiah," Jonar said, "before we decide what should be done."

What should be <u>done</u>? Julyiah's eye twitched, and she tugged on her hair. When would they get to the point so she could go home, curl up in bed, and cry?

"Julyiah," Jonar said, "Tomis brought his son in today, and the boy said he asked you some questions which you seemed unsure about. It is the reason for Tomli's questions that concern us." Jonar turned to Driscoll. "Jeris, please remind Julyiah of her statement at the Window viewing."

Driscoll's eyes grew wide. "She said, 'How long should we look?' and 'What about the Wind?' But I did not see anything wrong..."

"Of course you did not," Jonar responded. "It is easy to miss subtle mistakes; that is how clever the Lying Wind can be. Jeris, what did she say before that?"

Driscoll swallowed and he gave Julyiah an apologetic look. "She said, 'Look at those distant mountains.'"

An enraged voice exploded across the room again. "That was it! That was the one that destroyed him!" Tarni marched over to Julyiah, pointing a finger held at arm's length, his face distorted with rage.

"Tomli told me he would not have been interested in the Outside at all if it had not been for her statement." Tarni jerked his pointing finger several times on the word *her*. "Tomli came home jabbering about those mountains, all excited about what might be out there. I tried to tell him, 'No, Tomli! That is the Lying Wind—it makes you think bad things are good.' And it is all her fault." His pointing finger jabbed the air in front of Julyiah's nose. *"IT IS HER FAULT!"*

Julyiah could not breathe well. The room began to spin, the pit gaping below her. The smell was terrible, choking her. She could not tell where she was—in a dream, in her heart, or in the physical world. A door opened in her heart as though it was a way to escape, but something terrifying lurked there. She tried to shut the door; it would not budge.

Delwyn looked far away from her. He frowned at her, as though he could not believe she had done this terrible thing— that she had seen beauty on the Outside and had encouraged the children to look at it.

The flimsy thing she held on to above the pit gave way, and she felt herself sliding. Nausea threatened to make her sick, right there in front of everyone. The room closed in on her and grew darker as she started falling ... falling into the pit.

Was it the Silent Pit? It did not matter anymore, because at last her mind could rest, and her troubled heart would be at peace.

Chapter Eleven: Safety

♪

Julyiah lay awake in the hanging reed bed at her parents' house, wishing she had not agreed to spend the night. She dreaded talking to anyone and would rather have stayed in her own home. Trying to forget what had happened the evening before, she studied the stones in the walls, noticing the varied colors and patterns and watching the morning sunlight make interesting shadows on them as it streamed in through the window.

One corner of the room contained built-in stone shelves, where three flat rocks had been cemented in between other rocks on a somewhat level plane. Decorations sat on the shelves—little dolls Livi had made for Julyiah when she was a child and hardened clay animals that her father had made. How she loved to play with the dolls and toy animals outside in the dirt with her friends. Her favorite activity was to put the smallest doll on a toy horse and cause the horse to run around and jump over rocks.

Hushed voices in the next room told her that Livi had someone visiting. From the sound of the childlike voice, Julyiah assumed it was one of Livi's sewing students. Relieved, Julyiah hoped this would give her more time to herself.

As she rose to dress, Julyiah's thoughts rushed back to the previous evening with distressing speed. Again she tried to analyze Tarni's severity, Jonar's unusual behavior, and Delwyn's quizzical look before the room went black. Alternately blaming and defending herself over her so-called "mistake," she wondered how she could have known what to say or do at the Window Viewing that she had not done. She had asked Jonar ahead of time. If it was so important to say things exactly right, it seemed to her that one of the leaders should have done all the talking. But her biggest question was—*had* she made such a dreadful mistake?

On top of this confusion, the passage from Silia kept returning to mind: *The One sends Music, and the Voice sings the truth on the Breeze.* That was what she needed the most right now—truth. But she must not think about truth coming on the Breeze because trouble always rose within her heart at the thought.

Julyiah picked up her brush and checked her hair in the mirror. Taunting her even now, the closed door flashed in her mind.

That horrible door! Her experience in Jonar's office related to whatever she had seen behind that door, but she did not understand how. Her cliff nightmares threatened to return whenever it appeared in her heart again, and she was certain some kind of great height waited to terrorize her should she open the door.

The door would not shut the night before when she so desperately wanted to close it, but this morning it remained latched, hiding its secret. She clearly saw a brass handle and knew she could turn it if she wanted to. Something terrifying lurked behind that door—like standing on a high cliff that dropped off into an abyss. Whatever it was she did not want to see it again.

A loud knock stopped the conversation Livi was having with the child in the next room. Startled from her thoughts, Julyiah's heart swelled at Delwyn's voice.

"Hello, Del, come in," Livi greeted in a soft voice. "I am afraid Julyiah is not awake …."

Julyiah burst into the room, surprising everyone. Delwyn had left her the night before, saying he would come and take her to the Hall at the tenth hour. Livi and Harol generally went to a later meeting.

Julyiah headed straight for Delwyn, intending to leave with him. "But, you have not eaten," Livi complained as her kind eyes narrowed into a motherly warning for her daughter.

"Sorry, Mother, we will be late if I eat," Julyiah said.

"Sorry, Mother," Delwyn repeated, grinning and bringing a smile to Livi's face. The couple backed toward the doorway, nodding at the unfamiliar visitor.

♫

"Who was that girl?" Delwyn asked Julyiah, as they stepped outside and headed down the stone walkway toward the road. "She looked about twelve years old."

Julyiah squinted in the bright sunlight, shading her eyes so she could see Delwyn's face. "Probably one of Mother's sewing students. Why?"

"She must be from the Underground."

"Why would she be up here?"

"I do not know. But she looked Underground to me—all dirty and in a torn talia..."

"Was she? I did not notice." The girl in her mother's kitchen was the last thing on Julyiah's mind, and she responded to Delwyn's curiosity with irritation. Was he not worried about her after last night? Why had he not kissed her just now? He was eager to go to the Hall early—did he feel she needed more teaching from the leaders to avoid any more "mistakes"? Julyiah did not mind so much making a mistake as not knowing how to prevent it from happening again.

"Where are you today?" Delwyn asked her, searching her eyes with concern in his.

He does look worried. Julyiah felt a little better. "In a dark tunnel with many turns," she responded with honesty. "Where are you?"

"In a nice place. I thought we could hear Zuriel this morning and maybe come back for Delegar this evening. What do you think?"

Again, that eagerness to get her to the meetings. She should be eager also to hear the truth—should she not? "Whatever you think is best," she mumbled, staring at the dusty road and feeling alone in her confusion. *We need rain*, she mused as they approached a group of people waiting outside the Listening Hall.

Two Valley Law guards stood one on either side of the thick oak door that led into the Listening Hall. When the group of people grew in number, one of the guards knocked on the door and listened for a response. When there was a return knock, he nodded at the other guard, and they pulled on the heavy door to open it for those who had gathered outside. Entering the foyer, the people waited until a Door Keeper herded them to one side of the small room. Other visitors arrived until the room was full, and the outside guards shut the door.

A keeper opened a music box that rested inside an alcove, and all the people quieted down to wait for the safety check. When the room grew still except for the tune that came out of the box, the keeper held up one hand and turned it from side to side, checking for air movement. Nodding with satisfaction, he waited until the song ended before opening the door that led into the Listening Hall. "All is safe," he announced to the keeper who stood there.

The tenth hour listeners gathered in the Hall, trying to find the better of the one hundred stone seats that were not yet taken. Everyone dropped sokens in a leader's named box as they walked by. Since he was speaking, Leader Zuriel's box was filling up, but Leader Jonar's box was larger because he was the most popular speaker.

Delwyn took Julyiah's hand and led her toward the front. As they sat down, Julyiah began to sense the peace she often felt in the Listening Hall. The largest, most intricately carved music box was open, playing a familiar tune—one that was often played. The box showed wear in some places from years of use, and it had been repaired more than once. The music from this box reminded the listeners of the time long ago when the One sent His Voice to die, to save the people from Silence.

Julyiah had heard the Voice singing words from the books—in her heart. It was the most wonderful experience she had ever known. Many people told of these rare moments when the Voice sang to them through the words of the books. However, when someone said they heard something from the Voice that was not in the books, the leaders wanted to know so they could make sure it was not the Lying Wind. They taught the people that they knew best what the Voice meant to say to an individual, but Julyiah did not always tell them what she heard. She could see their point, but it meant too much to her, and sometimes she did not think they understood everything about someone else's personal songs.

Commotion arose near the foyer, grabbing Julyiah's attention. A Door Keeper rushed into the room and slammed the foyer door.

"Safety alert!" he cried just as the next group of listeners should have been admitted into the Listening Hall. A communal intake of breath rose from those who were seated, and some huddled together, glancing around fearfully, looking for any air movement.

Valley Law Guards rushed in from a side room. "Do not panic!" one called out as someone jumped up to run out of the room. The guards halted this person. "Please do not move around. We will call for Leader Jonar."

Those inside the foyer were not allowed to enter the Listening Hall while Jonar came from his office. When he arrived, several people looked relieved. They trusted that he would know whether or not the Lying Wind had been able to get through the safety zone. Jonar went into the foyer and shut the door while everyone remained still to prevent the air from shifting around them.

While they waited, one of Tomli's questions flashed in Julyiah's mind. *Miss Hartbrook, if people can be tricked by the Lying Wind from inside the wall, why do you worry about hearing it from the Outside?* Good question, Julyiah thought as her brow bunched in thought.

Jonar came back out of the foyer and stopped in the middle of the Listening Hall, raising one hand in the air in order to check the main listening area.

"It is safe," Jonar said, lowering his hand and smiling. Many let out a sigh of relief, and conversations resumed.

♪ ♪

Jonar continued to smile as he left the Listening Hall, but not because it was "safe." He shook his head, smiling with lips pressed together. The people were ridiculous! Never would he understand what the others were afraid of, but he would not say anything. The idea of the Lying Wind invading their air space was all nonsense, but as long as the people thought he had special knowledge regarding air safety, Jonar would continue to oblige them. He was the wisest person in the community, and he knew best. Making decisions did not bother him.

As he walked back into his office, Jonar asked Menila to get him a cup of herbal tea and some bread. The music boxes played in the Hall next to his office as he gazed out the window a moment, looking over the valley.

Perfect, Jonar thought. The gathering clouds outside had arrived as he had hoped, and a thrill of expectancy shot through him. This was the ideal day to enact his plan.

Chapter Twelve: The Books

♪

When Zuriel walked in precisely at the tenth hour, a keeper rose, closed the music box, and returned to his seat.

"We shall hear from the *Book of Silia,* passages twenty-four and thirty-four," Zuriel announced as he took a dignified stance in the center of the group.

All eyes turned toward another keeper who stood by a row of wooden pedestals with books on top. Moving toward one book, he opened it and sang the words from the book along with the tune coming from the box. "Who can capture Music? Who can say it is over here, or over there? For it comes when the One wills and does not conform to the wishes of man."

The keeper turned a few pages and continued singing. "What can compare to Music? Its sound travels from the rocks to the highlands, from the river to the mountains, from the valley to the sea."

When the music stopped, the keeper closed the box and opened another one. The melody filled the room, and Zuriel motioned for everyone to stand and sing along with the familiar song. When the song ended, the keeper shut the box and the people sat down again.

"Today we will study our music boxes. The Book Keeper has read about how genuine Music travels. Note that the first place from which it travels are the rocks. As you all know, Music was recorded on sound rocks before it was placed in these boxes. When light hits the rocks, the Music releases for us to hear. In the same way, this passage shows how Music travels *from* the rocks to other places. It does not come initially from some other place but must *first* come from the rocks.

"Even though music boxes were made four hundred years ago by our Librean ancestors, we know that this passage was prophetic, telling of the time that Music would eventually be recorded on the rocks. Obedient to the sacred *Book of Silia*, they recorded the true Music.

"In the first passage, Silia says, *Who can capture Music? Who can say it is over here or over there?* This should forever clear up any misconceptions that Music can be heard from another place than from the rocks. This makes it clear that man cannot say the Music might come from somewhere other than the rocks, for it was established where it would come from in the twenty-fourth passage. It comes *from the rocks.* Now let us hear another passage."

While the Book Keeper stepped over to another book, Julyiah puzzled over Zuriel's words. The passages did not seem to say what Zuriel said they did. She could not help feeling that the recorded music boxes themselves were an attempt to "capture" Music—even to control it. To use the passage to determine how Music travels only from rocks to other natural places was surely stretching the interpretation quite a bit.

Uncertain about her thoughts, Julyiah looked at Delwyn to see if he was bothered too, but his face showed a tolerant, bored expression.

"The eleventh passage of Ornae."

The keeper responded to the callout and read: "The foundation of Music will be set as in stone; it will be unchangeable."

Zuriel looked out at the group before him and smiled. "This, of course, is our primary guide. After the Libreans had heard everything they needed to hear from the Music on the Breeze, they realized that Music should be set in rock for all time, thus eliminating the error that might occur from man trying to hear it on the Breeze. What we have right now is *unchangeable*. Also, notice the passage speaks of a future time. These words are also prophetic. It is wonderful that we can now understand the only safe place to hear Music."

This also eliminates the idea of hearing any genuine truth directly from the One, Julyiah pondered. Was Zuriel saying an individual should no longer hear Music in their hearts either? This bothered her a great deal, since hearing the Voice's song in her heart was sacred to her.

Julyiah recalled the passage saying "set *as* in stone" not "set in stone," so the stone was surely a symbol of something that is unchangeable, not a final resting place for Music. Why had she never noticed this kind of issue before? Was she the only person in the room who felt this way?

The One sends Music, and the Voice sings the truth on the Breeze. The passage she had read the day before ran through her mind again. She pursed her lips, wanting to know the truth.

♪ ♪

Jonar sat at his polished wooden desk, admiring the fine craftsmanship evident in the golden hues reflecting from the light of his oil lamp. Menila had taken the office light rocks outside, insisting that the approaching storm would severely limit the sun-charging that day. He said all rocks should be put outside as soon as possible to take in all available rays and gave Jonar the oil lamp as a temporary light.

Standing, Jonar walked over to the tall glass case in one corner of his office. Inside were several volumes of ancient manuscripts, some encased by themselves due to their antiquity. Removing one, he looked at the gold-engraved leather cover which read, *The Refuge, by Jon.*

"One of the lesser ones," Jonar assured himself. "And there is another copy of it." He brought *The Refuge* over to his desk and laid it next to the lamp. Sitting down, he opened the book with care, noting the wonderful quality of paper that was available in the old days—such a rare commodity now. He began reading:

Gwenla arranged the books on the table before her, grateful there had still been some furniture in the fortress when they arrived so many years before. They had created their own little world inside the walls, with government, business, farms, and homes.

She was growing old—old, even for her. Gwenla examined the multitude of wrinkles on her hands and sighed. It was time. For the past ten years, she had been training a young man to replace her as Keeper of the Books. The position was not as powerful now— not since she had distributed her authority among the various officials of government. Still, the people must respect the chosen Keeper of the Books as well—a position as high as any official.

Gwenla pulled the bell rope by her side, and a white-robed servant appeared. "Destar, please tell Jon that I request his presence." A hundred creases lined her face when Gwenla smiled at the servant.

Destar's heart leaped as he rushed out the door and ran toward Jon's house. As Gwenla's most trusted servant and friend, Destar knew what she was planning. He had feared her frail body would not linger until she passed on her secrets.

"Today is the day," he marveled. Destar rounded the corner of the dirt road and strode up the steps to Jon's thin wooden door. He struck it loudly with the palm of his hand. "Jon," he cried as the door opened, "she wants you now."

Jon dashed down the steps, not waiting for his friend Destar. He had been training for a long time and tried to contain his excitement. Only Gwenla had the special information to pass on to him. Even though the morning was cool, he was perspiring by the time he arrived.

At Gwenla's door, Jon knocked lightly and paused a moment before opening it. Stepping inside, he felt the room was darker and colder than it should be. Something was wrong.

"What is happening here?" he asked.

A familiar face looked at Jon from the side of Gwenla's bed.

"I am sorry. She is dead."

Jon's gaze moved toward the books on the table. He was glad that Gwenla had given him her secret writings before she died, but although she told him to hide them, she had never explained them to him. Sorrow filled his heart as he sank into a chair.

A familiar face, Jonar read again. Yes, how familiar it would be to people even now—not the face, but the name. A gust of wind blew through his open window and scattered a few papers across his desk as fear rose within him. His anxiety was not due to the breeze but because of the words he saw before him. Examining the writing in the book, he noted the skillful manner in which something had been erased and something else written in. The writing still looked a little different from the rest. That handwriting had always bothered him, ever since he had first been told by his father, Donvan Suntar, about the Secrets of Gwenla.

"No one must ever know," Donvan had warned his son Jonar. "We have always kept at least one of the family in leadership to protect the Secrets. You see why it is so important."

"Yes," Jonar had said, shocked at the implications of the matter, but understanding his father's strong concern. "Yes, I see—"

And Jonar saw now. There had not been much of a threat before, but the issue with Julyiah might bring more intense inspection and study of the books. Whenever someone went astray there was always more focus on study and truth.

Julyiah had been a promising student last summer. Her complete willingness to follow was refreshing, as well as her open, pure honesty. But her honesty also made her ask questions. Jonar raised one eyebrow in frustration. He had seen it before. She would be a threat.

Jonar looked again at the rewritten passage before him and shivered in the breezy coolness creeping through his window. No one must ever know....

♪ ... ♪♫

"Did you see that?" the murky cloud asked the small gray wisp of smoke next to him. "He felt my presence."

"Yes, I saw it," muttered the smaller one, whirling himself in circles for amusement.

"You are jealous of my abilities," Murk said in a smug tone. "Admit it. Lord Zebul will be pleased when he hears how well I have done."

"You plan to tell him?" Gray asked in surprise, halting his movement. "What if he does not like how close you got to the man?"

"He will not be angry with me," Murk replied, puffing himself into a taller shape, "because Jonar is doing what the master wanted. The master will be happy with me, not angry."

"So you say," said the little one, going back to his circling motion. "But when a person suspects we are involved, they might realize what they are doing and stop their evil actions."

"Jonar does not know we exist. I doubt he cares if we do."

"Still, I would not take such a chance. Lord Zebul does not like it when we do things without his permission. And he could blow you into oblivion with a single breath. Or add your mass to his."

"That is why you will never grow larger," Murk said indignantly. "You understand nothing."

♪♪♪

In a cabin on the other side of Victory Valley, an old man took one of his books off of the stand and shuffled over to a chair by his stove. He opened to the beginning and read a well-loved passage, holding the book close to his light rock.

The old man closed the volume and put it back in the case with care. He knew what a treasure he had. No one else in the community had a personal copy of a Sacred Book. But he was getting old, and his son had no appreciation for books. Who should inherit the priceless item when he was gone?

Chapter Thirteen: Conflict

♪

When Zuriel finished his teaching, one of the leaders stepped forward. As he did, a keeper opened a music box again.

"Go to the music cells!" the man proclaimed in an encouraging voice. Julyiah recognized the familiar end to a meeting.

"Go and feed the hungry, as did Jeneniah of old."

"Go and clothe the poor, as did Dediakah."

Julyiah recalled her experience at the Hole. *We never actually do these things.*

"Go with joy, for those in a good place have heard Music."

The people slowly filed out of the Listening Hall, talking to one another about their places or activities as they walked out through the open foyer. *I wonder why they do not worry about safety on the way out like they do on the way in.* Julyiah's mind seemed prone to questions today. She raised her eyebrows, wondering why.

Many headed toward the music cells or to put money in the boxes near the door. Some of these funds went toward hiring workers from the Underground to tend the orchards, forests, or farms that the leaders owned. Providing jobs for those from below was considered feeding the hungry and clothing the poor— essential commands on the Breeze thousands of years before. Most valley folk did not know the actual conditions below them and did not want to know. Julyiah realized she had never sought to find out. *We assume the leaders take care of everything with the donated sokens to fulfill all the obligations to these commands in the books.*

Outside, skies were darkening to the north as an incoming storm moved over the upper end of the community. Julyiah and Delwyn observed the building billows of moisture.

"They will be rushing to plow today," Delwyn predicted. "The soil is probably dried out enough from the last storm." Gusts of wind blew dust and debris by them as the couple walked with others along Main Street. Some people near them increased their pace as they eyed the windy scene.

"Julyiah! Julyiah, dear!" The high-pitched, nasal voice grated Julyiah's nerves as she turned toward the speaker. Julyiah gave Ruti Suntar a polite smile when the woman approached, tugging Lisiya along behind her. Julyiah hoped Jonar's sister-in-law was not going to bring up the hair-pulling incident. Was that mischief she saw in Lisiya's eyes?

The round-cheeked woman bustled over to the waiting couple, the lacy edges of her puffy, embroidered talia bouncing around her. Her hair, pulled up in a tight twist on her head, allowed a few long, loose curls to dangle on one side in a style that was too young for her. Julyiah pictured Ruti's maid arranging her coiffure in obedient reluctance.

A frillier than usual Lisiya skipped along behind Ruti. The child's hair was a mass of curls so high and wide that it looked like a wig intended for a much larger person. Lisiya's talia was new, with a bright sash tied at the waist and huge bows all around the bottom that flopped as she walked. Two matching bows adorned her large hairdo. Julyiah stared at the pair in wonder, unable to overlook the gaudiness.

"*Dear* Julyiah..." Ruti came to a stop in front of the couple, halting their progress. Ruti's emphasis on "dear" in her greeting was an obvious attempt to dramatize her sympathy. "Julyiah, I heard you were disciplined by the leaders over a grave mistake you made in your class. Are you all right? They said you fainted."

Julyiah was not deceived by the apparent concern. She nodded without responding.

"Are you sure?" Ruti went on. "Well, I... did not hear much... but I *do* hope it is resolved." Julyiah did not miss the note of warning. She looked at Delwyn with a pursed smile.

♫

Delwyn frowned at the woman's insinuations and responded for his fiancée. "We are working it out, thank you, Mrs. Suntar."

Ruti smiled and asked with sickening sweetness: "We? Were you also involved in the problem, Delwyn?"

Delwyn wanted to strike the woman a silencing blow. How often, he wondered, had her wagging tongue brought sorrow and discord? How many had been hurt by this gossipy woman? And here she was attempting to obtain more missiles of information for her verbal arsenal.

"Yes, *we*," Delwyn replied with an intense scowl.

Undaunted, Ruti continued. "Well... I heard that poor little Tomli Tarni has been deceived by the Wind, and his father is just devastated." Her gaze darted around her with a frown, as the stormy breezes continued their unwanted interruptions. "It seems they feel it was your fault, Julyiah. My *dear,* it must be horrible for you, knowing what you have done to that unfortunate boy. I do not think I could take it as bravely as you are. I would not be surprised if little Tomli ended up in the Silent Pit—the Underground at least."

Julyiah stared at the woman with fiery eyes, before she turned toward her fiancé with a helpless expression. Delwyn knew he should not utter the words he wished to say to Ruti. Taking a deep breath, he let it out before speaking in as civil a tone as he could muster.

"Mrs. Suntar," Delwyn said, "what *have you not* heard? We do not like to think about where Tomli may or may not go. Such predictions do not seem healthy."

"Dear boy!" Ruti said with phony shock. "Perhaps thinking ahead would be a good idea, especially before one makes a critical error, eh?"

"Um—, " Delwyn grunted, trying not to respond with words. It was safer.

"Thank you for your concern," Julyiah interjected before Delwyn could say anything.

Noticing with glee that the unsettled air blew the woman's curls into disarray, Delwyn smiled as he took Julyiah's arm to leave. "Have a nice place, Mrs. Suntar."

"Oh, Julyiah, one more thing..." The voice called out behind the retreating couple. "Do *please* take strong precautions when my Lisiya is around, will you not? Such a travesty in her case could be... well, let us say it could be more *costly* than that of Tomli Tarni."

Julyiah whipped around, and Delwyn recognized a biting response ready to pounce out of her mouth. He touched her arm. "Do not speak," he whispered.

Julyiah grunted and turned away.

Ruti, looking satisfied that she had made her point, smiled after them pleasantly before she turned to leave.

♪ ♪

"Help! Keeper!" Jonar ran to his office door, making a great disturbance as he called out: "Fire! Fire!"

Fire—a dreaded word where wood was of such tremendous value. The keeper's eyes grew wide as he rushed into the office where Jonar beat at the flames with an old cloak.

"Quick! Get water!" Jonar cried. "It is one of the books—an ancient manuscript. It will be lost. Hurry!"

The keeper gasped and raced out the door, while Jonar turned back to the dwindling fire, which had turned to mostly smoke. Jonar examined the "accident" in a calm manner, while practicing a look of poignant sorrow. The broken oil lamp was lying across the open pages of *The Refuge* where it had fallen, spilling its slow-burning fuel rapidly across the spot Jonar had intended. The desk remained unharmed. *Good.*

Jonar glanced outside at the rising wind that preceded the storm and smiled. The Secrets of Gwenla were still protected.

♫

When Julyiah grabbed Delwyn's hand and pulled him down Main Street, he assumed she wanted to get as far away from Ruti as possible. "That woman is... is..."

"A Hekian toad?" Delwyn prompted. Julyiah nodded, giggling. The toads were known for obnoxious behavior toward any creature in their proximity.

"That is perfect! Did you see poor Lisiya's hair? And what she was wearing? No wonder she is disliked."

"Yes," Delwyn agreed. "Unfortunately, she will probably grow into another Ruti. Normally, I can ignore that woman, but when she waves my fiancée's faults around for all to see …."

Julyiah stopped laughing and stood still on the busy street, staring at the ground before her. The shops had closed and storm clouds spread throughout the sky, growing darker by the minute. The wind surged, blowing Julyiah's talia and hair sideways on her rigid body.

Julyiah turned flaming eyes on Delwyn.

Delwyn figured he had said the wrong thing but was not certain what it was, so he tried smiling away the problem.

"You are beautiful when you are angry," he said with a dreamy look deep into her eyes, hoping a compliment would help.

"Are you saying you think I made this 'horrible' mistake?" Julyiah remained in a defensive position, and her expression had turned to ice. "Do you agree with Ruti?"

Delwyn's chuckle had a nervous ring to it now, but the truth was that her demanding tone was irritating. He swallowed an insensitive reply. "I assumed you had taken the blame," he said quietly. "You seemed to feel guilty. I do not agree with the way you were spoken to last night—as though you were on trial. But what am I to think except that you made an error? Of course you did not mean to do anything wrong. Everyone understands that," Delwyn humphed, "except Mrs. Ruti Suntar."

Hoping his dismissal of Ruti would soften Julyiah's reception of his words, Delwyn gritted his teeth. Julyiah had been considering ideas that went against accepted teachings. What on earth was she thinking—that she did nothing wrong?

Hot tears drizzled down Julyiah's angry face, and she continued walking. Delwyn followed until she stopped again. When Julyiah's pain-filled eyes looked at him, Delwyn wanted to comfort her but had no idea how. If she could not accept her mistake, there could be a rough road ahead—both for her and for him.

"I... I... am going to a music cell," she sputtered, sounding furious.

Delwyn drew back in surprise. "But, should we not talk about this? And what about your meal? You still have not eaten this morning."

"Does it matter?" she blurted out and spun around, heading toward the music cells. Delwyn blinked in confusion, but before he could respond, Julyiah came back, her face scrunched in obvious bewilderment. "Do you have a couple of sokens I can borrow?"

Delwyn saw her predicament—especially if she still thought she was correct—but he was unsure about a verbal response. He reached into his dekat pocket and pulled out the money. Perhaps it was best that she went to study the books. Maybe she would be humbled, and they could both get back to normal.

Julyiah took the coins and stared at them a moment. "Thank you," she said, gazing up into his eyes with gratefulness until he gave her a puzzled smile. The sound of distant thunder could be heard as Julyiah turned toward the music cells.

♪ ... ♪♫

Unable to get closer to her, an invisible mass quivered near Julyiah. After she parted from Delwyn, the enormous blackness swirled upward, shooting out streaks of shadowy substance that settled over and around Julyiah's head. She glanced around, shook her head in confusion, and continued walking. The shadows dissipated without gaining entrance.

Other unseen creatures observed the scene. A tiny, slithery one came forward. "She is guarded, Lord Zebul," he said.

Zebul grunted.

"Obviously," Murk snorted in reply to the miniscule being before turning toward his master. "At least they appear to be successfully divided, sir."

Undaunted by the larger entities, the miniature snake coiled into a threatening posture to make up for his size. "She has been in the pit for some time, sir," he announced.

The enormous black fog groaned in disdain. "Not in the pit— on the edge." He rose heavily, slogging off toward the North Wall until he disappeared.

Several infinitesimal entities followed Julyiah, but they could not penetrate the luminous colors surrounding her. The iridescent hues flowed in circles around her head before bursting into a glorious spray like water hitting rocks.

The dark beings dispersed, avoiding the color but pressing in around it, trying without success to break through the vibrant barrier to reach Julyiah.

Large drops of water fell from the sky to moisten the dry earth, as Julyiah approached the music cells.

Chapter Fourteen: Riddles

♪

Julyiah had forgotten how crowded the music cells would be on Listening Day. Many people came from across the community for a meeting and wanted to get their music cell study done at the same time. Julyiah had to wait in line but discovered she did not care. In her heart, she hovered over the smelly muck of the pit, feeling invisible slimy things grabbing at her feet.

It did not seem to matter where she was in the physical world. Nothing made sense anyway, and not having to discuss it with anyone was a relief. Julyiah hoped she would not run into anyone who wanted to talk.

New gusts of wind subdued the chattering crowd. A few observed the swirling leaves and dust with apprehension and left the line, hurrying off toward their homes. Julyiah did not mind the storm. If the Lying Wind was stirring about, what difference would it make? Apparently, she was already deceived by it.

Julyiah opened the door to enter the tiny music cell station, hoping to squeeze in behind a man who was next in line. A pile of Teka leaves tried to escape the keeper's pedestal with Julyiah's blustery entrance, and he glared at her until she closed the door.

"Music cell?" the keeper asked the man in front of Julyiah. When the visitor in front of her was escorted to a music cell, Julyiah stepped forward and realized with a start that she was next. Certain that her face was vacant of expression, Julyiah attempted to pull her thoughts together.

"Music cell?" the keeper asked in an irritated tone. The stocky man looked over the long line outside with an impatient grimace. Pushing up the sleeves on his hairy arms, he straightened his Teka leaf records and jogged them noisily into order before stopping to stare at Julyiah.

When he began drumming his fingers on the pedestal, Julyiah remembered what book she wanted to read the most. "Silia," she said.

The keeper sighed and rolled his eyes as though he had had this conversation many times that day. "Silia is occupied. Do you wish to wait?"

Julyiah tried to think of another book she might enjoy reading that day, but her mind refused to concentrate when her heart was lingering over the muck… the mire…the smell…. *And what are those slippery things around my feet?*

"Do you wish to wait?" the keeper repeated, indicating the long stone bench outside that was filled with people huddling in the wind. "I do not recommend it. A party of ten went into the Silia music cell just now, and it will probably be an hour or more before they come out. Two more people are waiting for Silia. Jashgar will be open in a few minutes. I do not believe it will be much longer for Crata or Elia…."

"What is open *now*?" Julyiah interrupted with increasing desperation, dreading further conversation.

"The *Book of Secrets* is the only music cell with no waiting," the keeper replied, chuckling as he picked at some lint on one bushy arm. "Like I said, Jashgar will be open in a few minutes. You may stand to the side and wait for that one, if you wish."

"The *Book of Secrets*? Gwenla's Riddles?"

The keeper chuckled. "Yes, riddles they are, for sure. It has not been occupied all day."

Julyiah did not want to read the *Book of Secrets*. No one understood it, least of all her, and she was tired of reading the book she had found and thought would be so special in her life. However, at the moment she did not care so much which music cell she went to as long as she did not have to talk to anyone.

"Very well," Julyiah said. Another keeper of the music cells hurried over to escort her inside the room for the *Book of Secrets,* and the next person in line entered the music cell station.

♫

"Livi! Harol!"

Julyiah's parents sauntered out of Delegar's fifteenth hour meeting. Delwyn ran up behind them, his shoes splattering in mud puddles.

"Have you seen Julyiah?" Delwyn shouted, trying to be heard above the rain and wind.

"No, we thought she was with you," Harol replied, adjusting the wide-brimmed reed hat which pushed his gray hair over his ears. He held onto the hat as he turned, the wind blowing against the brim, and the rain hitting his face. "Were you not together today?"

Delwyn winced. He should not have let her go without talking with her more. "We were, but she went to the music cells alone. I should have gone with her …."

"I am confident that she is fine." Livi smiled at him with reassurance as she shifted her hat to ward off the wetness.

Delwyn pushed wet wisps of hair across the deep lines in his forehead as he glanced toward the music cells. "She could not still be in there, could she?" he asked with concern, blinking raindrops out of his eyes. "It was right after Zuriel's meeting that she went in."

"I hardly think so," Harol snorted, pulling the brim of his hat down for better rain cover. "I do not know anyone quite that devout. Why do you not try her house?"

Delwyn pressed his lips together before responding. "I waited there all afternoon."

"I am sorry, we have to get out of this wind and rain, son." Harol held his hand over his eyes to assist in keeping out the penetrating wetness. "I am sorry we cannot help. Maybe she went to Katia's."

"Come home with us and have a meal," Livi suggested.

"No, thank you. You are kind." Delwyn could not bear the thought of sitting to chat with someone else when he was so concerned about Julyiah. "I will keep looking."

Harol grinned, and Livi tilted her head sideways with a sweet smile.

"Have a nice place," Delwyn told them.

"Have a nice place, Del." Harol returned as they both turned toward home.

Delwyn left the area to continue his search, uncertain where to look, his apprehension building with each step.

♪

Julyiah sat in the music cell of *Secrets* for some time, wishing that the riddles in the book were distracting enough to draw her mind and heart away from her misery. But the riddles made no sense at all. The painting on the wall of a stream flowing through a meadow looked old and lifeless. The music coming from the box in the room was actually irritating, repeating the same tune over and over.

Somehow, though, Julyiah could not leave, and no one interrupted her. The keeper had left for duties in other music cells which were much busier than this one. In a desperate attempt for more quiet, Julyiah reached over and shut the lid to the music box, wondering if this were an act fit to send her to the Silent Pit.

As she sat again in the reed chair, Julyiah's gaze shifted from the lifeless painting in front of her to the stones lining the walls of the small chamber. To her surprise, they incorporated more color and depth than anything else in the room.

Julyiah's heart wandered through chilly tunnels with no light. It was a better place than she had just been in—a passageway that ended either on a terrifying cliff edge or clinging to the edge of the smelly pit of depressing slime. When she attempted to climb out of the pit, her feet constantly slipped on the muddy walls, as though invisible forces weighed her down. At the cliff, she faced rocks which moved to close the distance to the rim, attempting to shove her off into a vast unknown expanse. No other end presented itself in her heart wanderings. She did not know how long she could continue hanging onto the edge of the pit, and the distance between the pit and the cliff ledge was smaller every time she traveled the dark tunnel, as though her heart choices were becoming narrower.

Julyiah felt her heart sinking toward the murky pit of discouragement. Tired of the ordeal, she worked with great resolve to struggle out of the pit and back into the dim but safe tunnel. But whenever she went back to the tunnel from the pit, she always found herself on the edge of the deep chasm again. The tunnel started shrinking, and the pit approached from where the tunnel used to be, indicating a choice now limited to the pit or the cliff. It was as though she must decide which horrible death for her heart to die.

The One sends Music, and the Voice sings the truth on the Breeze. Could she trust that the One would send her truth? Would she be glad she found it? Perhaps it was better not to know … but she yearned to know the truth more than she feared the unknown.

The dim tunnel and pit faded, when Julyiah sought truth over safety. The cliff loomed in front of her, its depths calling to her. Reaching out to claw at the loose rocks that would allow no handhold, Julyiah fought to stay on the ledge overhanging the abyss behind her. She dared not look into whatever lay beyond the rim that rapidly approached her feet, as though seeing it could make her fall off the edge.

Astonished, Julyiah realized that the disgusting pit was familiar, but the world beyond the precipice was still a mystery, because she had been afraid to look. Curiosity gave her hope. What if death did not lie in the depths below? As the pit of muck grew closer again, Julyiah turned away from the wall behind her to face the open air on the precarious ledge.

Right away she feared falling. Imagining that only empty space and doom lay before her, she almost lost her resolve. Trying to turn back, her foot slipped, for the ledge on which she stood had grown too small to turn around.

Light streaked from the sky in front of her through calm white clouds that were unaffected by the great height. The driving wind turned into a gentle breeze, and the cliff rocks grew still. A closed door appeared in the space in front of her, and a key glistened in the lock. Flashes of turquoise, teal, and gold darted back and forth in front of the door. Barely perceptible, they pointed at the door as though inviting her to enter.

The *Book of Secrets* still lay on the pedestal underneath her hands. Focusing on the words before her, she read:

The key to truth will yet be found
When one is open to the sound
Of Music flowing on the Breeze.
From there, one will find all the keys.

A thrill of expectancy shot through Julyiah like a lightning bolt. Desperation for the truth overwhelmed her. "I want truth," she declared. "I want to hear Music and the truth that comes on the Breeze." No longer fearful, she felt her heart open up to hearing the Music and the Voice of the One.

A tiny dent marred the doorknob on the door that floated in space, and her heart jolted. This was the door she had seen just before she went into Jonar's office that night! Not Jonar's door but this one. Certain she was meant to open it, she reached out into the space and grasped the key, not even considering that she would fall in doing so. As her feet left the rim, the door lay down flat, catching her. It opened up, and Julyiah fell right through it into open space.

An unearthly thrill coursed through Julyiah. Flying rather than falling, she drifted on the beautiful melody that carried her through the sky and clouds. Sensations of peace and love surrounded her like great cushions against any fear of the heights. Flashes of countless colors that sang flew alongside her. The Voice spoke to her on the Breeze of her bravery and how she would be used for a special task.

The terrible cliff Julyiah had feared was a wonderful stepping-off point into inexplicable adventures with the Music. Julyiah's heart rejoiced, bathing in the comfortable wrappings of Music on the peaceful Breeze.

Julyiah threw out her arms like a soaring bird as the Breeze carried her through the clouds. Bursting from the billowing white puffs, she gasped with joy.

Mountains! Snow-capped, tree-lined peaks rose below her as she swept through the cool, fresh air. Laughing in ecstasy until the tears came, Julyiah blinked them away so she would not miss anything.

Minutes later, Julyiah opened the next section in the *Book of Secrets*, eager to read more. The next passage burst through her soul: "You search the books and trust their truth, but you are afraid to hear the Voice of the One who inspired the words." Now this part made sense!

Julyiah's heart jumped for joy. *The Voice still sings on the Breeze to those who trust Him.* The reality of the truth filled her heart with expectation for what was yet to come. Humming the melody she had heard on the Breeze, she examined more passages, understanding many truths and riddles that were written and exulting in the knowledge she gained. Pulling out a few Teka leaves that she always carried in her pocket, she hurried to copy whole passages on them.

By the time Julyiah left the music cell, it was dark and stormy outside, but she paid no heed. Delwyn needed to know what she had discovered.

Chapter Fifteen: The Truth

♫

The sun had gone down, but the rain continued to fall outside. Delwyn had tried Katia's and the Hartbrooks' houses again. Now he waited at Julyiah's place for his beloved to come home.

Hearing a noise he jumped, his heart beating rapidly. Was it Julyiah, at last? Rehearsing again in his mind his apology, he rushed over to the door and flung it open.

Julyiah hurried inside dripping wet, and Delwyn took her shoulders to hold her close as he shut the door. He kissed her and held her a long time, whispering how sorry he was to have hurt her.

A light rock Delwyn had placed on the table illuminated the immediate area, dissipating into the far corners of the room. Julyiah pulled back and brought out the bundle of Teka leaves from inside her shawl, setting them reverently on the table by the light. Her affectionate smile melted Delwyn's heart.

"Hello, Del."

"Are you all right?" Delwyn forgot everything else he wanted to say and only knew he loved her and was glad she was safe. As it often had in the past, her unpredictable personality lured his heart with a thrill of adventure. He ran a drying cloth over her wet, stringy hair, wanting to wrap his arms around her again.

"I am all right—just tired and a little shaky." Julyiah sank into a reed chair by the warm hearth, still holding his hand. At length, she let go of his hand, took the cloth he held, and rubbed her head with it in brisk motions before setting it down.

As Julyiah took off her wet shawl, Delwyn brought over a wool blanket and draped her with it, hugging it around her chilled body.

"Are you sick?"

"I have not eaten all day and have been busy."

Delwyn's heart jerked in alarm. What was happening to the one he loved? He rushed over to her cold box and opened the door, but the food was spoiled. Julyiah had never changed the stone inside. Turning up his nose and looking around, he spotted her bread. Knowing this should still be good, he brought it and a glass of water over and set them on the table next to her.

"Oh, thank you," she said, glassy-eyed. She turned the chair toward the table and stared at the Teka leaves in front of her as she began to eat.

Delwyn had not paid much attention to the leaves. He reached down and shuffled through them curiously, being careful not to smear the charcoal. "What are these?"

Julyiah chewed some bread and looked at the leaves as though at a treasure. Swallowing her bite, she looked up at him, her tired eyes now flashing with excitement.

"I have been copying passages all afternoon in the music cells, mostly from the *Book of Secrets*." Julyiah took another bite of bread and drank some water.

"*Secrets*? Why that book?" Delwyn's heart thumped. *Something is wrong!* "Why, Julyiah? I mean, I know the writings are special to you, but no one understands those riddles. Zuriel told me if it was not for the fact that Gwenla so often heard directly from the One, the *Book of Secrets* would never have been accepted as sacred."

"The riddles are prophetic," Julyiah said, her eyes dancing. "They have not been understood because they were for the future."

How could she know anything about the writings in that book? She was merely the person who found it, not a specialist on its meaning. Memories of Zuriel's message that morning wafted through Delwyn's consciousness as he attempted to grasp Julyiah's words. She took another bite of bread and chewed it, looking back at the stack of leaves as though she could not wait to read them again.

Delwyn held his breath a moment and exhaled in exasperation. He felt torn between his love for Julyiah and the way he had been raised. Why did she have to pursue this strange path all of a sudden? Yet the explorer in Julyiah appealed to him, as it so often had before.

An oak door appeared in Delwyn's heart, beautifully carved with Teka leaves. At first it seemed real, considering there was a pile of the leaves on the table in front of him, but the bright metal doorknob twinkled, as though inviting him to turn it. The Teka leaves on the door displayed writing that glowed, as though the words were important.

What does it mean?

"Look," Julyiah ate the last big bite of bread and reached for the Teka leaves. "Look here. Listen to this one:"

After the season is done;
After the rocks fall;
After the shadows flee;
Music will be heard again;
Indeed, even before this.

"You see? *Music will be heard again* it says. We are going to hear Music again."

"Yes, but that might refer to the time after the Great Silence long ago."

"No, no.... it cannot be that! Gwenla wrote this passage. She was not even born yet and it says 'will,' speaking of a time in the future."

"We do hear Music," Delwyn pointed out, ignoring her argument, "from the music boxes."

"Boxed music—because we have been told by the leaders to listen to it that way," Julyiah said, jumping up. She walked over to a nearby window, where the bright light rock at the Listening Hall shone on her face. "The One is a living Person who loves us," Julyiah protested. "The Music He sends is not limited to boxes. The books say nothing about music boxes. Did you not ever wonder where that idea came from?"

Delwyn was aghast. It was worse than he had thought—she was deceived by the Lying Wind! Rising to glance out the window, he looked for anyone who might have heard her heretical statements. Seeing no one, he pulled her toward him, looking straight into her eyes with a warning in his.

"You are misinformed, Julyiah. The Lying Wind has tricked you. You must fight this."

Julyiah smiled like a child, looking down while fingering the ends of her drying, tangled hair. "I am sorry, Del. I have realized truth today that I cannot ignore—through the books themselves and in my heart. The truth is there but... Del, it is not being taught." Her intense eyes held his gaze. *"The truth... is... not... being... taught!"*

Delwyn drew back, shocked at her assertiveness. This was not like her at all. "What is not being taught?" He mumbled in subdued response, his voice sounding small in a room that screamed with confusion. The oak door appeared to him again, and this time the words on the bright leaf carvings danced in place, enticing him to read them. Staring at Julyiah in wonder, he felt his heart question what he had been taught, wanting to know the truth.

♪

Julyiah came back to the table, sat across from him, and spread out the Teka leaves. She compared in her mind the difference between the repetitive sounds in the music boxes and the elaborate, ever-changing symphony she had heard on the Breeze. Somehow she had to convince Delwyn.

"Remember the *Secrets of Gwenla*?" She let this question settle in his mind while she stacked the leaves in small piles. She selected one in particular to begin with, leaning across the table in great anticipation.

Delwyn's eyes and mouth wrinkled in a grin at her question. "I may have heard that somewhere."

"*The Refuge* tells about them. As a schoolteacher, I read that book to the children. We had it read to us. Gwenla died before her secrets could be made known."

"Oh... yes, I have heard that," Delwyn said, swallowing hard.

He seems to be struggling. That could be good. "Listen to what Gwenla says in her book," Julyiah continued:

My secrets now cannot be known
Until to one these things are shown.
They will be seen again one day;
A child will surely lead the way.

"Do you see? Gwenla's secrets were meant to become known some day. She must have known she would die and not be able to share those secrets. Look how it says *will be seen again one day.* Is that not interesting? It sounds like far into the future, and a child is involved."

Julyiah slapped the leaves down on the table and stood up again, too excited to sit.

"Del, do you know when this all started?"

Delwyn's interest piqued.

"It started when I was reading a book the Suntar Clan loaned to me for school: *Captain Suntar.* The children enjoy it. It is the story of how the Captain led our ancestors to the fortress and got settled here in the valley. I have heard there is a question about its accuracy since it was written by a member of the Suntar family—the Captain's son in fact. But it still tells some interesting facts about the construction of the wall."

"Yes, I believe it was read to us in school too," Delwyn said, one eyebrow up.

"After I read it to the children the other day, Tomli asked his first question," Julyiah said. "'Miss Hartbrook, what does it look like on the other side of the wall?' The question itself had a tremendous impact on my heart. It threw me directly to that cliff edge I told you about."

"A bad place."

"I thought so at first—and I was in bad places all day. But the cliff was not a bad place, Del. The Lying Wind was trying to keep me from seeing the truth."

Delwyn groaned and leaned back in his chair. Julyiah saw that she was losing him, so she rearranged her thoughts.

"But is it not interesting," she asked pointedly, "that a *child* started all of this? Look at the words."

Delwyn leaned forward, moaning as though being forced to look once more at the sketchy words on the Teka leaf.

"You see?" Julyiah prompted. "Her secrets will be lost for awhile, but a child will lead the way back to them."

"That could mean anything," he said, shaking his head and looking at the floor.

Julyiah frowned and puffed in sudden irritation. "Well, what do *you* think it means?"

Delwyn smirked as he read over it again. "I do not know. It could mean a lot of things. Maybe she thought they would be shown to Jon, but she died."

Julyiah feared that Delwyn was listening out of politeness and not interest. There was no certain way to convince him with words because he was not open to hearing the Music on the Breeze, just as she had not been. She paused, trying to hear the Voice in her heart for what to say.

"Well, it has to mean what I said," Julyiah insisted, "because... I now know one of Gwenla's secrets."

Delwyn looked astonished, as though wondering what new foolishness she was adding to the conversation. Julyiah shoved nearly all of the leaves aside, leaving one in the middle of the table. She picked it up and waved it about dramatically.

"This... this will show you!" she exclaimed, feeling re-armed for battle. Flopping it down in front of him, she pointed to the first passage on it. "Read this—out loud." *Perhaps hearing his own voice speaking the truth will make a difference.*

♫

Julyiah's manner amused Delwyn, although sincerity encompassed her voice. The door in his heart came closer and brightened. He reached out to touch the knob as he read the passage:

The key to truth will yet be found,

When one is open to the sound
Of Music flowing on the Breeze.
From there, one will find all the keys.
He stopped, looked up, and stared at her.

"Listen, Del. I know this is going to sound strange."

He nodded with a puzzled expression.

"The past two days a passage I had read kept coming back to me," she said, leaning forward in her chair for the tale. "It was from the *Book of Silia*. I read this: *The One sends Music, and the Voice sings the truth on the Breeze.* I longed for the truth; I was in so much confusion."

Delwyn could readily agree with that and nodded with vigor.

"I kept trying to see truth in my heart," Julyiah went on, "but all I could see were bleak tunnels, a terrifying cliff, and mucky pits. I was afraid of all these things, but the Wind makes us afraid—afraid to be open to the Breeze and hear the truth. That is why the leaders teach us to listen to music from the boxes—they think that is the only safe way to hear music because they are *afraid.*

"Look at this passage from Silia: *The Lying Wind of Zebul brings fear, but the Breeze brings trust.* We should not be afraid of anything the One wants to bring to us. Fear is not from the One." Julyiah paused, took a deep breath, and told Delwyn of her experience on the cliff with the Music.

"The Voice was flying with me, Delwyn—singing to me. Music surrounded me with peace, even as the books tell us. I have never felt so close to the Voice. It was... how can I describe it? It was like color and Music all mixed together. It was wonderful!" Julyiah laughed in delight.

Delwyn felt his insides being torn apart. "But..." Delwyn asked with care, "you said you heard it the other day too, and how do you know it was the Voice you heard? It could have been..."

"No, it could not have been the Wind. The books say we should never be afraid to ask for truth from the One. I asked for truth and He gave it to me. Oh, Del—do not be afraid! His truth is beautiful. These were *real* places I saw, Del, not the paintings in the music cells. I flew over the top of a mountain covered with snow. You...cannot *imagine*, Del. It is so *thrilling* up there!"

She closed her eyes and danced around the room, singing.

Delwyn's heart hopped from bad places to good places and back again, afraid of choosing the wrong way. His mind sorted information like a vast network, compiling facts and sorting, then re-sorting, but he knew he could not go on facts alone. Seeing his own fear, he felt he must look past logic and tradition. He stared at the Teka-leaf carved door, trying to see behind it, but he would not know what was back there, until he opened it.

Drawing the Teka leaves toward him, Delwyn began reading again. He wanted to open the oak door, suddenly noticing that it had scratches down one side. Those scratches looked familiar....

♪

Delwyn grew silent, and Julyiah hoped he was considering what he had read without traditional influences. As she waited, Julyiah recalled the melody she heard when she stepped off the cliff. She began singing words to the song.

Delwyn looked up, listening to the tune and the words with apparent interest, but when he glanced toward her front door, Julyiah worried that he might leave. He stood and walked toward it, and she hurried to his side.

"Del—wait!"

Delwyn paid no heed but stared at the door. Julyiah squinted at his activity, wondering why he studied the scratches on the wood. Opening the door, Delwyn revealed the storm. As he gazed out into the rain, he did not leave but stood in the doorway, letting the raindrops blow on him.

"Del?" Julyiah whispered, unable to say it louder. A faint sound grew louder until a charge of something like wind with thunder burst through the open doorway. Julyiah was surprised they were still standing. Music followed the startling sound, carried on a strong Breeze. Melody filled the room, bringing peace and joy with it. As with Delwyn, the moist air blew on Julyiah's face, renewing her heart.

Exhilarated, she saw her beloved with his arms stretched out into the Breeze, an expression of ecstasy on his face as he began to sing with the Music. Julyiah knew he was hearing the Voice of the One and going to incredible places—places he had never been to before but now knew with a certainty were out there.

Chapter Sixteen: Pain

♫

"We've got a job to do."

Delwyn shuffled through the Teka leaves on Julyiah's table. After hearing the Music, he wanted to read every one of the passages Julyiah had copied. The words he had heard throughout his lifetime suddenly held new insight.

Why did I not see all of this before?

Julyiah had fallen asleep with her head on the table, her excitement and stress from the busy day had caught up with her. Startled at Delwyn's voice, she peered at him groggily. "Mm?"

"We need to find the other keys."

"Other keys?"

"Yes... it says here, 'from there one will find all the keys....'"

Julyiah blinked with a sleepy grin. "Let's start tomorrow," she suggested, stretching her arms and kneading a kink in her neck.

Delwyn almost allowed a disagreement to escape his lips. His whole being burned with a new purpose that he was eager to pursue. But he knew it was late, and they both had to get up early for work.

"Tomorrow then," he agreed. "I think we should go talk to Zuriel about this."

Julyiah's eyes widened, apprehension replacing the sleepy face. "Zuriel? Will he understand? This morning he was speaking so adamantly about music coming only from the boxes. What if he does not see the truth like we do?"

"We have to try. He is our friend, and a leader."

♪

The next day, Julyiah had a hard time concentrating on schoolwork. Throughout the day, her gaze wandered to the schoolroom window, where she longed to stare at the walls and dream about what might be in the places that lay beyond them. Contentment washed over her as her heart filled with magnificent mountains and tall trees. Later, as she hung up her wash outdoors, her heart dwelt on the rim of a cliff—this time not with fear but with awe at the vast space. What a relief to see such beautiful places in her heart!

Delwyn came by Julyiah's house for the evening meal after a long day of driving the horses. He carried the Teka leaves, which he had taken along to read in the Transport Wagon while he drove the horses. The two of them set out walking to their friend Zuriel's house in the North Wall. Delwyn seemed much more confident about talking to Zuriel than Julyiah felt.

"Zuriel is available," the keeper told them at the doorway of the Listening Hall. "Right this way."

They followed the blue uniform up the outside spiral staircase that brought them to the balcony above the Listening Hall. From there they could see the entire valley and the tips of the mountains far off to the south. The peaks were too far away to spot anything interesting, but Julyiah had seen them in her heart the day of the viewing out the South Window. How thankful she was that seeing them was not a bad thing!

They passed a couple of wooden doors, lots of windows, and several groups of potted herbs that had been placed out on the stone walkway to catch some sun. Arriving at Zuriel's door, the keeper knocked.

"My good friends!" Zuriel greeted with a warm smile as the couple entered the well-lit, richly decorated room. Light rocks set into the walls shone brightly among other stones of many colors and sizes. The daily sunrays automatically charged them unless it was too cloudy outside to gather much light. Engraved wooden chairs, painted clay ornaments, and embroidered woolen rugs rested upon oak floors and shelves, adding to the warmth of the room.

Zuriel gave the Teka leaves a curious glance but said nothing as Delwyn set them on a small table near the most comfortable chairs. Zuriel asked if anyone would like refreshment and when the couple declined, the keeper closed the door and left.

Julyiah smiled at Zuriel's newly grown beard, which matched his dark, curly hair. It made him look much older than his twenty-eight years. In his position he needed to appear older and authoritative.

Delwyn lost no time as he explained to Zuriel with enthusiasm the new truth he and Julyiah had seen in the *Book of Secrets*. Spreading out the Teka leaves, Delwyn repeated several of the same points Julyiah had spoken to him the night before. Zuriel listened with an occasional nod of his head, and Julyiah said *Yes* now and then to indicate her agreement on several of Delwyn's key points.

♫

When Delwyn finished, the room felt quiet, and he looked to Zuriel, expecting a response. Delwyn was confident that something understood as truth by two of Zuriel's trusted friends would have more impact on him than one person alone. But Zuriel's expression was indecipherable as he rose with a thoughtful expression and crossed the room to a small group of reading materials that rested on a carved bookshelf among some light rocks. He selected two and brought them over to the waiting couple, opening one to a well-worn spot. To Delwyn's dismay, Zuriel read the same passages he had preached from the day before, emphasizing his points about where Music now comes from—sound rocks. When he was done with one book, he opened the other and proceeded with the same argument.

His heart sinking, Delwyn realized that years of tradition and study among the other leaders had assured Zuriel this was the only truth about where Music comes from. Zuriel needed more than argument; he needed to hear the Music.

"Zuriel, I heard the Music," Julyiah said, "and it was this that helped me to see the truth in the *Book of Secrets*...."

Delwyn cringed. Although they had planned to talk about the passages in the books, they had agreed not to bring up their actual experiences with Music until Zuriel seemed ready for it.

"You *what*?" Zuriel interrupted, staring at her with horror in his eyes. He jumped to his feet and paced the room, shaking his head in silent disapproval. Julyiah's helpless gaze told Delwyn that she thought her words would be convincing.

"That was not Music," Zuriel said, stopping to gape at her in shock. He looked at Julyiah with intensity, as though he could stare her into submission.

"Of course it was Music," Julyiah insisted. "I was inside the music cell at the time—a safe place. What else could it have been? Do you think I am crazy?"

Zuriel had reacted without malice at first, but his expression quickly escalated to wide-eyed anger. He shook his head in apparent bewilderment. Delwyn wondered if the leader had no answer to what Julyiah had said.

"Whatever has entered your minds?" Zuriel asked. "After all the sound teaching you have received, why would you allow yourselves to be led astray? Our ways and teachings have been accepted for hundreds of years—can you not see that?"

Yes, we can see that quite well, Delwyn thought with a quirky smile.

Zuriel continued pacing the room with well-placed steps that emphasized every point he made. "The books themselves speak for us. Music no longer comes on the Breeze. The One knew that era could not last. He knew it *should not* last; there was too much deception—deception of this type." Zuriel paused in his pacing to direct his gaze at them both. "How many were lost to the Lying Wind during that time? The One brought us a better way—a safer way—the wall, the boxes, and the leaders."

"Zuriel," Delwyn countered, rising from his seat with flashing eyes. "Why then does it say in the *Book of Secrets* that Music will be heard again? This was the time of Gwenla, not the Great Silence. The Music was often heard on the Breeze at that time, so why would she say it would be heard again? It was because she spoke of another silent time—*this time*—when we would shut up Music in a box and play it whenever we want to. You read yesterday that Music comes when the One wills and *does not conform to the wishes of man*. This is Music, Zuriel—this *is* the One. His Voice should not be confined to a box."

♪

With apprehension Julyiah observed Zuriel's face filling with disdain for what Delwyn said. When Delwyn finished, he did not back down from his assertive stance, and Zuriel had such agitated displeasure written all over him that Julyiah was afraid he might resort to physical violence with Delwyn.

With a noisy exhale, Zuriel dropped his arms to his sides, making a loud *slap*. He strode to his door and opened it with a jerk, shaking and waving the couple out. Delwyn, the wind knocked out of his words, complied with shoulders sagging. Julyiah trailed behind him, wondering at what price they had shared their news with Zuriel.

"Wait! Wait right there," Zuriel sputtered, his red face contorted with rage when the couple reached the threshold. "Delwyn..." Zuriel paused and took a deep breath in an obvious effort to calm down, despair shadowing his face. "Del, have you … also heard this other music?"

"It is not *other* music," Delwyn replied in a gentle voice.

"HAVE YOU HEARD IT?" roared Zuriel, striking the solid doorframe with his fist.

Julyiah jumped, startled at the vehement question. Delwyn's face took on a visible wince at the sound of his best friend's irate voice.

"Yes," Delwyn said. Julyiah figured he wanted to tell more, but the fact that he was in an open doorway at the time he heard the Music would not help Zuriel believe it. That would not be considered a "safe" place to hear Music at all.

In the silence that followed, the couple slipped dejectedly out the doorway. Zuriel stepped back and slammed the heavy door in their faces. From within Julyiah could hear him moaning, his voice filled with anguish as though someone had died.

Julyiah walked through the cool stone hallway in shock, following Delwyn through the early evening air back down the spiral staircase. Grief overwhelmed her, and she knew Delwyn felt the same way, if not worse. Grateful no one else was nearby, she wept in silence. Reaching for Delwyn's hand, she squeezed rather than spoke her sympathy, as they trod the familiar road home.

"The traditional view is strong about hearing Music on the Breeze," Delwyn choked out. "Very strong."

A few minutes later as they shuffled through Julyiah's front door, she turned to face Delwyn. "I do not wish to bring up more problems, but what if the other leaders find out?"

Delwyn shrugged and went to get a drink of water from Julyiah's stone water pitcher.

Julyiah sat near the comforting heat of the hearth, staring at a cluster of warming stones that emitted an amber glow. But her heart resided deep within the fire as she struggled with the consequences of hearing Music on the Breeze. *What if everyone reacts the same way that Zuriel did?*

A knock on the door caused Julyiah's heart to leap into her throat and every pounding beat became painful. *They are already coming!* She could not face another uncomfortable confrontation right now.

Delwyn opened the door to reveal Dawnli, the young girl from the Underground. Julyiah's mother, the tenderhearted soul that she was, had taken Dawnli in to teach her how to sew so she could make a living for herself. The girl had come to the valley to escape her mother's wretched life in the evil taverns of the dark world below, but Dawnli did not have a chance to remain in the community without a way to earn sokens.

"Why, hello, Dawnli," Delwyn greeted with caution.

"Hello, I...would like to speak to Julyiah." The girl's sad eyes were offset by a natural beauty that had yet to blossom. Her blonde hair was long, but thin and dull, which Julyiah considered lack of proper nourishment.

"Of course," Delwyn said, glancing at Julyiah with concern before waving Dawnli through the door. "Please ... come in." This was an unwelcome interruption. Julyiah did not feel up to conversation with a stranger.

Dawnli entered the house, looking around the room in a nervous way. She tossed her waist-length hair out of her face and stood staring at the couple. Refusing a chair, she looked from Julyiah to Delwyn and back again.

"Would you like something to drink?" Julyiah offered, mystified by the girl's presence.

"I am sorry to interrupt you," Dawnli said, wringing her hands. "I came over here for another reason, but... I need to ask something. I thought... I mean I am fairly certain you have heard Music on the Breeze, is that correct?"

Julyiah and Delwyn's eyes came together like a magnet, Julyiah's heart racing. *Uh-oh. Dawnli heard us talking!* Julyiah wanted to deny it but knew that it would be denial of the One and his Voice.

"May I ask why you wish to know?" Delwyn asked in a careful tone.

Good response, Del! Julyiah held her breath.

Dawnli swallowed. "Because, I thought... I thought it was forbidden. That is what I have been told, but...."

Julyiah felt from these words that they could trust this girl, but fear held her back from a reply.

"Is it bad to talk about it?" Dawnli's voice remained hesitant.

Delwyn looked at the floor while Julyiah focused on breathing normally. They would be wading in deep waters if they told this young girl the truth. She was young enough to influence and old enough to get them into trouble. Julyiah's parents might be upset with her if they discovered what was happening. As her new guardians, they had been working to teach the girl acceptable valley ways, and listening to Music on the Breeze was not one of them.

Dawnli shifted her weight in the silence and looked at Julyiah with trembling lips.

"B… Because…" Dawnli faltered. "I have heard this Music."

Time seemed to stop.

Chapter Seventeen: Friends

♪

"Wha… what did you say?" Julyiah asked, making the girl repeat the amazing news.

Dawnli's eyes widened, and she bit her lower lip. "It is not acceptable, is it?" she asked in a trembling voice. "I am sorry, but I could not help it when the Music came to me." A slight smile curved at the edges of her mouth. "It was so beautiful! Maybe you could explain to me why it is a bad thing?" Dawnli pressed her lips together tightly. Delwyn brought a chair over, which Dawnli accepted, sitting with her hands together in her lap.

"Yes, we were talking about the Music on the Breeze," Julyiah blurted out with a lilt to her voice that she hoped would sound reassuring.

Delwyn's brow furrowed and he grimaced as though unsure whether this was a good idea.

Dawnli paused a moment, studying their faces. "Have you also heard Music on the Breeze, or have I been incorrect?"

"Yes, we have," Julyiah said, smiling. "This is wonderful! How did you hear the Music?"

Dawnli's face brightened, and her trembling subsided. "In the pine trees, down by the Hole." The girl took a deep breath, letting it out at length.

"When I first came up here, no one ever spoke of living Music, only what was in the music boxes. I thought that was better than no music at all, but it was nothing like what I had heard in the trees." Dawnli's face radiated joy as she talked.

"Livi did not like it when I told her—she thought it was something I learned from living in the Underground. I told her there was nothing so wonderful down there. Some people do sing, but not with good words." She made a face. "And some play musical instruments in the taverns…. Oh, and there is a music box in the Under Hall."

Dawnli frowned. "I do not understand. Can you tell me why no one else talks about real Music and they only listen to music that comes from boxes?"

For the next few hours, Julyiah and Delwyn explained the community traditions to Dawnli and told her about their experiences. Julyiah was encouraged to find another person who understood living Music, and was certain Delwyn did also, especially after their encounter with Zuriel. Dawnli showed great relief in discovering she was not alone.

When Dawnli was about to go out the door that evening, she stopped and laughed. "I forgot to ask you—are you attached to that white stone in your berry box outside? I wondered if I might have it."

"I am sure you can have it," Julyiah responded with a grin. "There is no lack of stones in this valley. But why that one?"

"I felt drawn to come over here today," Dawnli said, "and as I looked at that stone, I was taken to a place with many rocks and rushing water."

Julyiah brightened. "You have gone through the Understanding."

"Yes, when I heard the Music," Dawnli said.

"Oh! What a superb way to go through the Understanding," Julyiah chortled in delight. "My Understanding was not nice at all. How old are you, Dawnli?"

"I thought I was twelve," Dawnli said, playing with her hair on one side, "but your mother thinks I might be older."

"I imagine you are," Julyiah agreed.

"When I saw the rocks and stream in my heart," Dawnli continued, "I realized a good lesson of how we need to become smooth stones, not rough, for the water to flow well. I felt that we must let go of our bad desires and pride to become like the smooth stones."

"Maybe that is why the Music has not been flowing freely on the Breeze," Julyiah said. "We have been like rough stones—hindering the Breeze and scattering our thoughts with our selfishness. I could not hear the Music until I let go of my fear. If we cling to our fears and desires, focusing on self, we hinder the Breeze and do not hear the Music."

"Yes!" Dawnli agreed, her eyes lighting up.

Together the three went outside and found the stone. As Dawnli tried to pick it up, she had to dig deeper, for there was a lot more to it than what appeared on the surface. A long, thin part was buried in the dirt. Pulling it all out at last, she brushed the dirt off, but Julyiah and Delwyn gasped when they saw the form of it.

"It is a key!" Julyiah exclaimed and reached for the stone. "May I?" Julyiah examined it. The round end at the top was like a handle, but that was a small part of the object. The rest had been below the surface—a long section with perpendicular prongs—a definite key shape. Julyiah was certain it could not have been there when she planted the tinit berries in the box, or she would have noticed it.

"But what does it open?" Dawnli asked.

"We do not know," Delwyn replied. His eyes lit up with an adventurous glow. "We will have to find out."

♪ ♪

Jonar paced back and forth in front of his bookcase as Zuriel described to him the encounter with Julyiah and Delwyn. The respected leader paused occasionally to study the distraught younger man, noting the lack of ability to remain calm in a distressing situation. *He will certainly have to learn more composure*, Jonar thought to himself, *or he will never be one of the great ones. Be nervous on the inside if you must—even terrified— but certainly never show it.*

"This is disturbing news, friend," Jonar agreed, sitting at his desk and looking at Zuriel with patient understanding. "It is apparent that we have had a problem brewing for some time.

Somehow the Lying Wind has deceived Julyiah and she in turn has deceived others. It is unfortunate that they are your friends, but it must be stopped. We will have to take definite action."

Zuriel's brow furrowed. "Action?"

"Yes...yes. This ability to persuade is most disturbing."

"But, how can we stop her from speaking about it, unless...." Zuriel's eyes grew wide.

Jonar laughed, "Come now, Zuriel. We do not live in such a sinister time as that. There are other ways than violence to shut people's mouths."

The High Leader rose to his feet and made his way over to a clay calendar, gazing with interest at the events of the next few weeks.

"I have it!" he exclaimed. "They were to be married, is that correct?"

"Yes," Zuriel replied, confused. "I am to join them together myself." He smiled.

"We will cancel it!" Jonar declared, striking his hand on the calendar. "There will be no wedding."

♫♪

Zuriel's heart pounded in pain and wrenched, as he tried to hide his distaste for Jonar's idea. Shaking his head in dismay, Zuriel felt the impact of what he was doing to his friends. For the first time he wondered if he should have come to Jonar's office. The other leaders always went along with Jonar's plans, so there would be nothing Zuriel could do about Jonar's decision.

"But, what will it accomplish?" Zuriel asked, hoping Jonar might change his mind.

Jonar whipped around to face Zuriel, his eyes alight with ideas. "It will show them we mean business." He gazed at Zuriel, appearing to assess the younger man's reactions. "We are concerned for them, of course. We will take Julyiah off her teaching duties and suggest they do daily music cell studies, apart from each other. They need to seek and find the truth again before they are united. With no teaching job and the wedding cancelled, Julyiah will no doubt reconsider some of these ridiculous ideas." Jonar tilted his head and waved his hand through the air as though to clear away the disruption as easily.

"But, what of Delwyn? This may anger him and cause further rebellion."

Jonar chuckled again. "Oh, Delwyn. I can assure you he is no problem. He changes his mind on a whim, flitting here and there to different ideas, never settling on anything. With the threat of no marriage, he will also come back to the truth."

With growing pain and unease, Zuriel observed Jonar's confident smile over his plans. Delwyn and Julyiah were not likely to change their minds, Zuriel was certain of it. Although he had been torn apart by their turn away from the truth, they were people of great character. He had been close to them all of his life, and after what he had seen in his conversation the day before, he did not think Jonar's plan would work.

♪

In her assigned music cell of Zemar, Julyiah read again the passages suggested by Jonar. She smiled as the words not only failed to persuade her back to the traditional way, but instead emphasized the truth she and Delwyn had seen in the *Book of Secrets* the week before.

The painting on the wall in the much-traveled music cell portrayed some snow-covered mountaintops. Julyiah knew that the picture was inaccurate, painted a hundred years ago from the artist's imagination after reading about mountains and seeing them at a great distance. The rocky peaks were out of perspective, much too close for the trees in the foreground. She wondered at her previous admiration of the painting. The simulated display meant to show something beautiful now disgusted her.

With a sigh Julyiah wished she could go read the *Book of Silia* for words of comfort. She had been away from Delwyn too long and longed to be with him. With no wedding coming up or a teaching position to occupy her, her heart remained inside a lonely room, surrounded by stone.

Like this room I am forced to come to every day.

Julyiah was glad to have established a secret written communication with Delwyn through Dawnli, who served as a go-between. Dawnli pulled a note from Julyiah's berry box each morning, exchanging it for a note from Delwyn. Delwyn came into town every day after work for his assigned music cell, meeting Dawnli at the food market on the way. Dawnli met Delwyn behind a great stack of dried grain bags that hid them from the storeowner's view, where she gave Delwyn the note from Julyiah and took the note he wanted to send to his fiancée.

Julyiah's parents, distressed about the shunning that Jonar asked of them, spoke to Julyiah in secret as well. The leaders did not post any guards to enforce their restrictions, and since their daughter lived next door, it was easy to sneak over after dark and see her. But Livi and Harol spent a lot of time trying to convince Julyiah to give in to Jonar's demands. The meetings with her parents were not always pleasant for Julyiah.

As Julyiah flipped through more pages of Zemar, she still had doubts that she might be deceived after all. She had heard no more Music since the first day, and her heart was trapped within walls of stone. There was no one else who could marry her and Delwyn except the leaders, and they would not do it as long as the couple insisted on taking this stance.

Zuriel's betrayal also brought upon Julyiah feelings of pain and anger. How could Zuriel have done this to them?

And Poor Tomli. The boy's father had him under strict observation and no longer allowed Tomli to speak to anyone unless his father was present. He forced the boy to go to every meeting in the Listening Hall as well as to conduct daily study of the books in the music cells. Since Tomli loved the outdoors, Julyiah was certain he hated the routine, but there was nothing she could do.

"Remember the white stone," a voice said in her heart as she considered her trials.

Sparkling, silver-blue flashes accompanied the words, unseen above Julyiah's head. The glittery light shot out and upward.

"Did the lesson go into her heart?" another voice asked, followed by a lovely yellow streak, "as it did Dawnli's?"

"Not yet," the other replied. "Dawnli was fortunate, having suffered all her life, but Julyiah will remember. The lesson takes time."

"Yes, the people avoid suffering. They do not see its value."

"It is in their nature to avoid it. They need to remember that they will suffer, even as the Voice suffered."

The silver sparkles multiplied like fireworks before they disappeared.

Seeing she was getting nowhere holding a grudge, Julyiah laid aside her anger towards Zuriel. He was, after all, merely deceived as she had been. Her frustration with him had not helped anything, but it hurt her.

As she had seen before, it was in letting go of these bad thoughts that she felt better. Maybe she would be able to hear the Music again. Dwelling on evil thoughts and actions created a wall in her heart that blocked the Music.

Walls in my heart…

Julyiah's heart became lighter once more as the walls began to fade away. *The truth about the sacrifice of our natural desires is difficult to comprehend and accept. It defies our natural way of thinking.*

Staring at the *Book of Zemar* with unseeing eyes, Julyiah's mind attempted to grasp how pain could be good. The words on the page before her came into focus, and she read them out loud: "The Lying Wind may seem to bring a pleasant sound, but it will lead to Silence. Music may seem to bring death in the present, but it will lead to life most full."

Julyiah's understanding took hold. The suffering she went through often felt like death. Maybe the Music brought death before it brought life, and this was the way to joy. Did not the

Voice of the One also have to suffer and be silenced before He could sing again?

Julyiah shook her head in wonder at what she saw in the passage. Who could understand this? As the keeper came into the room, Julyiah made a mental note to study this part of Zemar further.

"Time to go now," the keeper said, maintaining the schedule the leaders had defined. Julyiah was to study afternoons and Delwyn evenings so that they would not run into each other. "I have a message from Leader Zuriel," the keeper added as the two walked back to the outside. "He wishes to speak to you this evening."

At the mention of Zuriel, frustration rushed back into Julyiah's heart. Perhaps this was the chance to speak her mind, so she pondered how to confront him.

But the walls returned to enclose her heart, and Julyiah saw that her ideas were not good. Shoving away the intense desire to be angry, she determined to dwell on compassion for her friend. As long as Zuriel did not believe in hearing Music on the Breeze, he would miss out on the truth. This was what she needed to remember.

Julyiah's heart felt lighter as the keeper escorted her up the stairs to Zuriel's home. She pictured herself walking into the room with Zuriel trying to argue with her, staring at her in animosity while she shot back her own explosive responses. Somehow she needed to hold her tongue and greet him in love, no matter what he said.

Taken aback when Zuriel greeted her with a smile, Julyiah blinked away her confusion. Zuriel maintained a mischievous expression as he invited her inside. Uncertain about his manner, Julyiah remained silent as she stepped into the room. About to ask what Zuriel's purpose was in bringing her there, Julyiah turned to see the keeper shutting the door and Delwyn stepping in from another room.

Chapter Eighteen: The Plan

♫

"Delwyn!"

Delwyn met Julyiah mid-room, and they greeted each other as engaged couples do, Zuriel looking on in pleased agreement. When they disengaged their kissing and hugging, Delwyn drew Julyiah with him to sit on some chairs, as close together as possible. Delwyn managed to turn his gaze from his loved one long enough to speak to Zuriel. "So, what do you think, friend?"

Zuriel's smile changed to a frown, and Julyiah looked from one to the other curiously.

"It would be a great risk, Delwyn," Zuriel said. "What would you do for a living?"

"Keenar has agreed to let me be one of the herders on the ranch if I disguise myself. Maybe after a while things will quiet down, and we can move back to the valley."

"Wait a moment," Julyiah interrupted in an impatient voice. "What are you talking about?"

Zuriel looked at Delwyn. "You have not told her?"

"Told me what?" Julyiah demanded.

Delwyn faced his wife-to-be. "Julyiah, I have a plan. It is... a rather unpleasant prospect in some ways but seems to be our only option. Zuriel does not believe as we do, but he also does not feel it is right to keep us apart. All the leaders have agreed we cannot be married as long as we believe this way."

"But, we cannot ever marry?" Tears came into Julyiah's eyes, and her lips quivered.

"Shh, sweet girl…" Delwyn touched her lips with one gentle finger. "Zuriel has agreed to join us in marriage, if it is kept secret."

♪

Julyiah's expression changed from confusion to surprise, just before her heart surged with joy. "Zuriel, you would do this for us?"

"On one condition," the leader said with a twist of his mouth. "That you and Delwyn move to the Underground. No one must know what I have done for as long as possible."

"Run away?" Julyiah asked, clinging to Delwyn's arm for support as the impact of this idea hit her. What were the consequences? No fancy wedding talia, no celebration with friends, and no forest visit afterwards as they had looked forward to for so long. Instead they would go directly to the depressing, wretched Underground. Dawnli had told many stories about the place, and these unwelcome thoughts now rushed back to mind.

Yet, Julyiah had been drawn to go to the Underground ever since the day she rode in the wagon and passed the Hole. She had felt destined to go, except she had thought it would be for a visit. Was she ready to face living there? What kind of life would a newly married couple have?

"One more problem," Zuriel said. "There has to be a witness at the wedding and I know of no one we can trust. We can try to use my personal servant Daish as a witness, but it is risky...."

Julyiah glanced at Delwyn. "We can produce a witness, I think," she said, "but how old does the witness have to be?"

"At least twelve."

A look of relief crossed Delwyn's face. "Fine, we have one. Dawnli, from the Underground. She lives with Julyiah's parents. The Music came to her when she first arrived in the community, and it was why she stayed. Dawnli would be a safe witness for our marriage."

♫♪

Zuriel was silent as he stared at Delwyn and Julyiah, who discussed their marriage plans in obvious excitement. Some confusion had entered his mind when Delwyn mentioned Dawnli's experience. After a moment, Zuriel shook his head to dislodge any unorthodox ideas, and he forced his attention on the marriage. There was a lot to do.

♪

The secret wedding was set for the next day, and Julyiah was both excited and apprehensive as the time approached. Julyiah, Delwyn, and Zuriel each arrived at the music cells at a separate time, in order to convene later inside the music cell of Zemar. Zuriel had special passes and keys for the doors in the music cells, so he was able to arrange for them to be together in one cell. The keeper was told they were holding a special teaching on Zemar to reinforce community ways. Zuriel had requested of Livi and Harol that Dawnli come also, since she was new to the valley and needed extra teaching from the books. Jonar was not told. Zuriel feared Jonar would stop it for some reason they had not thought of.

Julyiah was sorry she had to be married in front of something so fake as she looked at the bad painting of the mountains. Picturing the original wedding plans and the forest, the tears wanted to come. They might never go to the forest! Standing next to Delwyn in a plain, white cotton talia, Julyiah wore no beautiful wedding talia today. Unable to do anything special to her appearance lest they look suspicious, Julyiah struggled with emotional turmoil. Was it worth it?

The lesson of the white stone came back to Julyiah's mind, and she sighed in acceptance. They would learn the ways of true Music through their suffering, even as the Voice suffered and died in Silence. They would find the keys and unlock the Secrets of Gwenla. It was worth the pain; it had to be.

The ceremony was brief, held in the dimming illumination of light rocks that had been charged the day before. The music box in the cell was open, playing its pleasant little song as Zuriel presided, and the couple exchanged vows.

"Delwyn and Julyiah Sarroll," Zuriel pronounced, and Delwyn kissed his bride.

As they turned to sign the official marriage document, Dawnli revealed that she did not yet know how to write her own name. Zuriel gave her a brief lesson, letting her copy from what he printed on a Teka leaf. Dawnli practiced awhile, making a poor representation at first, but she remained determined. In the interim, Julyiah copied down more passages from the *Book of Zemar* to take with her to the Underground.

A keeper came in once to exchange a couple of light rocks, and Julyiah held her breath. But Zuriel hid the marriage document and acted as though he were teaching the group. The keeper left.

Finally Dawnli was able to make a legible scrawl of her name, obviously elated at the fact. They had been in the music cell for over two hours, and it was time to go.

"One more thing," Dawnli said, teary-eyed as everyone hugged one another before Julyiah and Delwyn's departure. "I want to give you this." She pulled out the white stone key, and handed it to Julyiah and Delwyn. "It is a wedding present—the only valuable thing I own."

Julyiah glanced at Zuriel sideways as she accepted the gift with a gracious smile to Dawnli.

"Thank you, Dawnli. We know what this meant to you and will treasure it," Julyiah said.

"And maybe find the lock it goes to," Dawnli replied, smiling.

Julyiah figured Zuriel was about to ask what this was all about, when Delwyn held the stone up to the nearest light rock in a curious examination. "There is something carved in this key— Z...e...n... No, that is an em. Then there is a hole, and I cannot make out what follows." He squinted and studied it closer. "And there are numbers...6...8...2."

"Zemar 682!" Julyiah shouted. "The key is for the *Book of Zemar,* and it is right here in front of us." Opening the book again, she searched the pages, certain that Zuriel was bewildered by now. She reached the 682nd passage of Zemar and read it aloud: *A bad place is death to a man; but a good place brings him life.*

Silence filled the room. Julyiah frowned. She felt nothing.
Delwyn shrugged and scrunched his nose.

Zuriel grinned, and Julyiah pursed her lips at his scorn of their
excitement. No doubt he was wondering what they expected to
happen, and of course, nothing did.

"I cannot read or write," Dawnli said, breaking in on the silent
thoughts. "But I do know some numbers, and I think the number in
the middle is a three not an eight."

Delwyn's eyes grew wide as he held up the stone key again.
"Yes, you are right! It is 632."

Julyiah feverishly searched back a couple of pages for the new
passage, noticing it was one of those sections where the
pages looked new and untouched because it was not often read.
She even had a little trouble getting the pages to open. When she
found the passage, she read:

*Men build walls and shut out Music, thinking they are shutting
out the Lying Wind. But Music will come again to those who seek.*

This time the words resulted in activity. Bright bursts of light
and color streaked into the room, visible to all. Julyiah noticed that
even Zuriel's eyes followed the colors around the room. The music
that had been droning on from the music box stopped in an instant.
Julyiah recalled the night that Delwyn heard music the first time at
her house and how the air felt. Something incredible was about to
happen.

Zuriel stepped over to the *Book of Zemar* and read with
reverence the words of the 632nd passage again out loud.

Dawnli gasped, and Delwyn stepped back as though afraid.

Julyiah's sensation of an imminent encounter grew stronger.

A loud *CRACK!* from the box made Julyiah jump and cry out.
All eyes turned to the box, and Julyiah expected music to come out
like never before. Instead a dark line appeared in the box's wooden
side, a gap which grew larger every second. A sound like a huge
boulder hitting another vibrated through the room as the box
exploded, scattering debris everywhere. They covered their faces,

and Julyiah was surprised when nothing hit her. Looking up she saw that no one had been harmed.

A myriad of sounds streamed into the room like tiny, singing insects, weaving themselves into Music. The Music on the Breeze blew into faces and encircled them like soft whirlwinds. Beautiful colors flowed with the Music, and Julyiah was taken away to a lovely forest setting, hearing the Voice singing to her about patience when waiting for the Music to come.

When Julyiah returned to the room, she could tell that Zuriel also had experienced the ecstasy of the moment. When it was all over, the four of them sat on the floor, catching their breath.

"Wow!" Delwyn whispered. "It has never been like that before. It keeps getting better."

"I think it had something to do with the music box breaking," Dawnli commented.

All turned toward Zuriel. "You heard it too?" Delwyn asked.

♫♪

Zuriel could not speak at first, so overwhelmed was he at his experience with the Music. He stared at his friends as though he had never seen them before. Feeling like jelly, he could not move but remained breathless and exhilarated.

"The... places," he whispered in awe. "So many places! So magnificent! They are... all out there." He waved his hand, indicating with a simple gesture the world beyond the fortress. "I went to a huge forest where a fall of water rushed down over towering rocks and spilled into a waterfall high above me. It splashed upon giant boulders right in front of me like thunder. I thought I would perish with joy.

"The Music was beautiful—so unique, yet familiar... and the Voice sang to me." Zuriel closed his eyes and his voice caught with emotion before he continued. "His song told me that he wants me to be a strong leader of the people—all the people. Not only the people in this community but in the Underground as well."

"Yes! You could do that, Zuriel." Julyiah said. "You are a good speaker and leader."

"And did you see a door?" Delwyn asked.

Zuriel looked at his friend, startled. "Yes! How did you know? Someone knocked, and I opened the door."

Julyiah and Delwyn smiled at each other. "We went through doors too," Delwyn told him.

"You have to make a decision to set aside your old ways before you can hear the Music," Julyiah said.

"I need to tell you all something." Dawnli swept aside her long hair as she stepped forward to speak. "I saw some words in the Underground that were carved in stone over a doorway—a man read them to me once. The words were in the shape of a key. It was those words that led me up to this valley where I first heard the Music."

"There is another key!" Excitement was evident in Delwyn's voice. "There is a key in the Underground where we are going, and the One must be telling us to go down and find that key."

"What were the words?" Julyiah asked.

Dawnli closed her eyes and recited:

Follow the death,
Come up from the under,
Music flows free,
Breaking Silence asunder.

"I would like to go back some day," Dawnli said, "but I believe the One wants me to stay in the valley awhile."

Julyiah smiled. "We will meet again."

"And it might not be safe to go down there right now," Zuriel warned Dawnli as he rose to his feet. "The leaders will wonder why you are following the Sarrolls. I want to go down too, but later. I want to look for the keys with you."

"And the Secrets of Gwenla," Julyiah added.

Zuriel's head shot up and he looked at the others with conviction on his face. He smiled—a broad grin that showed he was now with them all the way in their beliefs.

"Yes... and the Secrets of Gwenla!"

Part Two

The enemy has persecuted my soul;
He has beaten my life down to the ground;
He has made me dwell in darkness,
As those that have long been dead.
Psalms 143:3

Chapter Nineteen: The Underground

♪

"Try over there, Rashi," Julyiah called out to her three-year-old daughter. "See where the sun is on the Teka bush?"

"Thith one?" Rashella asked, pointing her tiny finger at a diasia plant.

"No, hon, over there." Julyiah grinned, recalling her own enjoyment looking for bugs when she was young. Her daughter took after Julyiah's love for any kind of creature, and children always found ways to play, no matter how dismal the surroundings.

Standing in her small garden in the dim world of the Underground, Julyiah patted her dog Shep's furry brown head as she ran her other hand across her forehead. Looking at her hand, she frowned. *Now I have smeared the dust into the sweat.* Her eyes squinted at the sun popping out from behind a pinnacle surrounding the jagged *Durnee Break* high over her head.

Similar to the Hole above the waterfall, the Break vented to the Outside instead of to the valley. Bright light shone through the opening, with rays of sunlight spreading over a wide area on the Underground floor, but it only lasted a short time. Julyiah liked to be outside so that she and Rashella could catch a little sun, no matter how hot it was. The sunny spot lit up the few plants that managed to grow before the beams moved on across the huge cavern. From the start, Julyiah had been astonished that anything would grow in her tiny garden.

Barely enough energy to survive, Julyiah thought. *Like us.*

"Shep," Julyiah spoke to her shaggy dog in an urgent tone as she pointed to a leaf that had moved in the garden, "there is a mouse!"

The dog let out an excited yip and sped across the garden, bounding over the plants in his faithful search to keep rodents from invading his mistress's garden. If he found one, he also had the joy of a small snack for the day. His main course would come home with Delwyn when he brought scrap fat and bones from his ranch work in the valley.

The year they arrived in the Underground Julyiah had been grateful to find a little house so close to this sunlit section of the vast subterranean cavern. Though it was tiny, with a dirt floor, the house had higher rent because of the available garden area.

Leaning on the hoe she had been using to oust some inedible weeds, Julyiah waved to a neighbor woman, who had come out into her garden. Julyiah enjoyed talking to an adult once in a while, and some families had children who came over to play or learn something from her lessons in reading.

Some of their neighbors were not so friendly, but they kept to themselves, and for that Julyiah was grateful. Most of the people in the houses worked in the Durnee tavern, gambling house, or hotel, where no law prevented those of evil intent from carrying out their plans of darkness. A man named Darse owned all of the buildings in Durnee, and he lived in a richly decorated section of the hotel, or so Julyiah had heard. She had heard stories about his dark manner and did not like to think about what kind of activities he managed in his buildings.

Having neighbors they could trust had become essential, especially if Delwyn was working above, or if they had to leave their home. All of the houses under the Durnee Break were situated in a wide circle around the area where sunlight shone through, in order to allow garden space in the center. The layout also helped guard the garden from unwanted invaders.

Shep pounced under a diasia plant and bit at something between his paws, his brown fur shivering with his movements. Julyiah assumed he caught his mouse. "Good boy!" she called out, observing the dog's tail wagging in acknowledgement. His head did not turn, indicating he was busy with his catch. Minutes later, he jumped up and ran to Julyiah with a skinny tail hanging out of his mouth. She laid a loving hand on his head. "Good boy! What would we have done down here without you?" Julyiah told him. Shep yipped through his mouthful before trotting over to Rashella.

"Good dog!" Rashella declared. Shep's tail wagged in furious receipt of her praise before he lay down to enjoy his snack.

The nicer setting of their house did have a catch—endless dirt falling from above. On the other end of the Underground, the water spilled through the Hole in a spectacular waterfall, the constant spray settling the dusty air. The Durnee Break, on the other hand, did not open to the green valley but to the Outside, near the West Wall. The constant winds on the Outside blew dust over the edge of the opening, where it settled without end on the inhabitants below. In addition, extra strong winds blowing from the desert sometimes blasted against the West Wall, causing the fine particles to pile up at the base, where they spilled through the Durnee Break like a sandy waterfall.

The sun moved on all too soon, and Julyiah now stood in a shadow on the edge of the green area, studying her plants. Rain fell through the hole above and watered the spot on a regular basis, unless a drought afflicted them. The leafy diasia and root crops grew well, but she had to pollinate them by hand. Bees would not come to that end of Durnee, though a few buzzed over by the waterfall when the sun shone through the Hole. Julyiah had tried to grow a red smush plant her first year there. She smiled at the memory. The plants had grown into ridiculous-looking, long spindly vines with a bleak green color and no fruit. That type of plant needed more sun than they ever received in the Underground.

As Julyiah continued hoeing, she kept watch on Rashella, whose persistence in digging around the Teka bush encouraged Shep to join her. He kept pouncing where she dug, no doubt certain she had found something living. Julyiah was glad that Teka bushes did not mind someone digging around them.

Julyiah took her hoe and walked over to the prolific Teka bush with its many thin branches, each holding one large, pale green leaf. "Rashi, do you want to help me harvest some Teka leaves?"

Rashella jumped up, brushing the dirt off of her brown leggings. She pulled off several leaves that Julyiah pointed to. Examining them, Julyiah chose a few to be heat treated and flattened into writing material. The rest she stuffed into her talia pocket for rags and other uses.

Julyiah used her hoe for a walking stick as she took Rashella's hand with her free one and turned back to the house. Shep needed no invitation to follow them as he ran alongside. The dog had been a gift from Rikial Keenar, who was concerned about Julyiah's safety while Delwyn was working for him during the day. Keenar had been to the Underground a few times, and he knew of the numerous dangers that lurked in the darkness. "The dog will guard you and your home from ruffians and your garden from raiders."

How true! Julyiah shivered when she recalled her first week without Delwyn at home, cowering inside her house while Shep guarded the door with his furious barking. When he had stopped, still growling, Julyiah ventured to look out the window. In time to see two rough-looking men hurrying away, she could imagine what they were after. As for the garden, the mice and hungry people would have eaten or stolen it all before she could harvest, if it were not for the dog.

After Rashella was born, Julyiah was more grateful than ever to Keenar for giving them the dog for protection. Keenar also visited them once a month, which she felt was kind. Though he did not know they were married, he never spoke a word of judgment against them.

When she and Delwyn made the decision to marry in secret, Julyiah had not considered the pain and rejection that would follow. Thinking the couple had not been married at all but ran away to live together, her parents would not even speak to Julyiah for several months. It was not until she was pregnant that they had softened—long enough to help with her pregnancy and to see their grandchild Rashella after she was born. After Zuriel broke down and told Julyiah's parents the truth—that he had secretly joined the couple in matrimony—the relieved Hartbrooks agreed to tell no one else. Harol also met Delwyn once a week at the Hole to give the family some extra food and send notes from Livi to Julyiah.

Julyiah laid one hand on her stomach, now bulging with a second child. They also seldom saw their friends. Neither Zuriel nor Dawnli came often to the Underground, feeling they should stay in the valley.

Julyiah could not blame them. It was not a nice place to visit, but Zuriel had done his best to help them as he could without risking his position as a leader. "I should tell the other leaders the truth," Zuriel offered one day. "They do not know about the marriage. I will take whatever punishment I must endure."

The married couple glanced at each other. "No, Zuriel," Delwyn said. "Jul and I have discussed this. We do not feel it would make any difference in our lives if you spoke up. No one in the valley will accept us as friends after our disobedience, and you might be deposed as a leader."

"We would still have to live below regardless of what you told anyone," Julyiah agreed.

At first, the Sarrolls had investigated the caves of the destitute, excited to see the plaque in the shape of a key guarding the door as Dawnli had told them. Passing out food to the poor, they searched the caves until dark, but examination of every corner of the caves turned up nothing. After a time, having no further direction from the Voice and no longer hearing Music while in the Underground, the couple gave up the search.

Julyiah's focus turned toward the children in the Underground right away. Often hungry and neglected, the children ran wild, forming packs in order to fight over food. Taking Shep with her for protection, Julyiah befriended those who allowed her to talk to them and persuaded some to come to her house for school. Although they often missed school time due to illness, working, or searching for food, the children grew fond of Julyiah due to her unfailing kindness toward them. Luring them with a very thin but warm chakia soup each day, she taught those who came how to clean themselves and live better, and she hoped it made a difference. A few regular attendees also learned from her how to read and count. And since her only literature was what she had copied from the books, this writing was what they learned to read.

Julyiah wished she could feed the children more, but she had her own family to consider, and she knew that the leaders sent food down every week to all who came for it at the Under Hall. She decided that teaching the children how to fend for themselves was more important.

Daily survival overshadowed any previous desire Julyiah had to find new truth or fight tradition, and the misery of living in semi-darkness too often crowded out any further outreach to others in the Underground. Caring for her own little family was her primary goal.

♫♪

Zuriel observed a growing melancholy in Delwyn Sarroll every time they met each other at the Hole. Delwyn's life had become obvious drudgery—coming the long way to work in Keenar's herds each day, and going home tired, dirty, and depressed. Zuriel knew that Delwyn loved horses and missed his work with them—now he saw only sheep and goats.

Regardless of the Sarrolls' advice not to bring to light all that had happened, Zuriel thought his friends might have a chance at a better life if he spoke up. Although Delwyn's parents had died, he thought perhaps Julyiah's parents could house the little family. The leaders might continue to condemn the couple for their actions, and the people of the valley might follow their lead, but his friends would enjoy more comfort in life. It troubled him that he was carrying on with his life as though nothing had happened, while his friends in the Underground struggled so much. Still, Zuriel shuddered as he contemplated what might happen to him if he confessed to marrying the couple without permission. He could end up losing his position and the Sarrolls no better off.

Uneasiness also pressed on Zuriel as he continued teaching at the Listening Hall. He could not speak the truth about listening to

Music on the Breeze because it was certain he would be removed as a leader, bringing upon himself the wrath of the community. Traditional passages from the Books remained safe subjects for his teachings, but when he observed the complacency of those who came to the Listening Hall each week, Zuriel hated to continue.

Zuriel's primary joy in teaching anymore was the presence of Dawnli at the meetings. She soaked up every word he taught and shared his belief of hearing Music on the Breeze. Sensing an interest of a different kind in Dawnli as she grew older and more beautiful, Zuriel no longer saw Leadership as his only goal.

Between the people's attitudes and what the Voice had sung to him about being a leader, Zuriel became dissatisfied with his regular weekly teaching. Zuriel longed to teach those who yearned to hear instead of the bored crowds who came out of obligation. A smaller meeting place called the *Under Hall* had been built years ago in the Underground, and the youngest leader, Jesero, had been appointed as the new overseer. Zuriel felt certain he could help Jesero with the distribution of food to the poor. The leaders tended to despise the poor, and Jesero might welcome the help. While working at the Under Hall, Zuriel could visit the Sarrolls more often without suspicion. Perhaps he could even take over the work down there some day.

Zuriel felt this plan should work. At last, he could follow the calling he felt within and see more of his friends as he did so. He set out to make his request right away.

Chapter Twenty: The Storm

♪

"Sand storm!" someone called from the other side of the Underground. The phrase repeated as others called out the same warning, until shouts echoed throughout the huge Underground cavern. Julyiah rushed out of the tiny house and looked up at the Durnee Break. Clumps of dirt blew across the large hole overhead, hit the edge, and whirled down to the Underground.

"Come inside now, Rashi," Julyiah called out to the little girl who was busy stacking small rocks in front of the house.

"But I am building a goat shed," Rashella complained, dropping her shoulders in protest of the loss of precious time, gazing on her project with forlorn abjection.

Julyiah laughed softy. "I am sorry, Rashi," she soothed. "A storm is coming."

Rashella glanced at the Durnee Break, since that was her only known source of a *storm*. "Not coming thoon," Rashella said, pointing up to the opening where the wind had not yet blown clouds of sand on them. "Th'ee?" Turning back to her work, Rashella did not appear concerned.

"I see it is not here *yet*, but it *is* coming soon. Come now, please," Julyiah said in a more convincing voice. "I do not want you buried in sand."

"I can take a bath!" Rashella announced as though this idea would solve the problem. "May I th-tay outside?"

"Rashella Sarroll!" Julyiah's stern call alerted Rashella that Mama was not happy. The little girl jumped up, brushed off her brown talia, and ran toward the house.

"Coming, Mama."

When her daughter was inside, Julyiah locked the door behind them. A sand storm would dump several inches of dirt on her garden, leaving layers of the stuff on everything in the

Underground. She did not want any homeless people trying to barge their way in to find shelter. Hoping Delwyn would make it home before dark, Julyiah sat back with her bored three-year-old to wait out the storm.

♫

Delwyn assumed there had been a sand storm below ground that afternoon, when he heard the wind howling louder than usual outside the West Wall. He paused to listen to the wind, while leading a goat to the milking area at the Keenar Ranch. The high walls around the community protected it from the west winds, but the Underground got buried in a layer of dirt each time. The milk goat announced her desire to continue, so Delwyn patted her and walked forward, knowing he would have a lot more labor at his own house after his ranch work was done.

Picturing his home and garden covered with fine dirt, Delwyn gathered his belongings for the long walk to his house. Grateful for the strong muscles he gained from his daily walk and work among the herds, Delwyn shifted the multiple bundles on his shoulders, unable to leave anything behind due to its value at home.

Puffing, Delwyn approached the final leg of the switchback road at the base of the falls and observed people in the process of cleaning up. Shoveling mud from their front porches, those who dwelt in the preferred area near the waterfall grumbled at their plight. Delwyn waved as he passed but had no sympathy for them. The dwellings under the Durnee Break received the worst of the storm, and his family lived in one of those homes. Living with the incoming sand was part of the price they paid for their location.

Delwyn needed to reach the house before dark if he wanted to clean off the garden plants in the daylight. Rain followed the strong winds and turned the garden plants into little piles of mud that flattened them, if the dirt was not removed. Julyiah was in no condition for such hard labor, and everyone else would be busy cleaning up their own yards and homes. Most of all, Delwyn wanted to make sure his family was safe. The homeless or certain rough men often sought shelter during the storms, and he hoped his house was not one of the places they had invaded.

Walking through the tiny village of Durnee, Delwyn heard strands of music coming from Durnee Tavern and considered the loss of creativity. *Those stringed instruments could be playing something beautiful, if they did not have such foul words put to them.* Valley dwellers had not been allowed to play musical instruments. It was believed they would bring the Lying Wind to the community.

At last, Delwyn reached home and knocked on the door. "It is me!" he called out to Julyiah, who unlocked the door with a happy smile. Shep and Rashella also hurried over for their personal greetings of welcome.

After giving Delwyn a quick hug and kiss, Julyiah unloaded his many packages off his shoulders, setting them on their small table to unpack for him. Shep sniffed at one of them in eager anticipation.

"Shep, down!" Julyiah ordered, and the dog backed away with a hungry whine. Turning back to care for Delwyn, Julyiah handed him a drink of water inside a metal container.

"I am so sorry I cannot help you out there, Del. I do not think I can bend over much."

Delwyn patted her pregnant belly and grinned. "Do not worry, Jul. I can manage."

"I want to help Papa," Rashella announced. "He hath worked too hard today."

Rashella's admiration of him touched Delwyn's heart.

"Rashi, can you really help Papa?" he asked.

The little girl squealed with delight. "Help Papa? With what?"

"Come outside and see," he enticed, extending his hand toward her.

Rashella threw her arms up to be carried. Delwyn lifted her briefly but set her down again. He needed to conserve his strength for the task ahead.

"Come, we must clean up the dirt in the garden."

It was dark an hour later, but the garden plants had been unburied from the ravages of the sand storm. Delwyn and Rashella dragged back into the house, holding hands until they stepped inside, where Rashella rushed to hug Julyiah.

"Papa could not carry me, Mama," Rashella explained with short, hurried breaths. "He wath too tired." She let go of her mother and flopped onto the dirt floor next to Shep, who was chomping on his evening bone.

"Whew!" Rashella sighed in a loud demonstration of how much she had accomplished. "That wath hard work!"

"Good job, Rashi!" Julyiah said to Rashella. "I hope she was not too much trouble, Del," Julyiah whispered to her husband, grinning.

Delwyn shot back a weary smile as he sat down to recover. "She was a trooper," he said. "Rashi brushed off the garden leaves after I shoveled most of the sand away. I think she actually helped."

Delwyn looked over at his precious daughter, who had laid her head on Shep's side for a pillow, closing her eyes. His gaze drifted toward Julyiah, who handed him a bowl of soup she had prepared, no doubt enduring great pain in her final month of pregnancy to provide it for him.

Thanking the One for his wonderful, productive family, Delwyn set his exhausted body in a reed chair by the table to eat his dinner. He would sleep well tonight, unless the baby came. Whoever said the poor were always lazy had no idea what they were talking about.

♪

One week after the sand storm, Jesero sent a messenger around, announcing a meeting that would be held every week at the Under Hall. Excited to meet with others again, Julyiah and Delwyn went to the first gathering, thinking it was better than nothing. However, Jesero proved to be an inferior teacher, with a droning voice that focused on evil living. It was his obvious view that anyone living in the Underground was deceived. A music box was available for the group to sing to, but it was an old, worn out one that skipped notes. The Sarrolls could not wait to leave the Under Hall and did not intend to return.

One day after they went to the meeting, Jesero visited the Sarrolls. Julyiah greeted him with a polite smile at the door, hoping that he had come with compassion, not judgment.

"Where are you folks today?" he asked them, smiling.

"In a nice place," Julyiah replied. "Where are you? Will you not sit down, Leader Jesero?"

Delwyn echoed the greeting, but Julyiah could tell he wished their visitor had not come.

"Would you like some tea?" Julyiah asked.

"No, thank you," Jesero said, studying the drab living area with a table, where perhaps three adults could sit in a row. One doorway indicated a tiny bedroom. Julyiah regretted the dirt everywhere, but she could not help it.

"Do you enjoy living here? Do you enjoy being poor?" Jesero asked, sounding amused. "Why do you not return to the correct beliefs so you can get married and return to the valley?"

Julyiah and Delwyn looked at each other with widened eyes. *How can we possibly respond?* Julyiah wondered. If they mentioned that they were married, they would have to say who presided over the ceremony, betraying Zuriel. They could not get married a second time because they had no plans for meeting the prerequisite to deny the Music on the Breeze.

"We no longer have anywhere else to live," Delwyn pointed out. He had left his room at the Keenar Ranch in order to join Julyiah below, and Julyiah's house was occupied by someone else now. Julyiah knew Delwyn's answer was an attempt to stall.

"Julyiah's parents would surely house you," Jesero said. "They have room, even with Dawnli living there. If you denounced your silly beliefs, you could be married and accepted as though you never went astray."

"We have no intention of denouncing our *silly* beliefs," Delwyn said, his fiery eyes making his disgust clear. "Also, we do not make a habit of staying where we were not invited."

Julyiah hid a smirk in admiration of her husband's response, but she gritted her teeth when Jesero raised his eyebrows and shrugged his shoulders. Apparently, he felt Delwyn's answer relieved him of any further obligation to help the couple. He got up to leave, shaking his head as though he could not think of anyway to get through to such deluded people.

If they could admit they were married, it would make such encounters easier, but they could not. How glad Julyiah was that she had copied passages from the books before they came below! They no longer had anyone nearby who shared their beliefs, and she often drew comfort from the words of truth. The rest of the Underground continued to show that it had little to offer. Little Music. Little friendship. Little life.

♫♪

Dawnli sat in Livi and Harol's house with her benefactors and Zuriel, her chin resting in one hand as she tried to remember the month in which she was born. Zuriel scrutinized Dawnli's transformation into a lovely young woman, her now healthy, shiny blonde hair glowing in the sun that streamed through the window. Dawnli's other physical features had improved also, no doubt from years of better eating. Squinting, Dawnli moved her lips from side to side in thought as Zuriel crossed the room to sit next to her, relishing the closeness.

"What about your brother?" Zuriel suggested, trying to ignore his longing to hold her. "Do you remember his birth month?"

Dawnli's head tilted sideways as she looked at him, her hair falling softly off her cheek. His breath caught at her beauty, so he made a show of clearing his throat as though from the food they just ate.

"I remember mine was either Autia or Aptia—one of those. How would my brother's birth month help?" Dawnli asked, flinging her hair behind her with an impatient grunt.

"You said you are four years and two months older than your brother. Try to remember what kind of day it was. Was it cold, hot, raining? Perhaps he arrived in the fall—in the month of Nomem. Your birth month might be Aptia. If he was born in the summer, your birth month is probably Autia."

Dawnli brightened. "I remember that it was a hot day when Bobbiel was born. My birth month must have been Autia. You are right, Zuriel." Her smile of appreciation caused his heart to rejoice that he had assisted her.

"You are nineteen years?" Zuriel felt his pulse quicken in anticipation of what this might mean to him.

"Yes! I can hardly believe it!"

Zuriel agreed. He marveled that the skinny, homely girl that came up to the community five years ago had turned into such an attractive woman, but he was still nine years older than she was. Too timid to approach her with anything deeper than friendship, he had used any excuse he could to be with her. Absorbed with her circle of friends at the Listening Hall, Dawnli had faithfully attended in, learning more about the books and augmenting her social life in the process. Zuriel was delighted with her interest in study, but he was concerned about losing her attention to a man her own age.

Zuriel and Dawnli had both heard the Music at Julyiah and Delwyn's marriage, and this bound them together in a special way. They often reminisced about that wonderful day in the music cell of Zemar when Zuriel first heard the Music. As far as they knew, no one else in the community had ever heard real Music. Their one difference was that Dawnli still heard the Music often while Zuriel rarely did.

As Zuriel listened to Dawnli chat with Livi about a talia she was making, his heart beat quickened. He loved Dawnli, but he knew he could never ask her to marry him and go on some wonderful visit to the woods afterwards while his best friends still suffered below. He had unfinished business to take care of.

Chapter Twenty-One: The Under Hall

♫♪

Jonar and the other leaders were more than willing to let Zuriel take over the delivery of food to the poor, but they left it up to Jesero for the final decision. Jesero said he was relieved to have someone help, and his broad smile at Zuriel's desire to speak at the meeting in the Under Hall told Zuriel that eventually his entire plan would work out.

"Let us start with one duty at a time though," Jesero said, laughing at Zuriel's enthusiasm to get started. "I appreciate you taking over the food distribution first. That will be a big load off of me."

An excited Zuriel arrived at the Under Hall the following Listening Day, along with Jonar's personal Keeper Menila and a wagonload of food. The Under Hall was situated off of the Access Road, about halfway down to the cavern floor. Nestled into the stone wall, its rocky front and one heavy wooden door faced the waterfall. The horse pulled the wagon to a stop in front of the building, within a space that was barely large enough to hold such an ensemble.

Menila had told Zuriel of the chaos that always ensued with the distribution of food, so Zuriel had instructed Menila to help him combine the food into bundles before they loaded the wagon. Each bundle had the same amount so that no one would be left out or get envious. He hoped this would prevent the occasional fights that Menila had mentioned.

As they unloaded the wagon, the people crowded around, pressing in and holding out their hands to make sure they did not miss their share. But as they saw that each person would get the same amount, they calmed down and waited their turn. Zuriel enjoyed passing out the bundles of chakia, grain, and diasia to the eager crowd. He dreamed of them being as eager to hear him speak when the time came.

Jesero came out of the Under Hall building, looking surprised. "How well managed," he told Zuriel with approval. "And much quieter." Jesero went back inside, and a shiver of excitement rushed through Zuriel. Jesero had been impressed with his work! He admired Jesero because the man was so willing to come below and work among the poor. It appeared they would be getting along well together, and they had the same goals for the people who lived in the Underground.

As the food was distributed, Zuriel invited each person to come in and hear truth from the sacred books. He quoted passages as he sat and waited for them to eat, but not many looked interested. Jesero walked out and asked Menila to take buckets down to the river for water and bring them back for Zuriel to fill the many metal cups that were ready for the people to drink. Zuriel thought it odd that Jesero was coming up with more for him to do, but he so highly esteemed Jesero's work that he complied. Zuriel thought perhaps Jesero wanted to see if he was willing to do the small duties before he gave him anything more.

When Menila brought the water back, Zuriel went to get a bucket to fill cups, but Jesero stepped in ahead of him and began to do it himself. Zuriel marveled at Jesero's willingness to stoop to the level of a servant. He grabbed another bucket to follow Jesero's lead. Surely Jonar or another leader would make the Keepers do such work, not do it himself. They would consider menial labor beneath them. *Impressive!*

As the weeks went by, Zuriel became so active in helping Jesero with the poor that he did not mind so much listening to Jesero's singsong teaching voice that dwelled on what was wrong with everyone. His major problem with it was trying to stay awake. But he enjoyed going down to help, and he was certain that Jesero would see before long that Zuriel was serious and dedicated to the task. He figured that must be the reason Jesero had not invited him to speak yet, since that was Zuriel's most obvious talent. No doubt

Jesero wanted to make sure Zuriel would not start something he did not plan to finish.

One day as Zuriel was handing out the food bundles to each poor person that arrived, greeting the man, woman or child in person, Jesero came and stood nearby. Without warning, Jesero stepped over, grabbed the next bundle out of Zuriel's hands, opened it, and handed it to the next person. Jesero continued, opening the next bundle before handing it to the next person, ignoring Zuriel completely.

Taken aback, Zuriel blinked in confusion. *What is he doing?* But Jesero did not explain. Zuriel noticed the man in line looking as surprised as Zuriel was; he took the open bundle with hesitance. Zuriel had talked to this man and had built a relationship with him. Jesero spoke some kind words to him, and turned to the person behind him, but Zuriel had been hoping to speak to the man again himself.

Trying not to feel affronted by Jesero's actions, Zuriel stepped away from the wagon and stood by to watch. *Was he feeling jealous?* Zuriel did not think so, but he knew he was embarrassed standing around doing nothing.

A child who had sat down to eat something started to cry, and Zuriel hurried over to the boy. He appeared to be about six years old, and no adult was with him.

"What is wrong?" Zuriel asked the boy, squatting in order to be closer to his size.

The tear-streaked face peered up from under a wad of straggly, thin brown hair. "Someone took my chakia root when I was not looking."

Because his bundle had been open when he received it. "I will get you another," Zuriel told the boy, who gave him a hopeful smile. "And I will watch out for you until you can eat it."

"What is wrong?" Jesero asked Zuriel when he came back to the wagon and rummaged through the extra supplies under the blanket.

"Someone stole the boy's chakia root out of his bundle," Zuriel said in disgust. "Who would steal food from a child?" Zuriel wished he could have seen who it was so he could confront him.

"These things happen," Jesero replied without concern. "You will learn, and so will the boy."

Jesero's comments caused Zuriel to pause, fuming. He was not sure he had ever been so furious. Zuriel spun around, snatched up two chakia roots, and headed back to the boy, muttering to himself over and over: *You will learn... You will learn.* Jesero was several years younger than Zuriel and had not been helping in the Underground much longer than Zuriel. What experience did Jesero feel he had over Zuriel?

"Here, you can eat one now and take the other one home with you," Zuriel suggested to the boy.

"Oh thank you, sir," the boy said, smiling. The youngster took a bite of the raw, unpeeled food, grimaced at the taste of the bitter peel, and grinned as he reached the inside starch, closing his eyes as though he was eating a delicious dessert. He devoured the chakia in no time and began to tie up his bundle as Zuriel had suggested.

"That is much better if you peel it, you know," Zuriel said.

The boy smiled and nodded. "I know. But I was hungry."

After the boy left, Zuriel went inside the Under Hall. If Jesero wanted to hand out the food himself, what did he expect Zuriel to do now? Twisting his mouth sideways in consternation, Zuriel looked around. He had already swept and mopped the room, arranged the chairs into three rows, and replaced the light rocks. Wait... why was that light rock in a different place? Did Jesero not think Zuriel capable of placing light rocks properly? Was he planning to adjust them all?

What is going on? Zuriel's mind turned in circles as he wondered how to confront Jesero. At last, Jesero came into the room.

"Sitting down on the job?" Jesero commented, laughing.

That does it! "I am sorry?" Zuriel held back a sharp reply. "Why did you not let me pass out the food like I was before? Do you want to change the work I do?"

Jesero smiled as though he had been waiting for the query. "Because I wanted to do it differently. I felt the people needed to see what they were being given."

Zuriel could not believe his ears. After all the help he had given Jesero, why would he push his way in front of him like he did, unless he felt himself a superior person? Perhaps he did.

"You gave me a job to do," Zuriel said, trying to remain calm. "And I was doing it to the best of my ability."

"It is not your job to oversee the distribution of the food," Jesero explained, smiling as though he was happy to help Zuriel understand true Leadership. "I am still in charge of the food distribution. You are assisting, and I appreciate that. But I need to be able to make changes, and I felt a change was needed."

Zuriel's eyes widened and he shook his head in disbelief. "But why did you not ask me to change what I was doing instead of shoving your way in front of me, doing so while the people watched?"

Jesero smiled again. "I am sorry if you are jealous, but I am in charge and I need to remain in charge. The people need to know this too. You cannot dictate to me how to do this work; I dictate it to you.

"Now, if you do not mind, I have a meeting to start." Jesero walked away, leaving Zuriel in so much inner turmoil that he had to sit down to control his raging emotions. His heart plunged into a place where he was attempting to walk across a deep chasm on a narrow bridge with no handrails. He tried to sing himself out of the bad place, wishing the Voice would come and help him understand, but he could hear no response or direction.

As people came into the room and took a seat, Jesero continued to rearrange the light rocks Zuriel had placed. *Is he deliberately trying to irritate me?* Zuriel brooded. *Is he trying to demonstrate that I am not needed here?*

Jesero passed out Teka leaves and writing charcoal for the study he was preparing to give and did not appear to have any qualms about what he had done or said to Zuriel, nor did he act like he cared whether Zuriel was in the room.

Zuriel saw no point in staying to listen to Jesero's teaching. In the weeks that he had been helping, Zuriel had endured the droning voice out of respect, but that respect was waning. As Jesero continued to ignore him, Zuriel walked out the door, his shoulders sagging.

Later that evening, Zuriel sat at his desk in his beautiful home and wondered what he should do. He knew he needed to sing, but it was hard when he felt so low. At last he sang, asking for the Voice to bring him truth or some Music on the Breeze to comfort him. He wondered that he could be so certain where his life was headed a few weeks ago and now have no idea at all.

So subtle that he almost missed it, Music and beautiful shades of blue and green lights floated into the room from his open window on a refreshing Breeze. Zuriel saw himself sitting on grass by a quiet stream with a pleasant burbling sound. The Voice sang to him: "Do not be discouraged, Zuriel. You will speak to the poor and feed them. I want you to teach all of the people My ways, and you will start with the poor."

When he was back in his room, Zuriel sighed deeply, feeling at peace. Perhaps Jesero was merely having an off day—some type of personal problem that would pass. After all, he had so admired the man before. Zuriel decided he should not be so quick to dismiss Jesero but try getting along with his odd behavior. The man appeared to mean well.

"I have an idea," Zuriel told Jesero the next time Menila and Zuriel brought down the wagonload of food.

"Wonderful," Jesero replied, not looking up as he uncovered the bundles in the back of the wagon. "I am always glad to hear ideas. Menila, hand me those pieces of rope, will you?"

Zuriel hoped Jesero was still listening to him as he watched the other leader bustle about tying up the bundles of food. *Wait, what is he doing now?*

"I thought you wanted to leave the bundles open," Zuriel pointed out, frowning in confusion.

"I decided it was better to have them closed."

No acknowledgement of whose idea it was in the first place. Oh well, one always needs to learn humility, right? Zuriel swallowed his pride.

"What is your idea?" Jesero asked, pulling Zuriel out of his reverie.

"I could speak to the people while you are passing out the food," Zuriel said assertively, since he felt that the One wanted him to do this.

Jesero looked up with his usual noncommittal smile. "Oh, but I would like you to pass out the food again," Jesero said. "You enjoyed that, did you not?"

Zuriel's mind jolted as he squinted at Jesero and grimaced. "What?" he asked, unable to think of anything else to say. "What do you want me to do?"

"Today I want you to feed the people with a tied bundle as you did before. You can talk to them of course also, if you like," Jesero said. He hurried away as though he did not have another minute to spare.

Zuriel stood, dumbfounded, staring after Jesero until the other leader disappeared inside the Under Hall. Was the man playing with Zuriel's emotions on purpose? What could his intention be with this odd behavior? Jesero had no interest in how a person felt, as far as Zuriel could tell. Jesero often talked about how people felt, which would be an admirable characteristic if he cared, but what if he did not care? Jesero acted as though his service for the One was all that really mattered. Did he care for other people at all? Zuriel was not certain anymore.

Scenes of Jesero with himself and others came back to mind. Zuriel remembered Jesero saying something rude to one of the homeless people the week before, and Jesero had even shoved Menila aside once, because Jesero wanted to do something and Menila was in his way. The sacred books mentioned in several places that they needed to show other people love—that even a servant should be treated with love. Yet Jesero showed no shame over his actions. Now that Zuriel considered the whole picture, he could not remember Jesero apologizing for anything to anyone. *Does he not see his own actions as wrong?*

Zuriel tried not to let it bother him. After all, Jesero had said Zuriel could talk to the people while he passed out the food, and they were starting to line up. Zuriel shook the confusion out of his head and began to talk to each person or quote passages from the books. Again Jesero reappeared, with the music box that was kept in the Under Hall. He opened it and set it on the wagon seat. It played its little tune too loudly for anyone to hear what Zuriel was saying. It did appear that Jesero's intent was to sabotage anything Zuriel did, while acting out his part as a superior leader. Zuriel stopped talking to the people, too upset to continue, as he handed out the food.

In the days that followed, Jesero continued to behave the same way, changing Zuriel's every duty until Zuriel could no longer understand what he was supposed to do next. When Zuriel asked Jesero a question one day, Jesero smiled as though nothing was wrong but said, "You do not appear to enjoy this work any longer."

Zuriel stared at him, shaking his head. "How could I enjoy it?" he asked.

Jesero kept smiling but said nothing. Discouraged, Zuriel realized there was no reason to continue working at the Under Hall since he was making no difference. The poor would still be fed and taught the same way whether he was helping or not. Jesero would see to that, even if he had to do it all himself. Which he often did.

Relieved in a strange way, Zuriel turned to walk home, leaving Menila to bring the wagon up later. When Zuriel spoke to Jonar about the situation, he suggested Zuriel stick it out, even with Jesero's rude and unpredictable behavior. Perhaps things would change. Zuriel did not think so. Perhaps the One meant for Zuriel to speak to the people some other way, because he certainly was not allowed to do it at the Under Hall.

Chapter Twenty-Two: The Poor

♪

"Mama!" A merry face beamed with some exciting news as Rashella ran inside to her mother, panting and burbling some unintelligible words.

"What, hon? I cannot understand you." Julyiah wiped her hands off on a softened Teka leaf and patted the youngster's brown curls affectionately. It grew difficult to bend toward the girl with another little one growing larger inside Julyiah every day.

Rashella pressed her lips together and tried again. "I thed, Papa'th comin' acro'th Cherry Bridge!"

Julyiah smiled as she realized why she had not been able to understand her daughter the first time. "You may go meet him." She did not have the words out any sooner than Rashella sped back out the flimsy metal door, slamming it in her haste to run up the road to her father. Shep whined when he could not follow his charge outside, so Julyiah had to get up and open the door for him. With a joyous yap, the dog bolted out the door.

The bucket of vegetables refused to wash themselves. Julyiah turned back to the stone table and pulled up a dilapidated reed chair, arching and rubbing her back. She was tired. A nap had been helpful before picking the vegetables, but they needed washing right away, or they would wilt. It had been harder than Julyiah expected to bend over the bank of the river to fill the bucket, pull it up full of water, and cart it many steps uphill. *Too bad I cannot teach Shep how to wash vegetables,* she thought, smiling.

The pain in her back worsened as Julyiah sat and put out her arms to wash the leafy green diasia and crisp white chakia roots in the water. Frequent resting became necessary. *Delwyn's dinner will have to wait again,* she told herself. She could only do so much. When finished, she would have a three-day supply of vegetables stored in the cold box, and that would be a worthwhile accomplishment. Hoping the baby came before she had to do it again, Julyiah continued washing.

As she peeled the starchy roots for the usual dinner of chakasia stew, Julyiah looked around the featureless room. *I am tired of this place,* she realized. *I am tired of the dirt floor. I am tired of no cupboards and nothing to put in them. I am tired of bare walls, bare floor, and bare living. And I am tired of that big crack in the corner where the bugs hide.*

Sighing deeply, Julyiah gazed out the window a moment to relieve the painful ache in her heart—an ache stronger than the one in her back. Her eyes landed on the fake tree down the lane, near the bridge. Studying the brown rocks, piled and formed into a trunk and stocky, thick "branches," she smiled at the peeling green paint on the man-made metal leaves that stuck out unnaturally from the lifeless rocks. Many such fake trees abounded in the Underground, made by men who thought to add some greenery to the drabness.

Julyiah let out a short laugh, but tears came to her eyes as she remembered the real trees that grew above. How she and Delwyn loved trees! Yet they continued to live where no trees could grow, mocked by painted representations of them.

What had happened to their lives? Had not the One directed them as they had thought? Would he not want them to help the poor and proclaim the truth? Why did he not send the Music? Their hope and energy dwindled. She sometimes wondered how they could continue another day. Yet, she always wondered that, and onward they managed to go.

A beggar boy sat under the handmade tree, appealing to workers coming home from above. Julyiah watched as the weary men and women walked by the pleading child, ignoring him as best they could, even cursing him to be quiet.

Delwyn and Rashella walked hand in hand over the bridge, laughing in delight as they passed by the boy, but they did not see him since their focus was on each other, and Shep's attention was on them.

The boy looked at them, his eyes mournful, and he stopped asking for help. Putting his hands over his eyes, he started to cry. Julyiah could not take her eyes off the boy. He came from the abandoned mines, she decided. Maybe his mother or father was sick, and he had to do the begging. Or maybe he was already an orphan.

Julyiah's problems disappeared as she sought a way to help the boy. But they had so little themselves, and a baby was coming. They could not spare any more money or food than they already did, having decided from the start how much to give because it was too much to think about on a daily basis.

Unwilling to watch a child starve under a fake tree, Julyiah looked away. Maybe if his begging was unsuccessful, he would not come back tomorrow…. With horror, Julyiah realized she was hoping he would go away and die somewhere else, out of her sight. *What wretchedness are we doomed to that we not only turn away from starving people but wish we did not see them in the first place?*

Julyiah looked back at her pile of fist-sized chakia roots. It was a three-day supply for her family, but a few roots would not be greatly missed. They could also skip the sweet leaky roots they loved to chew on after dinner—their one "luxury" as they called it. Leaky roots had been so named due to the sweet-tasting sap that "leaked" from the roots. Foregoing leaky roots for a week would allow them to spare two sokens for this boy.

For a brief moment, Julyiah thought she heard music. Was someone whistling outside? She tried harder to listen, but Delwyn and Rashella's noisy arrival through the door disrupted any ability to hear sound from another source. Shep added to the commotion with a welcoming bark, and Delwyn stepped over to Julyiah for a welcoming kiss.

"I am sorry to be getting your dinner late again," Julyiah apologized as Delwyn sat wearily in one of the two reed chairs in the house. She straightened and rubbed her back again before pulling a small chunk of meat from Delwyn's leather tote to put into her stew. Continuing to peel the chalky rind off of the chakia, she cut the roots into small pieces and put them into a pot of water on some flat warming rocks that had started to glow with heat.

Shep whined at her feet. "Learn to wait a little longer," Julyiah said to the dog. She was glad Shep had caught a mouse that day, for there was no bone in Delwyn's bag. Tossing an extra chakia root into the water whole, Julyiah knew the meat-flavored chunk would help stave off his hunger. Perhaps he would find a few bugs around the house that evening as well. Otherwise, he would be chewing on a piece of old leather, as he often did. *It is either that or our shoes,* she thought with a smile.

"Mama, I am hungry," Rashella whined as she stood next to Delwyn's chair and helped him pull off his sandals. "When can I eat?" She raised her eyebrows and pushed her lips out toward Julyiah, as though her expression would assist in her request.

"You learn to wait a little longer too," Julyiah told her daughter with a smile.

"Shhhh, darling girl," Delwyn said, turning her toward him and holding up his hand. "Mama is tired because she has to carry two people around. Did you know that?"

Rashella looked at her mother and cocked her head, one wavy curl slipping over her eyes.

"I do not th'ee another perthon, just Mama," she said, pushing her hair back and placing hands on hips. "You do not mean it, Papa," she announced, leaning forward, peering up at his eyes.

Julyiah laughed at her daughter's antics.

"Oh, yes I do mean it," Delwyn countered, looking serious.

Rashella's smile faded and she examined her mother again. "Where ith another perthon?" She held up an arm on each side and cocked her head.

"She is carrying herself and the baby," Delwyn said, smiling. He held out his arms, inviting his daughter to come.

"Oh, I th'ee, the baby!" Rashella's face lit up as she climbed into Delwyn's lap.

"Del?" Julyiah glanced out the window to make sure the boy was still near the bridge. "Would you mind if we gave some food to that boy out there?"

Delwyn frowned. "Boy? A beggar?" he asked, standing and holding Rashella as he walked over to the window.

"By the bridge, see?" Julyiah pointed. "He saw you and Rashella walk by, and … he was crying. It was so sad. We should do something."

The admiration in his eyes almost answered for him as he smiled at her before turning to Rashella. "What do you think, sweet girl?" Delwyn asked his daughter. "Should we ask the boy to eat with us?"

Rashella answered with a resounding, "Yeth!"

♫

After dinner, Delwyn hurried along Circle Street with the boy, Johan. The road followed the river west and north around the far side of the Underground in a horseshoe shape, until it flowed down under the wall and out again. It was over two thousand paces to the abandoned mines where the child lived, and Delwyn wanted to make his delivery before dark. At times, groups of men formed bands in order to rob those walking down the road at night, and Delwyn did not want to take Shep away from the house where he could protect Julyiah and Rashella.

How did Julyiah always get him into these situations? Were they not almost as poor as these beggars and he already exhausted? They should have given Johan dinner and sent him on his way. When Delwyn glanced down at the boy who stumbled along with an eager grin, he knew their own life was much better than Johan's. The boy scampered beside him, no doubt dreaming of good food.

"This will make Mama well!" Johan nodded confidently. Delwyn had guessed wrong. The boy wanted good food for his ailing mother. Johan glanced up and smiled through a grimy face streaked with the tears he had shed earlier. Delwyn knew that

Julyiah had tried her best to persuade Johan to let her wash his face, but he had been aghast at the idea of wasting water on such an action. "Why, it will be all dirty again in an hour," he assured her. "And you would have to haul the water again. I can wash in the river."

Delwyn was impressed by the boy's thoughtfulness. "This goat dung should last you three days if you use it sparingly." Delwyn indicated the bucket he carried for the boy. "You do have a warming rock, do you not?"

Johan looked at him with disdain. "Of course! Everyone has a warming rock! It is the fire we do not have... or something to make it."

Delwyn felt the chill of the evening spring air. "Even in winter?"

"Of course. We are not better off in the winter."

"But how can you get by?"

The boy looked at Delwyn as though he must be the most ignorant person he had ever met, shrugging and kicking at a rock in the road. "You hope for spring."

Delwyn thought of his own family. They were always warm. They sat every evening around their little stone stove, warming rocks glowing with heat from the goat dung that Delwyn gathered freely from above—a bonus from Keenar. Well, he would simply have to gather more dung for this boy and his mother.

Approaching the caves, Delwyn's jaw dropped in amazement. Five years ago, there had been maybe twenty or thirty in these caves. But now he saw a group of one hundred or more. Nothing was left of the mines but the dingy caves, and just the poorest of the poor went there.

The population of the poor is growing. Times must be growing worse.

Some had fire and had scavenged a little food for the evening. Others stood a short ways off, looking on with longing. Many more were inside the caves, incapable of standing. As Delwyn and the boy approached, one man hobbled over to have a look, and others followed him. Delwyn hid the goat dung inside his coat to keep it for Johan.

"Food? Sokens?" they pleaded, and Delwyn sensed the frustration that Julyiah had felt earlier. Even as he was sharing with this boy what little they had, it was not enough—there were so many more that needed something. It looked hopeless.

Young Johan did not struggle to solve the problems of the masses. He handed over one of his precious chakia roots to the two nearest beggars and another to a sorrowful-looking young girl. "Take this to your Nana," he told her. Her face lit up with gratitude, and she ran inside with the little prize, a tattered part of her talia trailing along behind her in the dirt. The boy waved the others off. Perhaps they had eaten that day, Delwyn thought, and Johan knew it. Or maybe they were bullies.

The smell inside the caves assaulted Delwyn with the reality of poverty. With new insight, he realized that poor people who are sick have no money to hire a nurse to carry off their waste. And those who might do it themselves were too weak or discouraged to bother.

Delwyn had experienced some discouragement. Just a little. Still, it was real enough to teach him compassion. He cringed, remembering how he used to discuss among valley friends the reasons why people lacked sufficient money to live on: *They do not want to work. They gamble. They waste their money on wine or evil recreation.* But as he stood there, observing the sights, sounds, and smells of poverty, the reasons why people were poor no longer mattered. The books said these people should be helped; nowhere did it say they should be judged.

Johan's mother's eyes lit up when she saw the chakia roots and the goat dung. Lying on an old patchwork quilt that was pulling away at the seams, she smiled. The quilt stank terribly but was the only thing that spared her from the ground. Apparently too weak to raise her head, she mumbled a thank you to Delwyn.

Delwyn turned to the flat warming rocks that made up the tiny stove near the woman. Pulling out his flint, he struck it and lit the goat dung inside the grate under the rocks. Some warmth began to reach out to them. The fire would die out before long, but the rocks would retain the heat throughout the night. *What a blessing that warming rocks are so plentiful down here.*

Johan had left but returned with a bucket of water which he put on the stove. He dumped three large chakia roots into the pot, conserving the rest for the next couple of days.

When Delwyn thought he could stand the smells inside the cave no longer, he said goodbye. Outside, he stopped to gasp for fresh air, determined to preserve the entire scene in his mind.

A group of beggars by the road had given up for the night and lit some rank-smelling trash for heat. One man pulled out a bucket of the bitter chakia root peelings which were often discarded by wealthier folk.

"There are some diasia ends in there too," the beggar announced, appearing proud of his ability to scrounge. "I had to fight off the Wilsos, who always try to get Darse's garbage for their animals. I says, 'You going to give them scraps to goats? There are people starving where I live.'"

"You did good." One of the men nodded as he wolfed down a raw peeling, spitting out the sand he encountered.

"You know what I will do?" another said. "I will get out that piece of fat I found in the garbage yesterday, and I will *fry* these little treats on that piece of metal!"

"Mmmm," they all murmured.

Delwyn's eyes drifted to another group, who were not eating. These sad folks stared at their neighbors with envy, no doubt plotting how they would do better the next day. Delwyn figured they must have at least found some materials to make a fire, because they hovered around a small rock. Others retreated into the caves as the daylight faded, and some pulled their ragged coats and blankets around themselves to curl up in a quiet corner near the cave opening.

Deciding he had better get home to his family, Delwyn headed toward the road. After a few steps, he took one last glance back at the caves and spotted the plaque over the main entrance, in the shape of a key.

Follow the death,
Come up from the under,
Music flows free,
Breaking Silence asunder.

An eye-opening thought struck Delwyn as he looked at that key. In fact, for a moment he thought he heard music, but shook his head. "No, it could not be," he told himself. He had been imagining he heard music for years. He stared at the words on the sign, trying once again to understand what they could mean. But he was growing weary and realized he was ready to drop. Turning around, he put the caves and their problems behind him, heading for home.

♫♪

Zuriel was certain that no one in the group was listening to him read from the *Book of Silia* that he had brought to the Underground. He was sure it did not matter much, since just four people were present, and three of them were Julyiah, Delwyn and Rashella Sarroll. Julyiah was busy trying to keep Rashella quiet, while the other man who had come kept talking to Delwyn every few moments instead of paying attention to what Zuriel said.

After his episodes with Jesero at the Under Hall, Zuriel decided to come below and read from the books in the Underground to whoever wanted to come and hear him. He liked to read near the sunlit area under the Durnee Break so he could see the words better, and Delwyn had set up some rocks for the people to sit on. Zuriel and the Sarrolls had been excited about the idea at first, but Zuriel never had much of an audience.

Although Julyiah and Delwyn appreciated him coming all the way down there to read for them, Zuriel still did not feel he was doing much good. The people in the Underground were more in need of food than in listening to him talk. Zuriel always brought food. In fact, after Delwyn told him they were sharing food and sokens at the caves, Zuriel had brought more food down for his friends, so they never had to go without their delicious leaky root treat. Zuriel also visited the caves with food for the beggars and could distribute it the way he felt best.

Chapter Twenty-Three: The Pain

♫♪

It was so quiet that Zuriel could hear the strike of Jonar's pencil tapping as if in rhythm with his heart, except his heart was missing every other beat. Cisco got up and went to open a window. Zuriel could agree that the room was hot and stuffy after he had confessed what he had done and why. He ignored the others that waited in silence—Delegar, Jesero, and Keeper Menila over in the corner who always waited on Jonar hand and foot. Zuriel's attention was on Jonar, whom all else listened to and obeyed. Whatever Jonar decided, the others would follow.

♪ ♪

Jonar sat at his desk, staring at Zuriel with a blank expression, developing a plan for how to handle this unexpected interruption. More than ever people looked to him as the ultimate leader in Victory Valley. He had heard rumors of a plan to build a statue in front of the Listening Hall to honor him—Jonar, the Respected. His great wisdom had outwitted the most perplexing problems. His judgment had been impeccable. *Why*, he thought, *is it so difficult to curb this rising tide of heresy?*

"I seek counsel," the master leader said, turning to the others who were present. He stood up to begin his characteristic pacing around the room, rubbing one side of his head as though by this action he might persuade answers to come forth. "This is a problem to all of us. I made a decision over Delwyn and Julyiah years ago, and Zuriel chose to ignore it. Such action is punishable among the people, but among the leaders, it has been virtually unknown."

Jonar whipped around, and his eyes narrowed as he glared at Zuriel.

"You have broken many years of tradition. You have blemished the fine name by which we are called. *Respected* they call us. What will that mean now?"

♫♪

Jonar let out a partial moan as though in pain and sat down again, staring at Zuriel with hatred that the younger man had never seen in a person before.

Why did not I leave it alone? Zuriel asked himself. The answer came to him right away—the Voice sang to them. That was why he could not leave it alone. The Voice sent the Music on the Breeze and prompted him to join Delwyn and Julyiah in marriage. *It is His fault... wherever He is or has been for the last five years.* But even as these thoughts went through his mind, Zuriel knew he would not now choose another path if he could. Music was his life. He had dedicated his entire being to the service of the One and the continuation of Music. If he must be tested in this, so be it.

Delegar was slow to anger—in fact, slow to anything. He rose with a laborious grunt, his old, arthritic limbs creaking as he cleared his scratchy throat. Glancing around the room, he regarded each person with sad eyes in a gaunt face. Pausing for a lengthy look at Zuriel, Delegar let out a little cough before speaking.

"It seems to me that Zuriel has been led astray by love for his friends, Delwyn and Julyiah. He had long looked forward to their marriage, foreseeing it long ago and encouraging it since. They are the only family he has, his parents having died long ago."

"Yes," interrupted Cisco, catching Jonar's eye. "But can we allow love of friends—or even love of family—to get in the way of obedience to the One?"

"I did not disobey the One," Zuriel pointed out, receiving the piteous stares of all in the room, who no doubt considered him demented.

Jonar responded in a patronizing tone: "Disobedience to a High leader is equivalent to disobedience to the One." Zuriel noted Jonar's animosity.

"Do you not agree?" Jonar asked, looking at the others, daring them with his eyes.

"Most certainly," Cisco said right away. Jesero nodded. Delegar said nothing and sat down again, elbow propped with his head in his hands.

"What should be done to a leader who disobeys the One?" Jonar asked as though it was a group decision.

"He is cast over the wall," Jesero quoted from the books.

No one had been cast over the wall since the first years in the fortress. Jonar knew that Jesero had never liked Zuriel, having been jealous of his higher position and ability to speak. Jesero's recent dealings with Zuriel had confirmed this.

"No... no," Jonar chuckled as he laid one hand on his desk to pause. "Nothing so dramatic. We are a peaceful people. Such action is fit for murderers." Jonar grew thoughtful. "Or blasphemers." His eyes narrowed as he turned toward Zuriel. The brief silence that followed was broken only by Delegar's snoring.

"But it can be agreed, I am certain, that such disobedience calls for a strong response," Jesero countered.

"Yes, indeed," Jonar said, putting his hands together in a thoughtful prayer shape under his chin before continuing his pacing. "I recommend removing Zuriel from his position as a leader for the crime of direct disobedience to proper authority. He will be cast... over the wall, so to speak, of leadership, housing, and service. This will be temporary, of course."

Jesero smiled.

Cisco nodded.

Delegar woke up.

Zuriel heard no more. He barely comprehended the fact that the others agreed, for his mind blurred with echoes of "cast over the wall." *It is as I knew it would be. I have tried to help Delwyn and Julyiah and have condemned myself—and for what? A position I no longer have.*

167

♫♪

That evening, Zuriel shuffled out into the night air through the door of his apartment in the North Wall, to take a breather from the heart-wrenching task of packing his things. *Maybe I will be back soon*, he told himself, staring at a distant light rock. Grateful for the chill of the evening, he enjoyed its freshness compared to the despair engulfing his home.

Laughter rippled from below, and Zuriel peered over the stone railing of his balcony at the bright light of the nearby Listening Hall. A group of young people leaving the music cells appeared to be enjoying themselves. One of them caught his eye—Dawnli. She had gone to the music cells with her friends—two... no three boys... yes, and three girls. The girls always flirted with the boys, giggling in that ridiculous teen hysteria at everything the boys said. Zuriel noticed that Dawnli also joined in this play, giggling near that handsome son of Cisco's—Daleil. In spite of his disgust at her immature behavior, Zuriel felt painful twinges of jealousy.

Zuriel was about to turn away when Daleil leaned over and kissed Dawnli, who smiled with pleasure at the gesture of affection. Daleil took her hand, and the two of them walked on with the others. Zuriel wanted to see Dawnli wrench her hand away from Daleil, but instead they began swinging their arms and gazing into each other's eyes, smiling as they headed for the shops.

"One moment too late," Zuriel said aloud. "Why did not I look away sooner?" He reached up to stroke his face, regretting that he had shaved off his beard in order to look younger to Dawnli. *All for nothing—like everything else.*

Tears streaked down the deposed leader's face as he stared at the distant light rock. *I should have kept my eyes on that light.* Amazed at the strange calm in his heart, he sank further into the swampy pit he had been trying to avoid all afternoon. Turning, he walked back into the stuffy, stone room that was his home for one more night.

♪ ... ♪♫

Dark shadows followed the hissing and moaning sounds back and forth, back and forth. An occasional word could be heard from the thick cloud of blue-black substance. Two dark beings discussing something in an anguished whisper.

"They must not make it through this!"

"Surely they have lost hope."

"Yet Julyiah came so close to hearing the Music again today, I almost saw color."

Murk was silent for a moment, wondering what his master would want to hear most. "Close, my lord, but still so far away. Her circumstances consume her thoughts. Delwyn feels much worse this evening. Zuriel is close to complete despair. Those who serve our purpose are left alone to cause trouble."

The pacing stopped, and the giant settled into a flat pool, shrouded by a rising gray mist. A horrible silence full of imagined groaning filled the area. Hostility as keen as the edge of a knife shot inky goo out of the pool into bleak soggy patches. Slimy creatures appeared from nowhere and rushed toward the collections of muck.

"And without hope, they cannot survive."

♪

The Underground remained cool in the heat of summer, except when a series of one hundred degree days settled onto the area. It was in the middle of such a heat wave that Julyiah and Delwyn's son, Mikela, was born.

Delwyn mopped Julyiah's brow with cool water for hours while the midwife helped the younger woman bring another child into the world. After Julyiah's many screams of pain, the fitful cries of a baby boy rent the hot, still air at last. Relief washed over Julyiah when the terrible ordeal ended in a healthy birth. She wanted to hold him, but she was too weak to do more than admire him lying by her side.

"You will have to heat more water," the sturdy midwife instructed Delwyn, running an impatient hand across her sweaty, thick forehead as she packed her bag. "There is quite a mess to clean up."

The woman lacked any sympathy, Julyiah decided, wishing she had the energy to confront the midwife. She regretted the way the woman barked at poor Delwyn, who had worked all the previous day and came home to no sleep all night. Blinking his droopy eyes, Delwyn picked up a bucket and headed outside.

Julyiah's mother had insisted on a midwife. "I will not have you bearing another child with improper care," Livi had declared. "You take this money and hire the best midwife in the Underground."

Julyiah had laughed at her mother's concern, but now she was glad there had been help. The baby had been turned wrong, and the woman knew what to do.

"You are going to need a nurse, you know," the midwife informed Julyiah with a businesslike snap of her satchel.

"The money I gave you…."

"It covered the delivery."

"But..."

"What is it?" Delwyn asked, stepping back inside with his bucket of water.

"She needs a nurse." The woman took the baby and wrapped him in a blanket with efficient expertise, before laying him back at Julyiah's side. Gathering her remaining equipment, the midwife stood, bag in hand, ready to depart.

♪

Delwyn stared at the woman a moment. "I will take care of her," he asserted.

The midwife laughed, wiping the corner of her eye as though the statement was hilarious. "You hired, me, sir, on the basis that I know a bit more about this process than you do. Your wife has undergone a difficult labor and is exhausted. When you return to work—which I assume is in a few hours—she will be unable to care for herself, much less a baby. She is too weak to move...."

"That will do," Delwyn shushed the woman, trying to think. "How much for nursing?"

"Ten sokens a day, plus room and board somewhere of course. I cannot be expected to travel so far every day."

Delwyn stared at her a moment and burst out laughing. "Room and board? Ten sokens? What do you think—this is the valley? That we are the Suntar Clan?"

"Get it from her parents again," the woman advised. "Or do without. Makes no difference to me." She made a motion to leave.

Delwyn squinted at her in disbelief. "We will do without," he replied with a dismissing wave of his hand. "Thank you for your services." He wanted to say more as he followed the woman to the door, but he knew his anger would not create a good atmosphere for a recovering birth mother.

Returning to Julyiah, Delwyn watched Julyiah raise herself up a little to shift her position, but her arms flopped back on the blanket as though helpless. She sighed, looking at her baby with longing.

Delwyn hurried over to help Julyiah move her body. Relieved that Mikela had gone to sleep for the moment and Julyiah had closed her eyes as well, Delwyn headed out the door. Glancing at Rashella, who slept soundly on the floor near the table in the main room, he knew he had to do something.

♫♪

"Zuriel!" Delwyn woke his friend, who had fallen asleep in one of the reed chairs outside. Zuriel had hauled water several times that night for the expecting couple, figuring it was the least he could do after all the hospitality they had shown him the past few weeks. He had been planning to help them with their rent a little also, even though he slept on a dirt floor, but his new job working on a ranch did not pay enough. Not used to physical labor, Zuriel found the work exhausting. He could not work enough hours to help with more than the cost of his food because he had other financial responsibilities.

Zuriel squinted up at Delwyn, hoping this was a short interruption, and he could close his eyes again. "Is it morning?" he asked in a sleepy voice.

"Not yet. I have to go talk to Julyiah's parents—now. Can you stay here with her, Rashella, and the baby until I get back?"

"Sure, but why....?"

"Julyiah is exhausted and cannot take care of the children. Neither you nor I can stay all day with her because of our jobs, and I do not know what else to do. I have to ask her parents to take her and the children in to live with them...." Delwyn's voice drifted off with the last few words.

Zuriel's eyes grew wide. This was serious—no sleeping matter. His mind snapped to attention, yet he was not certain how to respond. "That is a good idea, but…"

"No time to discuss it," Delwyn said, turning away. "I will see if Dawnli can come and stay here today, and I will make arrangements at work to bring Julyiah up tomorrow. I am sure Keenar will loan me a horse and wagon."

Delwyn's words faded out as he hurried back the house to get ready. Zuriel told himself that he could go back to sleep for now, but it no longer appealed to him.

Dawnli was coming.

He had not seen her since that painful night when he lost his status as a leader. For a time, he hoped she would hear of his banishment and move to the Underground. *Surely she will at least visit when she hears of it.* A little voice reminded him that she appeared to love someone else and a stab of rejection cut into his heart at the memory. *Surely that was just a young girl flirting.*

Despondency threatened Zuriel once again. That feeling had become too familiar. In his heart, he sat for long hours alone in an unlit cave, doing nothing. He had never felt so depressed before. Understanding better what Delwyn had been feeling, Zuriel could identify with those who no longer wanted to live. Many important issues burned within him, yet he was helpless to do anything about them without his position as a leader. Why did life cause those who can do something not to care and those who cannot do anything to care with all their being?

Zuriel did a little for the poor, where he visited with food scraps or goat dung. He and Delwyn passed out what meager amounts they could bring. It should have been more, but Zuriel had a lesser job than Delwyn and was required by law to pay a monthly fee to reserve his home above the Listening Hall. Zuriel could still get it back if he was returned to his position, as long as he reserved the place by paying for it. Otherwise, it would be given to another some day.

Of course, he thought, *they may never reinstate me, and I may be paying it all for nothing.* But what would life be to him without Leadership? It was all he had known. He could not picture himself doing anything else for any length of time.

But what was life without Dawnli either?

Chapter Twenty-Four: The Move

♪

Julyiah did not enjoy the torturous ride in her weakened condition, but she managed to adjust herself so she could see through a crack in the wagon's side, hoping it would distract her from her pain. They passed by various landmarks—another fake tree, the store, the tavern, and the gambling hotel in the center of the Underground which made up the "town" of Durnee.

At last the sound of the waterfall grew closer. Excitement sprang up in Julyiah when the wagon shifted and angled in front, adjusting to the climb up the Access Road. With great effort, she turned over and searched for another crack to peek through. Yes! The abundant spray of water at the base of the falls glistened in the afternoon sunlight from above.

Hope continued to grow as the work horse exerted more force with his powerful muscles, pulling the wagon slowly up the incline. Julyiah heard Shep's familiar yip and knew the dog was excited to accompany them. The dog loved to travel up this road when he got the chance.

Unable to bear the prospect of life at her parents' house without Delwyn, Julyiah held onto the hope that they would have their own home again someday. Maybe they could get her old place back—Julyiah's parents owned the house. Someone else had rented it, but those people might be willing to move on. Now that all knew Julyiah and Delwyn had been married for five years, maybe circumstances would settle, and her life would return to the way it was.

The way it was...

While the road full of potholes and rocks jarred her body in too many places to count, Julyiah contemplated the past. Would she go back to life before hearing the Music if she could? Dreaming of peaceful afternoons teaching school, contented

Listening Days at the Hall visiting with friends, and weekly dinners at her parents' house brought tears to her eyes. It would still be that way if not for the Voice they had heard and the Music He sang.

Maybe the leaders were right. Maybe it had been the Lying Wind after all, disrupting their lives. It had brought pain, not just to Julyiah and Delwyn, but to her parents and to others. Was that not what the Wind did? The lesson of the white stone came to mind, but Julyiah ignored it, feeling she was in too much turmoil at the moment to welcome it for any reason.

The baby broke into a cry in Dawnli's arms as she carried him alongside the wagon. Julyiah's maternal instinct shoved out all other matters in her heart. It had been a while since Mikela had nursed, and her arms longed to hold her newborn again.

"We will have to stop," Dawnli called out to Delwyn, who had job of leading the harnessed horse up the steep road.

"There is no room here," Delwyn shot back, and Julyiah felt bad for him. His obvious frustration and humiliation tore at her heart. Julyiah often felt she could bear what happened to herself easier than what afflicted Delwyn.

Julyiah's face tingled from the mist, the roar of the falls growing louder as they drew closer to it. When the light went dim, Julyiah knew they had gone behind the waterfall—the last landmark before taking the final leg leading to the top.

At last, sunlight streamed in through the Hole and speckled the cavern walls. *The valley!* Julyiah and Delwyn had brought Rashella up to visit her grandparents a few times, meeting at a picnic area next to the Hole, to spend the day together. Julyiah looked forward to having the sun all day. The light grew stronger, and Julyiah squinted as she adjusted her eyes to the brightness.

The poor down below never see this wonderful light.

The leaders insisted that the poor chose their own way of life, but Julyiah knew better now that she had lived so close to a poverty level. Most of those people had not chosen to be poor. Other choices they made had played a part in it to be sure, but to stand up for the truth was hardly an offense punishable by poverty. There were many reasons the people found themselves in the Underground way of life. Some had made unwise choices, like gambling or an evil lifestyle, but others had become too sick to continue working or were hurt in an accident and had no friends to take care of them. Even those who despaired of finding a better life were to be pitied, in Julyiah's opinion. No one should be ignored because they lived in poverty, of that she was certain.

♫♪

The baby grew quiet in Zuriel's arms. He had taken the newborn when Dawnli offered him, and little Mikela had stopped crying. This result merited an admiring smile from Dawnli that melted Zuriel's heart. Something in Dawnli's manner disturbed him—she had changed. Also, an unseen barrier stood between her and her old friends, because she was not experiencing the same hardships that he and the others had. Why? Was it because she had grown up in so much suffering as a girl?

Dawnli still heard the Music on occasion and had told Zuriel she did not understand why they did not still hear it as well. Zuriel wished he knew. Also, Dawnli enjoyed the teaching at the Listening Hall, even though she did not agree with all of it. Zuriel hated going anymore, but he went in order to keep peace with the leaders and the people. Not going would assure his total rejection from everyone. The fact that he came up each Listening Day from the Underground was unheard of, but he had no intention of going to the Under Hall again. Zuriel spoke to valley folk of his work among the poor, hoping the leaders and Dawnli would recognize his worth.

Zuriel looked up as Dawnli tossed her hair back from her face to gaze up at the sunrays, unaware that the reddish tint of the setting sun caused each strand to glow with color and splendor. Zuriel's heart burst in awe as he relished the sight, while pain stabbed at his heart. How he loved her!

♫

Delwyn did not even notice the baby had changed hands, so intent was he on his destination. He wanted this ordeal to be over with as soon as possible. Going to Julyiah's parents and asking them to take her and the children in had been the hardest thing he had ever done. They were delighted to do so. Perhaps it was *how delighted they were* that had bothered him. Of course, they were happy. Now they would be able to care for her and the grandchildren themselves and do a better job than he had done.

The wagon hit something and stopped still, the horse straining to continue without success. Delwyn's harsh words toward the animal caught in his throat as Julyiah moaned. Shep barked at the holdup, impatient to continue up the road.

Snorting air instead of swearing, Delwyn patted the horse's foamy neck and side as he spoke to him. He decided the animal needed a breather. Delwyn walked cautiously back to the wagon, looking for whatever held up the wheels. When Shep tried to nose in for a stray hand to pet him, Delwyn pushed him aside with a gentle, "No, Shep," so he could look for the problem.

When he spotted something sticking out of the road in the way of a back wheel, Delwyn handed the horse's lead to Dawnli. He found the long edge of a rock that had sunk partially into clay and hardened. The metal wagon wheel was up against the rock and would not budge—at least not forward. Pulling out a pick from the wagon, Delwyn wielded it and loosened the object, kicking it to the side. Trudging back uphill the length of the wagon, Delwyn retrieved the lead from Dawnli and tugged on it, encouraging the horse to continue. The animal thrust its weight forward once again, and the wagon moved.

Delwyn's last scrap of pride had diminished that morning. Until today, he had hoped to reinstate his place in the community as a responsible person—as a responsible father and husband. He used to come home every day the hero and breadwinner. At least in the Underground his inability to provide better was hidden. Down there he did better than most, not worse. With Julyiah and the children living at her parents' house, his lack of success would be apparent to the entire community. His love for Julyiah and his children was the only thing holding him together now, but the relief that they would be better cared for was offset by the devastating knowledge that he was a failure.

If the Voice would send the Music again, he could hold his head up high no matter what the circumstances, knowing the Voice guided his way. However, of all the things about to happen, he was fairly certain that hearing Music again was not one of them.

♪♫

Dawnli glanced at Zuriel again with a half-hearted smile. *I should have told him before,* she thought, cringing inside. *He still loves me, I can tell.*

The wagon approached the trees by the Hole, and Dawnli noticed the pine needles sparkling in the sun's glow as the afternoon breeze moved them ever so slightly. This was where she first heard the Music, and even now she heard a hint of it in the treetops.

Why can the others not hear the Music anymore? They had never been disobedient, so far as she could tell. The white stone, smoothed over by so much washing, had meant so much because throughout her childhood she had suffered and hoped the trials had smoothed out her rough edges. Why had her suffering stopped but that of her friends continued?

Nothing was rough for Dawnli now, except what she still had to tell Zuriel. Daleil had asked her to marry him, and she told him yes. When she shared about hearing the Music on the Breeze, Daleil had been skeptical at first but later grew more interested. Dawnli was certain he would hear the Music any day now.

Why were the others all in such daily turmoil, rejected by everyone and struggling? And poor Zuriel—his life upside down! How could she tell him she was engaged to Daleil? *It will break his heart.*

The wagon continued on around the south end of the community up Town Road until the travelers approached the Hartbrooks' house. Harol and Livi rushed out to see their daughter and their new grandson.

"We are so glad you are coming to stay," Livi told Julyiah with an excited kiss to her cheek. Dawnli knew that Livi loved being a mother to anyone who would let her.

"We will be losing Dawnli soon to someone else," Livi went on. "Now I will have a daughter again!"

Livi continued to make over Julyiah, Rashella, and baby Mikela, while Delwyn and Harol carefully lifted Julyiah out of the wagon.

Dawnli was afraid to look at Zuriel. *How insensitive of Livi!* Dawnli had asked Livi to keep her engagement quiet until she could tell Zuriel. Dawnli hurried to lift belongings out of the wagon, knowing that she had to talk to Zuriel.

♫♪

The busy group headed toward the house while Zuriel began unloading the wagon alongside Dawnli, aware that she had remained behind on purpose. Noticing her grimace at Livi's remark about *losing Dawnli soon to someone else*, Zuriel's stomach tightened. Something was not right.

"Dawnli?"

Letting out a long breath, Dawnli turned around to face him. Zuriel was surprised to see her look guilty. The look gave him a strange, horrible feeling in his stomach. What did that look mean? It was as though ….

"I am sorry, Zuriel, that you had to find out this way."

"Find out what?" He played along with the conversation, though the knowledge of what she was about to say was becoming all too clear. Clinging to a hope that she did not know how he felt about her, he shoved aside the painful ideas that formed in his head.

Dawnli bit her lower lip and tossed her head to fling her hair out of her eyes. It refracted light from the rocks up the street and Zuriel stared, hypnotized.

"We have been such good friends, Zuriel. I... do not know how to say this. I meant to tell you earlier but I could not. I do not want to hurt you."

It must be bad, thought Zuriel. *Really bad.*

"T-tell me?" he stammered, clearing his throat. His side of the conversation sounded ridiculous. Why did he not think of something charming or witty to say? *As though something witty could change her mind about me.* He glanced at the bundle on the wagon, trying to appear unruffled and ready to get back to work. *Yes, go back to unloading the wagon so none of this conversation will have taken place. You are just dreaming, that is all.*

♪♫

Dawnli studied him with as sympathetic of a look as she could muster. Exhausted, his dark hair was tousled, his clothes dirty from working in the herds that day and helping Delwyn move. The lack of a beard made him look younger, she decided, knowing full well why he had shaved it off. She pictured him the way he looked the first day she heard him speak at the Listening Hall—wearing a white, long-sleeved dekat, hair neatly combed, moustache and beard trimmed, and a sparkle of fire in his eyes. She cared about him so much, but... just as a friend. A year ago, she noticed his growing love for her, and she would have told him the truth had the subject ever come up. But now—the time had come.

"I am... leaving here soon." She looked down, unable to watch the pain with her next statement. "Daleil and I are getting married." To her surprise, she was fighting tears.

Dawnli looked up but was sorry she did. All the color had drained from Zuriel's face. He stared at her, frozen in time as though not moving could prevent her words from being true. Certain that he faced loneliness and despair, her heart ached with a desire to take back the hurtful words.

♫♪

Wrenching, searing agony ripped through Zuriel's heart. He thought he had been ready for this possibility. Surely his imagination had considered everything. So why did the news hit him with devastating grief? Why was it shocking, as though it had never occurred to him? Nothing could be worse than the suffering he had endured when he lost his position as a leader, could it? And he had already seen Dawnli with Daleil, but this—this was intense anguish. Desperate for a way to escape the torture in his heart, how could he cause the words Dawnli said to fade away? *There has to be a way out. I cannot live with this truth.*

Through a wall of blackness, Zuriel smiled at Dawnli and said, "Congratulations."

"Thank you. Zuriel, I... I am so sorry...."

He tried to ignore his heart—a cold, lonely cave. Total silence. Nothing good—no, not ever again. Some repulsive creatures started grabbing at him in the cave—tearing at his heart—pulling, yanking on him. They kept ripping away layers of him and would not stop. He was certain they would not stop for a long time.

Zuriel yanked one of the weightier objects out of the wagon, groaning gratefully under the burden. In turning toward the house, he caught a glimpse of the brightly-lit Listening Hall not far away. Everything he loved was out of reach. Dawnli was marrying another. Was anything left for him now?

No matter. The grabbing creatures were tearing out his insides and he would die soon—physically, mentally, and emotionally. The torment was too great.

A few dark clouds appeared in the sky, standing out again the white puffs that floated overhead. Zuriel felt the appearance of black clouds was all too appropriate right now. Shaking his head, he did not care what clouds might gather in the sky—it did not matter where he was going.

A large shadow huddled unseen near Zuriel, dark tendrils swirling around his lowered head. The churning darkness continued to burst its filth at Zuriel's head as he hefted a small bag of possessions onto his shoulder. Zuriel trembled with the knowledge of his only remaining option as he stumbled down the road, heading south toward the Hole.

Chapter Twenty-Five: The Death

♫♪

Zuriel looked up at the ancient inscription with a weak smile.
Follow the death;
Come up from the under.
Music flows free,
Breaking Silence asunder.

"Follow the death...." He contemplated the story Dawnli told them of how she came to this place of death when she was young. She had come to die but had been drawn up to the valley instead. Now Zuriel had come to die, and he saw no possible rescue.

Some of the poor people at the caves recognized Zuriel when he arrived and hurried over, hoping for a handout. Zuriel did not disappoint them. He had come prepared, with all the sokens and food he had brought with him. Glancing around, he doled them out, knowing who needed what the most because he had been there so many times. The beggars looked over their handouts in delight before they shuffled away, holding onto their new treasures with joyful expressions, mumbling "Thank you." Zuriel watched a few moments, feeling a little better about himself.

Unwilling to move from the spot, Zuriel studied the cavern walls, allowing his thoughts to ramble. *I was depressed the day I was deposed as a leader, but now my despair is much deeper, and I am truly ready to die. It will take a long time to starve, but maybe I can bring comfort to those around me. At last I will be talking to them more as the Voice instructed me. Perhaps this is what He had in mind all along.*

Zuriel's gaze wandered up to the inscription carved above the entrance to the caves. *Music flows free...* He recalled the Music and how much it had meant to him. How he longed to hear it again! The short time he had heard the Voice sing to him was not enough to sustain him further.

How could I have helped the deceived when I must be deceived myself? The One blesses those he loves—everyone knows that. I am certainly cursed.

Follow the death.

The inscription above the cave opening was carved in a stone, in the shape of a key. He watched people wandering in and out of the cave.

Follow the death.

How many times had they searched that cave, looking for something—anything that could be a key? Whatever it was, he thought it must be gone. This was the cave of death, and they had tried to follow it, but to no avail. The mining caves carved into the Underground cavern walls were not deep, nor did they have many corners or crevices. He and the Sarrolls had searched the caves. Maybe whatever was there before was now gone.

Zuriel heard people talking inside the caves somewhere. A small crowd made its way out of the cave entrance, followed by a young boy who was crying in hysteria. *It is the boy that Delwyn befriended—Johan.* The people were bringing out a woman who was obviously dead. Zuriel's heart went out to the boy as he witnessed the scene, and in that moment he forgot his own problems.

"Mama! Mama!" Johan screamed, his heart-rending cries echoing through the Underground. Johan hurried to keep pace with the group of makeshift pallbearers, who half-carried, half-dragged the poor woman's body toward the river. With so many dying and nowhere to bury them either above or below the ground, the river remained the common burial site. A continuous whirlpool near the caves sucked the water down to go under a manmade, brick barrier. The swirling water pulled the bodies down, where they disappeared forever.

The valley also used this burial site, having nowhere else to bury someone, although they always brought the Valley Law with them to chase away the beggars so the mourners would not be disturbed. It was called the *Tunnel of the Dead.* Running under the wall to the Outside, the river carried the bodies to an unknown location where they were never seen again.

A couple of the more devout people in the crowd muttered a few words over Johan's mother as they paused on the bridge. Zuriel joined them, quietly muttering phrases which had been a part of his occupation as a leader.

How many dead have been thrown in over the years? Zuriel wondered. *Where do they end up? Perhaps I will find out before I die.*

Follow the death.

With little reverence, Johan's mother was thrown in, and Johan began screaming again. He wiggled violently in the protective arms of a man who spoke gentle words to him. The others shook their heads in sorrow. Zuriel knew what they were thinking: *Another orphan... another hungry mouth... another lonely heart.* The people ambled away.

Zuriel, Johan, and the man holding the boy remained—all still staring into the water where the body had vanished into the tunnel. Johan grew quieter, though still sobbing, and his benefactor began to release his tight grip. The boy could not be more than seven years old, Zuriel decided.

Johan took the opportunity of the man's loosened grip and broke away from him, leaping over the bridge railing into the water. In horror, Zuriel saw the grief-stricken child sucked into the eddy.

Follow the death.

Zuriel felt an inexplicable tug at his heart. Had he not come to die himself? There was nothing left for him in life. In one incredible moment, he made the decision of a lifetime. This boy would be his final mission. A few seconds after Johan jumped in, Zuriel followed him, diving into the watery grave.

♫♪♪

The kind stranger who had held Johan saw Zuriel dive into the river. Though the man waited a long time, he did not see anyone come up again. Shaking his head, the man found it difficult to care. The weight of his own survival was upon him. If others chose to die, there was nothing he could do. He had not eaten in three days and had missed Zuriel's handouts. There was begging to do. He turned with a sigh and left.

♫♪

Zuriel could see nothing in the gloomy, wet world but was grateful that the water was not freezing cold due to the summer heat. He groped about under the water as it carried him along. How long he could hold his breath? His hope was to find Johan and hold him while they died. At least the boy would not be alone. Zuriel wondered why he did not feel alone either. It made no sense, but nothing made sense anymore.

Zuriel ran into something like flesh, and for one horrible moment he wondered whether it was dead or alive. A struggling arm revealed that it was the boy. He pulled Johan closer and wrapped his arms around him, satisfied that his last mission in life was successful, and his life, as well as his death, would not be in vain.

After another couple of minutes, Zuriel found it difficult to continue holding his breath, and the boy's body felt limp. The end was just a few heartbeats away.

They struck soft ground, like a sand dune, and stuck there a moment. Zuriel reached out and felt the well-worn, slippery branch of a tree. Tired of being forced along in the current, he grabbed hold of the branch with one hand, still holding the boy with the other. Zuriel thought Johan had already drowned but did not want to let go of him in case he awoke.

Zuriel groped his way along the tree branch, which gradually rose in height. In seconds, his hand broke the surface of the water. Surging upward, he drew himself out of the water and sucked in gulps of air in the darkness. Extracting the boy from the water also, Zuriel drew his arm tightly around Johan's middle. The boy sputtered and coughed as water gushed from his lungs, and he gasped for more air.

Silence enveloped them except for the lapping of the river against the rock walls. Shivering and crying in the darkness, Johan grabbed hold of Zuriel.

"I am... scared, mister. It is... dark. Who are you?" His small voice did not echo, so Zuriel assumed there was not a lot of space overhead. He reached up and touched the tunnel ceiling.

"I am Zuriel, and I am going to try to find a way out of here, son. Are you ready? Hang on to me...."

The boy seemed willing, so Zuriel waved his arms about, looking for he knew not what. All felt like empty space except for the ceiling. The tree was the only other solid object within their grasp, and just a small branch was sticking out of the water. In dismay, Zuriel realized they might be out in the middle of the river with no rock or land close enough to reach. However, new courage surged through Zuriel with the challenge before him. He told himself to get the boy out of the water. In his heart, he heard Music again and thought about how the One could take him and the boy out of this mess just as the Music took people to good places on the Breeze. Hope rose within him.

Zuriel reached into a pocket and pulled out a tiny light rock. He had brought it to keep him company in the caves, and it still glowed with dim, green light. The soft light shown out into the cave, and Zuriel marveled at the blessing of sight.

He had guessed right—they were in the middle of the river, and land could not be seen nearby— just vertical rock walls. But downriver Zuriel could see a beach. Since this was the only safety in view he realized he would have to swim to the beach in the swift current, towing a small boy. In order to see where they were going, someone would have to hold the light rock above their heads as he swam. Zuriel needed his hands to swim and his mouth to breathe— only the boy would be available to hold the light. What if he dropped it?

Chapter Twenty-Six: Light

♫♪

Zuriel pondered all angles of the situation, but when Johan's entire body shook all over, Zuriel knew the boy's life could be in danger. Johan had been through a lot in a short time—nearly drowning, plus witnessing the death of his mother. A sense of urgency shot through Zuriel.

"Johan, do you see that sandy beach up ahead?"

"Y-y-yes," the boy stuttered, his teeth clicking together uncontrollably.

"We will have to swim for it. Do you think you can hold onto my back?"

Johan was silent.

"Johan, we have to swim. Here, get around in back of me, and put your arms up...."

Zuriel maneuvered the boy into position, instructing him not to squeeze around Zuriel's neck should he lose his grip on his shoulders. The light rock was in the boy's uppermost hand so it would shine where Zuriel needed to see. Zuriel hoped it would be above the surface of the river at least part of the time so he would not lose his bearings in the water.

"Do not drop it, Johan, or we will be in the dark again."

The boy mumbled something and shook. Zuriel wondered whether it was possible for Johan to hold onto the rock when he was trembling so much.

"Do not let go of me," Zuriel coached. "If you ever cannot hold onto both me and the rock, you must let go of the rock."

"Yesss....sir."

With the boy's arms around Zuriel's shoulders and the light rock held high, the two set off for the sandy beach.

The expedition went wrong from the start. Zuriel was an inexperienced swimmer, and the child on his back presented an alarming situation for which both were unprepared. Zuriel repeatedly went underwater while at the same time attempting to fight the current and head for the beach. In response to Zuriel's disappearing head, Johan panicked and grabbed for higher ground, which turned out to be Zuriel's eyes or hair. Once, Johan shoved the light rock into Zuriel's right eye, blinding him, dim though it was. At intervals, Zuriel managed to spot the sandy beach ahead and attempt to aim for it. Unfortunately, all his efforts failed due to the current, and the two drifted right by the intended landing zone.

"The beach…" Johan pointed a shaky finger at their goal as they floated past.

"It is all right," Zuriel said. "We will find another one."

By this time, Zuriel had learned better how to swim in the current with a struggling boy on his back. The muscles and stamina he had built up in his recent manual labors had taken on new value. He kept his head above water and searched for more shoreline, but the light rock revealed no new place to stop, and the river continued to flow.

We should be on the Outside by now, Zuriel thought, feeling weary. He spotted a different object ahead—a fallen pillar that projected out over the top of the river. About an arm's length in diameter, the octagonal pillar jutted out from behind a stone wall, a manmade one.

When he noticed Johan's grip was less secure, Zuriel swam for the signs of civilization, surprised at the remaining strength he was able to muster.

"Hang on, Johan. I see something." Zuriel felt the boy's arms tighten around his head as Zuriel reached out, catching the end of the pillar. A mere hand's breadth of space lay between the pillar and the water, and the current tried to pull them underneath it. For a few desperate minutes, Zuriel's cold, tired hands grabbed at the slick pillar, slipping several times until he had a better hold.

Feeling the boy's hold loosening again, Zuriel grabbed Johan's arm with one hand as he lunged with his other arm clear over the top of the pillar and held on.

Spotting more ruins off to their right, Zuriel thought he saw a small room. But Zuriel's final launch onto the pillar had knocked the light rock out of the boy's hand. It fell onto the pillar, and slid into the water, causing all light to fade. The tiny green light sank and drifted off with the current. The gravity of the situation stunned him. They had no light.

"I am sorry," Johan said through chattering teeth. The boy sounded exhausted, and Zuriel worried whether he would survive.

"It is all right, Johan. You did what I told you to do. There is a room here, and we will be able to get out of the water. Maybe there will be some light nearby, too." Zuriel knew this was not likely since the entire area looked black. Yet after his eyes adjusted, he began to see it was not completely dark. A faint light from somewhere revealed a few large objects in the room.

Coaxing Johan from his back, Zuriel pulled him around to the front and placed him on the pillar. As he and the boy straddled the pillar, Zuriel scooted along the top toward shore, steadily moving Johan ahead of him.

Zuriel searched for the source of light. Were they near the Outside? Was it sunlight or an artificial light source?

At last, the two reached the end of the pillar, and Johan collapsed on the sandy stone floor of the old chamber. Amazed that the room was not cold, Zuriel hoped that the source of light was the sun. The days had been hot. Speaking some encouraging words to the boy, Zuriel made his way across the room alone, heading for what looked like a brighter spot.

Coming around the far corner of the room, Zuriel saw the light source. Large stones had crumbled, leaving gaping holes in the walls. Deep cracks in the thick wall permitted a little light to come in from the Outside. Studying the rocks, Zuriel gasped with the realization that they were at the base of the North Wall.

Scrambling over to the broken stones, Zuriel put his eye to any cracks that might reveal what was on this northern end of the Outside. No one had seen outside the north end of the wall in 400 years. Yet all Zuriel saw was more rock. The many stone blocks that made up the North Wall widened at the foundation—about fifteen paces across, and the stones were staggered to each other, making it impossible to see a straight view to the Outside. Through one opening he saw farther out and decided he must be viewing one of the stones in the last row on the Outside. To his astonishment, the stone was in such disrepair that it looked like it would crumble at any moment.

Zuriel looked through every crevice, memorizing what he saw. Debris and chinks still filled most of the fissures. Why were the wall stones crumbling? What did it mean? He called out to Johan to let the boy know where he was, before he turned and spotted stairs in the ruins. Zuriel shoved a wooden beam aside and brushed away some debris. Yes, there were stairs, and he was certain they went up to the valley.

Another fallen pillar blocked the upper section of the staircase, and this had prevented him from seeing it sooner. As he stepped up and ducked under the leaning pillar, he saw that most of the stairway was clear, but dark. Could they go up the stairs with no light?

A tremendous weariness overcame Zuriel as he made his way back to Johan. There was nothing they could do right now except to rest. Zuriel settled himself down next to the tired boy, telling him about the light coming through the cracks and the stairs he found. Johan yawned and fell asleep. Zuriel followed his example.

♫♪♫

No one noticed the warm Breeze that drifted in through the fractures in the North Wall and over the sleeping figures. No one saw the rich colors that accompanied the Breeze. No one heard the voices in the unseen world.

"They do not know that their work among the poor has been a key that crumbles the wall?"

"No. They do not even know the wall needs to come down."

"Why did they continue?"

"This one almost did not."

The two beings observed the man and boy sleeping side by side, warmed now by the Breeze that dried their clothes and flitted in and out of their hair. Warm yellows and ambers eddied with the Breeze, and settled on a nearby rock.

"It will not be long now, will it?" a yellow streak asked.

"No, but a lot of pain is still to come." A fountain of colors surrounded the second voice. "I remember how difficult it was for me when my goal was so close. I knew it would be over before long, but when I lost my Voice, the Music died in the Silent Terror. A terrible thing happened that day, yet it was necessary in order for the people to be saved from Silence."

The melodic fountain of color made it difficult for the listeners to distinguish the Voice from the Music.

"They do not realize how important pain is, do they?" the amber asked.

"No," the Voice answered. "They rarely understand that pain is the door to the fullest life or that if they do not suffer now, they will suffer in Silence. Silence is the worst pain one can imagine, even as Music is the greatest joy."

Chapter Twenty-Seven: The Tyrea

♪ ... ♪♫

"He is interfering again—the other," a sinister voice rumbled in the dark. "They reject the life he gave them, and instead of letting me claim what is rightfully mine, he comes and breathes new life into them."

"Why does he let them suffer so much?" A wisp of gray moved carefully to avoid disturbing the larger, unstable force.

"It is how he deceives them. "They come to him thinking he will make their lives easier. When they find out what he requires they lose heart. That is when we have the most opportunity. But those that make it through this kind of discouragement are dangerous— very dangerous." Angry spurts of wind burst from the giant black mass.

The smaller puff of gray smoke drew closer. "What is the next step, my lord?"

"Work on Delwyn. He is overcome with bitterness due to lack of money. If he despairs out of bitterness, we have a tight hold. The other does not tend to rescue one who chooses such a path. If Delwyn will not listen for the Music, he will never hear it when the other sends it."

"What about the wife? Julyiah has influenced him before."

"Afflict her with weakness and depression. Maybe she will not have the motivation to speak about anything good. Her life will be full of childcare for a time. Make it as difficult as the other will allow. In caring for her children and herself, she will not have any love left for her husband."

"And in his bitterness, he will have nothing left for her."

"Exactly."

♪ ♪

"Julyiah is back in the valley," Jonar said as he twirled one of his precious wooden pencils between his fingers. Cisco sat in

Jonar's office, hoping for a chance to get the great leader's attention. If Cisco came up with a good plan, he might obtain increasing favor from Jonar. For years, he had been working his way into Jonar's confidence and had the privilege of being a sounding board at times when needed. Cisco longed for a higher position like Jonar, but the more Cisco agreed with Jonar, the less power he had himself.

"Yes," Cisco agreed, "and we have no laws against Julyiah being in the community, just disfavor. If they had not legally married ...."

"But they did!" Jonar roared, bursting from his chair to begin his characteristic pacing. He paused now and then to twirl the pencil. "Zuriel's plot."

"What could be Zuriel's purpose in such a plot?" Cisco asked, surprised when Jonar laughed in reply and shook his head as though it was a ridiculous question.

"Purpose? To get even, of course," Jonar said, still chuckling. "Zuriel's purpose is the same as it is for the rest of us. We are leaders—we want a following. When we took that away, he developed a plan of his own. Zuriel mumbles about helping the poor, but he is actually regrouping his followers. I have a feeling that Dawnli is involved as well. You had best keep her away from Daleil."

"But they are to be married ...." Cisco eyed the pacing Jonar with irritation. The Most Respected leader always walked the length of a room in an obvious attempt to intimidate all who were present. However, Cisco's fear of Jonar kept him from a negative comment about the other man's habits.

As Jonar continued his monologue, Cisco glanced away, admiring the beautiful antique displays in Jonar's office—at least twenty old manuscripts inside a wooden case—musical instruments from the time of Gwenla that were never played. Most of them had wooden arms of some kind, with strings. He wondered if the music from such instruments would sound like the music from the boxes. In his heart, he played the strings on one of them, but he stopped. Playing musical instruments had been forbidden long ago. Blinking, he could no longer remember any reason written in the books, nor any reason given by Gwenla. Pushing his mouth up on one side, he wished he could understand things better.

Cisco looked back to see Jonar glaring at Cisco's absent-minded perusal of the room and considered Jonar's discussion of those who had rebelled against authority. *Jonar's authority.*

"Zuriel is not doing much damage, is he?" Cisco said so that Jonar would know he had been listening. "Just a few have heard this *other* music. I think Zuriel may give up. I do not believe his heart is in it anymore."

"I have seen the look in his eyes," Jonar insisted. "His position has been his primary purpose in life. Without leadership, he would have to resort to another following of some kind. He will continue leading people astray even if he has just a few followers."

"What will we do?" Cisco asked himself as much as Jonar, hoping there would be a way out for Dawnli since he had grown to love her as a daughter. Cisco stared at the twirling pencil in Jonar's hand, wondering if he would ever own such a rare object.

"I have a plan," Jonar announced with a mysterious smile. "It is a plan that has not been used since the time of Gwenla." A gusty breeze blew in Jonar's office window as Cisco waited expectantly, but Jonar revealed no more of his ideas.

♫

Delwyn walked into the little hut where he and his family had been living the past five years. He spotted the warming stones in the corner and smiled, wishing it was not summer and he could light a fire under them. It sounded less lonely. He had Shep with him, and the dog provided some warmth of spirit as well as a slobbery kiss now and then.

Thinking he might haul up some water and have a bath, Delwyn humphed. For what reason? Who would care—the dirt and bugs? The goats he herded the next day? Shep liked him better dirty. Still, Delwyn always enjoyed getting the sticky grime and smells off of his body in the evening. *A swim in the river would cool me off and be more enjoyable than bathing from a bowl,* he decided.

Delwyn scrounged through the cold box searching for something to eat, while Shep stood at his heels, hoping for a scrap. Sitting in a reed chair near the door so he could feel the breeze blowing through, Delwyn opened a Teka leaf with bread inside. When Shep whined, Delwyn pulled a bare bone out of the bag he had brought home from work. "Sorry Shep—this is all I could get today." But the dog seized the bone with an eager click of his teeth and lay down to work on it.

As he savored the last of Julyiah's bread, Delwyn stared at a crevice in the wall—one Julyiah always hated because she knew bugs hid in there and crept out at night. Delwyn had never fixed the hole. Maybe he would do it now, to feel better about himself.

Jumping up to fill in the hole, Delwyn started to jam the Teka leaf wrapper into the opening, but something metallic glinted inside. Curious, he reached in to see if the object would move, and to his surprise, it came right out.

Examining the article, Delwyn did not think he had ever seen one before. Small holes ran up and down the sides of the forearm-length object, with two prongs sticking out at an angle on one end and a curved holding bar at the other. A thin slit near the holding bar invited one to blow. With a rush of wonder, Delwyn realized it was a musical instrument in the shape of a key.

Delwyn's heart raced as he remembered something he had read before in the *Book of Silia*: "When the tyrea is played, the fortress of Silence will fall." The leaders had different ideas about what this meant and often argued about it. The problem was that no one knew for sure what a tyrea was. Could this unknown instrument be a tyrea?

Most community folk had never heard musical instruments playing songs, though some had heard descriptions of the music they played or seen the instruments that were locked in the viewing cases in Jonar's office. It was forbidden to play them for as long as Delwyn could remember.

A sudden thought entered Delwyn's consciousness: *What if the fortress of Silence in this passage meant the old fortress wall that surrounded the valley?* If so, could the fortress wall could be the "wall of silence"—intended to keep out the Lying Wind but also keeping out the Music on the Breeze. Everyone knew it was erected to prevent the Lying Wind from coming inside, but was it meant to stay in place forever?

Delwyn retrieved Julyiah's notes from the books that she had let him keep. Remembering that the tyrea was mentioned also in another place in the books, Delwyn searched the Teka leaves. The word "tyrea" stood out at last—in one of Gwenla's riddles. Delwyn read the words out loud in the otherwise quiet room.

"In later years, some will come who are like me but not like me. They will speak the words of the Voice, play the tyrea, and sing the songs of Music on the Breeze."

The warm air coming through the doorway blew harder. Delwyn began to shake all over and had a strong urge to play the tyrea. Overcome with anticipation, he put the flute-like instrument to his lips, and out came one beautiful melody after another, even though he had never before played an instrument. The sweet notes flowed into the room, as though he had been playing a tyrea all of his life.

As Delwyn played, his heart soared with joy, and he found himself in a beautiful meadow where horses ran free. A sleek bay stallion stopped, neighed in his direction in an obvious greeting, and trotted up next to a large rock. The horse had a bridle on and tossed his head at his own back, and then at Delwyn, gazing at him intently with his large, expressive eyes, as though inviting him to climb on and ride. Feeling exhilarated, Delwyn ran over and leaped onto the horse.

The stallion took off at a gallop, running through a stand of trees so tall that they dwarfed everything in sight. Colorful strands of mist flew alongside them, as the horse sped along the forest

trail. Brilliant hues darted about, apparently producing the power
that caused the horse and rider to move through the incredible
scenery. Figures like people appeared along the trail, holding
stringed instruments and playing music. Each musical device
played a different sound, but all of them blended into a symphony.
Each figure held his instrument toward Delwyn when he passed
by, as though inviting him to play the music. Tears threatened his
eyes as Delwyn took in the spectacular sights around him.

When Delwyn came back to the Underground shack, he
looked around the wretched place and wondered why he wanted to
stay there when his wife and children were in the valley above. He
could think of no reason but pride. With great resolve, he picked
up the few belongings that had not already gone with Julyiah,
made sure he had his new instrument, and left the deteriorating
room and furniture behind. As he headed out the door with Shep
by his side, Delwyn brought the tyrea to his lips and started to play
it for all the Underground to hear.

To Delwyn's surprise, three men hurried out of the Durnee
Tavern to follow, playing stringed instruments and joining in the
song with a variety of tones. A woman ran out of her house
grinning and carrying her small drum, and another man came with
a large horn made out of metal. Others joined in, humming and
singing. One man brought a small drum lined with metal cups that
clattered together in a delightful ringing when he struck it. The
jingles resounded in time with the other instruments whenever the
melody picked up to a rhythmic beat.

Before long, Delwyn was surrounded by musicians, children,
and a beautiful mixture of sound and chorus that blended together.
Caught up in the ecstasy of playing in the group, Delwyn moved to
the rhythm as he walked and played the tyrea, until the entire
assembly was dancing, singing, and playing their song, like a high-
sounding parade that could not be ignored.

Chapter Twenty-Eight: Cracks

♫♪

Zuriel and Johan slept through the night.

When Zuriel woke, the room was much brighter than the evening before. While Johan stretched and yawned, Zuriel hurried to look through the cracks in the foundation stones. The rifts were wider, and light streamed in through one tiny hole. Zuriel put his eye to the gap and saw the blue sky and... *what is that? Green?* Seeing an object of color, he strained to identify it. The green moved, as in a breeze. *Those are leaves... leaves of a bush or a tree!* Did foliage exist to the north outside the wall?

Zuriel felt weak from lack of food and this new discovery. *A tree... a tree...?* Breathing in and out slowly, he sat down. His mind struggled to find the significance in this unexpected revelation. There was life outside the North Wall—there was a tree. What else was out there? Perhaps more trees.

Perhaps not, he told himself as he rose to look through the hole again. Maybe a single tree grew near the river outside the North Wall, and he happened to see the only one out there.

Zuriel returned to Johan, and the two got a drink from the river, leaning out over the edge of the stone floor. Zuriel observed how the river swept beneath the stone floor they sat upon and wondered about its travels beneath them and what supported the floor. The river held less water here than at the caves, indicating it must have branched off in another direction as well as this one. That might account for not finding any bodies....

A little wooden box floated near the shore, having made its way under the pillar. Zuriel reached out and grabbed it. *What on earth ...?* How could something so valuable have fallen over the waterfall from the valley and drifted with the river through the Underground without being seen? Unless it came from these ruins.

If that was the case, what could have disturbed it to float down the river at that moment?

The box looked like a food storage container for the rich—something to hold cheese or bread perhaps—and it was sealed with beeswax. Zuriel opened it, breaking the seal. A round of cheese lay in the box, wrapped in cloth. Food! Thankful, Zuriel found a stone to scrape off the mold on one side, so that he and Johan could eat several bites of the tasty, sharp cheese. It was large enough to save a portion until later, so after eating, Zuriel re-wrapped the cheese and put it in the box. Johan put the box inside a large, empty pocket in his dekat.

Moments after eating, Zuriel's eye caught something shimmering on the stone floor near where they had slept. Zuriel went closer and found a light rock—the same light rock Johan had dropped. How had it come back up out of the depths of the river? Whatever the reason, they now would be able to go up the gloomy staircase and perhaps find an old, hidden door to one of the music cells above.

"Someone is watching over us," he told Johan, who nodded with a knowing gaze, as the two headed for the staircase.

Zuriel and Johan had to climb ten flights of stone stairs before they came to the top. Panting for breath, they felt a strange vibration under their feet as though something was shaking the staircase. At the top, a wooden door stopped them. Light shone around its edges, inspiring hope for a way out. The shaking was strong at the landing by the door, and they could hear a loud, steady roar on the other side of it, like a torrent of water.

Excited, Zuriel tried the latch but discovered the door was locked. While he tried pushing, pulling, banging, and knocking on the door, Johan sat on the stairs and complained that he was hungry. "I want Mama," Johan said, tears running down his face.

Zuriel reluctantly gave up on the door and sat down to comfort Johan, while trying to think of a way through the immovable wooden object behind them. Light shone through the tiny keyhole. *There must be a key to this door.*

Yes, a key! Keys had been significant ever since he had heard the Music. Maybe the key to this problem was nearby.

"Quick, Johan, help me find the key to the door." The boy cheered up a little with the activity, while they searched the stairwell, the stairs, and the door itself. They stopped looking, and Zuriel sat down with his head in his hands in discouragement.

Johan pulled out the box of cheese, no doubt ready for the comfort of food. Zuriel turned toward the boy, stretching out his hand in request for a piece. Johan broke some off, balancing the box on his knee. As Zuriel reached for the cheese, a sparkle caught his eye near the ceiling of the room. The tiny stream of light coming from the keyhole highlighted a shiny object. Something metallic hung from the rock roof overhanging the stairs.

Zuriel jumped to his feet and rushed down, stumbling in his haste. *Is it possible?* Reaching up for the glinting piece of metal, he pulled out a key. Wasting no time, he ran back up the stairs where a wide-eyed Johan watched him fit it into the keyhole with no resistance. Without delay, Zuriel opened the door.

Warm breezes hit them full in the face, along with bright daylight. To the immediate right and left were more stone walls, but farther ahead to the left was a direct opening to the Outside. A waterfall thundered nearby, unseen. It was so close that a misty roar rose up to greet them from the dark depths of a drop-off directly in their path. The walls on either side of them and in front of them were sheer rock with no way to see out the opening on the left, even though it was a mere ten steps away.

They had come too far to stop now—there had to be a way to see out that opening! Zuriel searched the wall to the right, which was made out of smaller stones than most of the other walls. "This was added later," he said, "probably to seal off this window." He wondered what was behind it. They had come up far enough to be at the valley floor level.

Johan found a broken chunk of stone which had fallen from the ceiling long ago. It was hard as metal with a rather pointed end. "We can pound a hole in the wall," Johan suggested.

Johan's idea was odd, but Zuriel took the sharp rock from Johan and began attacking the wall, slamming the makeshift hammer against a group of smaller stones with all his might. *Perhaps there is a weak spot somewhere. The mortar is old by now.*

As he struck the wall, Zuriel was startled to see little gusts of colored mist blow against it, tearing at the wall also, as though assisting him. Drawing back, he stared at the strange phenomenon. But when he stopped the colors disappeared and some odd-looking gray puffs of smoke momentarily blurred his vision. When he continued pounding against the wall, the smoke drifted up into his eyes, but the wispy colors returned as well and blew holes through the smoke so that he could see. He began coughing and blinking back tears, but he tried to ignore the interference, determined to keep working on the wall.

Under Zuriel's persistent hand, the mortar began to crumble. Striking the wall with new vigor in spite of his raspy cough, he brought the sharp-edged stone against the wall again and again. The smoke grew thicker, but the colored breezes came to blow it away.

A few stones moved away from the shattered mortar, and Zuriel could make deeper thrusts. His arms grew heavy, and he had to stop and rest. Johan offered to help, and Zuriel noticed that the breezes helped the child's efforts as they had helped him.

Sheer determination prevailed, and Zuriel broke through the wall. He had been working around a large stone, and with a final blow this heavy object fell away from him, having lost the substance that had held it upright. A large hole was now in the midst of the thick wall.

Zuriel and Johan peered into the next room to see the shocked expressions of many faces in the Listening Hall.

Chapter Twenty-Nine: The Breakthrough

♫♪

When Zuriel broke through the wall, several things happened in rapid succession. First, the Breeze rushed through the open hole and blew Teka leaves and people's hair askew throughout the Listening Hall.

"Safety Alert!" shouted a Keeper, barely heard amidst the cries and screams in the room. Music rushed into the Listening Hall on the Breeze, even as it did that day in the music cell of Zemar.

After the commotion started, crackling noises sounded from a few of the music boxes in the Listening Hall. The boxes creaked, split, and burst open, the wood scattering in all directions. Shrieking in fear, some people rushed to the Door Keepers and begged to get out. The Keepers hurried to oblige, no doubt wanting to get away themselves.

Elated by hearing the Music again, Zuriel's heart rushed to a high cliff, where he wielded a sword against evil beasts that were somewhat transparent. The shadowy forms of mud-like existence proved to be susceptible to Zuriel's bright sword, which glowed with colors he had never seen before. Each monster moaned and fled with every strike of the shining two-edged weapon.

When he came back to the Hall, joy filled Zuriel as he saw people in the building listening to the Music for the first time, Johan among them. Many were terrified of the Music and the Breeze alike, apparently thinking the Wind had broken through the wall. Some stood transfixed, observing everything in wonder, while a few did not appear to hear or see anything unusual and stared at the chaotic assembly with puzzled expressions.

♪♫♪

As Music surrounded him, Tomli's heart raced in ecstasy, traveling to the beautiful green mountains he had seen when he looked out the South Window at the age of eight. As he flew high above trees, flowers and streams, several shades of blue and red streaked around him. The Voice sang to him from the midst of the colors: "Sing to the people, and I will speak through you."

When he returned to the room, Tomli cried out for joy. *The Understanding!* His heart had opened to see places, and he now saw them in abundance. Glancing about for someone to share with about his experience, he found that the tumult in the room was too great. All were either terrified or ecstatic, except for the two leaders—Jonar and Delegar. They did not appear to hear the Music, but seemed more concerned with the disruption to the Listening Hall. Jonar dispatched Keepers to capture Zuriel and Johan, and Delegar told the people to remain calm, as the Keepers led Zuriel and Johan away to Jonar's office.

Tomli was thirteen now and had been to a meeting at the Listening Hall every week for the past five years. He also went often to the music cells to study the sacred books. Gaining a good deal of knowledge about the books in his required studies over the years, he enjoyed the ancient passages that revealed the errors taught by tradition. The Voice whispered in his heart as he read the truth from the books, at an age much younger than usual. Several passages from the books came to his mind now, about how the Music came on the Breeze in the past and how it would come again. After hearing the Voice sing to him, Tomli felt a surge of boldness deep within that fought past any fears he may have felt before.

The Voice wanted him to sing to the people!

♫♪

Zuriel stumbled along between his two guards, no longer caring what happened to him. He had heard the Music again; nothing else mattered. Johan had heard it too, and Zuriel was happy that he was able to share something so wonderful with the boy.

Two Valley Law guards and a Keeper hurried to cover the hole in the wall with a large wooden table standing on end. The Breeze and the Music dwindled, and the chaos in the room subsided. People whispered in small groups, trying to understand what had happened. Some were excited and others were upset, although the most fearful among them had fled the building.

Zuriel still held the hard, narrow chunk of stone he had used to break through the wall. It had worn down to a squatty shape through its usage that day, but he held it up for a closer look. Before a guard snatched it away, Zuriel perceived that the stone resembled a key.

♪

Seven days after Mikela entered the world, Julyiah woke stronger, but irritable, depressed, and suffering from new mother blues. The active baby stayed awake late at night and kept Julyiah occupied with his care. Although Grandma Livi was helping, Julyiah never got enough rest. In her heart, she wandered in a barren desert, searching for water.

The weather in the valley had cooled off, and Julyiah took pleasure in a pleasant breeze that fluttered the leaves on the napcot tree outside and blew in the window to refresh her body and soul. Soon the tree would be loaded with ripening napcots.

Julyiah took a deep breath, focusing on Mikela's safe birth, her family's comfortable condition, and her now repaired relationship with her parents. Julyiah recalled her apology to her mother the day before that she had not worn the wedding talia Livi had spent so much time making for her. It had been a good talk— mother and daughter—like old times. Livi supervised Rashella that morning so that Julyiah could rest.

As Julyiah worked on her attitude, her desert rippled like water in the distance. *A mirage again*, she thought, for she had seen many illusions in this desert place for years. Why bother to hope for more? She longed to hear Music again and go to scenic places, not this desert. This was the true "water" she looked for—

hearing the Voice and the Music. Many times she had been hopeful, but nothing had come of it. The water always disappeared from her desert place whenever she drew closer. The mirage looked different, but had she not thought that before? She hated this part where she stumbled wearily through the heat toward the shimmering blue pool just to discover it was not real.

Julyiah staggered over a hot sand dune. Yes, it was a mirage—nothing but searing hot, dry sand. Julyiah sighed but did not feel disheartened. How often in the past had she exploded in disappointment and rage, wondering why the One made her go through this over and over and why the Voice did not speak or sing to her? This time she felt resigned and ready to persevere. Hope somehow rose that she would find water in her parched heart. Trust welled up within her. Yes, some day the Music would return, she was sure of it.

Julyiah reached for the glass of water by her bed and drank. If only the thirst in her spirit could be so easily quenched! At last, she grew sleepy and turned away from the window to take a nap since Mikela had fallen asleep nursing.

Minutes later she heard something in the stillness—a unique, faraway sound. Julyiah woke up, wondering what it was.

Music!

A mysterious spot formed in the dry sand in her heart.

Water!

Since the Music was outside the house, Julyiah left Mikela asleep, asked Livi to watch him, and rushed to the door. When she opened it, the Music was louder. Water bubbled up in the wet spot inside her—a spring in the midst of the desert.

Music drifted toward her from the south, and Julyiah turned her head. Bewildered, she saw Delwyn walking up the dusty road, playing a musical instrument with a huge cloth sack tied onto his back. Several people followed behind him, waving their arms, singing, and dancing to the song.

Joy flooded Julyiah's heart as she ran inside, picked up Mikela and rushed back out to meet the group, falling in step at Delwyn's side. In her heart, grass and lush green ferns began to grow. Trees rose wherever the spring of water flowed in the desert sand. It spread outward from the bubbling spring and did not appear it would cease for some time.

Delwyn smiled at Julyiah with his eyes, dropped his sack in front of the house, and continued his march. The happy group followed close behind him as he headed toward the Listening Hall.

As they drew closer, Julyiah saw some people running from the building, screaming in fear, and others shaking their heads as though a tragedy had struck them. When the group of singers and dancers approached the Hall, Dawnli appeared from among them and rushed up to Delwyn and Julyiah, worry marking her features. The entire procession halted and grew quiet.

"Delwyn! Julyiah! They have taken Zuriel to Jonar's office." Dawnli's manner portrayed extreme agitation.

"What? Why?" Julyiah asked.

♪♫

Dawnli attempted to catch her breath and sort through her feelings. After hearing Music and knowing Daleil heard it too, she had been elated. But Zuriel's captivity was excruciating.

"He... he broke through the wall! In... in the Listening Hall— from the Outside," Dawnli explained in distracted snatches.

"From the *Outside*?" gasped Delwyn. "How?"

"I...I do not know," Dawnli said, trying to calm down so she could speak. "It was hard to tell. We could not see anything except more wall behind them. A boy from the Underground came with him. Music came in through the hole, and some of the music boxes broke apart, like that day we were in the music cell of *Zemar*. Some people thought the Lying Wind had come in. Jonar's face turned purple, he was so mad. I do not think he heard the Music at all. Or Delegar either. The Keepers covered the hole and took Zuriel and the boy to Jonar's office. I am worried about them."

"Some cannot hear the Music?" Delwyn grew thoughtful. "But others did hear it?"

"Never mind that now," Dawnli interrupted. "We need to help Zuriel. We do not know what Jonar might do."

♫

Zuriel. Alarm rushed through Delwyn as he remembered the night Jonar interrogated Julyiah after her insignificant "mistake." What might be done to Zuriel for such a deed as this?

"Come!" he told the small crowd behind him, gesturing north. "On to the Hall!"

The entire group of people who had followed Delwyn moved with him toward the Listening Hall. Inside, the place buzzed with activity and the heavy door in the front was open, unguarded, as an increasing number of people left. Delwyn and his group walked right in.

Jesero and Cisco argued in one corner. Delwyn thought one of them must have heard the Music from what he could hear of the conversation, but neither seemed happy about it. He spotted people sitting on the seats talking among themselves. A few Keepers attempted to fill in the last cracks of the hole in the wall behind the table blockade. Some crowded around Jonar's closed office door where a Keeper stood guard. Menila held Johan outside the office, and Delwyn could not imagine why the boy was present.

At that moment, Tomli made his way to the center of the room, stood on a bench, and announced: "The time has come!" Then he began to sing the same words.

Delwyn did not know what Tomli meant, but as the words were sung, Delwyn knew what he must do. He led his followers toward Jonar's office door and pressed in through the crowd. The people made way for Delwyn, recognizing him as a friend of Zuriel's.

"I stand with my friend," Delwyn declared to Menila.

Chapter Thirty: The Stand

♪

Julyiah gasped.

A reverent hush flashed through the noisy assembly.

"Did he say he stands with Zuriel?" someone asked in a suspicious voice.

"He did! He did!" Others asserted. All was silent again as the crowd held a collective breath, waiting for the outcome of Delwyn's declaration.

Menila stared at Delwyn in dismay. "Are you aware of what you are saying?" he asked, looking shocked. "Zuriel is likely to be sentenced to death for this."

"I stand with Zuriel too," Dawnli said.

"So do I," Julyiah added, amazed at her own courage. Daleil announced he took the stand with Zuriel also, winning a smile from Dawnli.

"I too," said someone who had come up with Delwyn, and many joined in the resistance, until all of Delwyn's group and several of those who had heard Music in the Hall also declared they would stand with Zuriel.

Tomli rushed over, made his way to the front by Jonar's office door and sang out, "We all stand with Zuriel!" The crowd blinked in surprise at Tomli's authoritative manner, and they cheered.

Wide-eyed by this point, Menila grew unsteady. He reached back and grabbed the doorknob to Jonar's office, jerked open the door, and ran inside as though chased by wild animals.

♫ ♫

Jonar manifested red-faced, shaking rage when Menila burst into the tension-filled room, and it became evident to the servant that he was interrupting the High leader in the middle of his interrogation of Zuriel. Jonar whipped around, glaring at the Keeper, who shut the door at once, not wanting those outside to witness the scene. Menila's apprehension escalated when he observed Cisco and Delegar also trembling. Having seen Jonar's temper before, Menila could picture him releasing angry outbursts into the room moments before the unsuspecting Keeper came in.

Zuriel lay face down on the floor, his head swollen and bleeding as though he had been kicked. Menila stared at the scene, stunned. The Keeper had never seen the High leader resort to violence before—not toward a person anyway.

"What are you doing?" roared Jonar in obvious fury. Menila thought for a moment of running back to the crowd outside, for safety.

"Y...y...your servant," bowed Menila submissively, an approach often used with irate leaders. "The people—all the people—the entire crowd outside the door says..."

"I do not *care* what they say!" Jonar bellowed, slamming his fist against the back of a chair. "I must deal with this... this... *filth!*" He spat on Zuriel. The wet projectile hit Zuriel's tender face, and he winced.

"But... sir..." Menila ventured further, trying not to show his distaste for Jonar's approach to Zuriel's rebellion. "They want to stand with him—all of them!"

A unified gasp escaped every other person in the room. Cisco and Delegar slumped into their chairs, looking sick. Jonar jerked back as though struck.

♪ ♪

"What...? What?" Jonar asked, fear gripping his heart. Staggering over to the chair he had sent sliding across the room, he shook his head. *What have I done? Have I gone too far with this?*

"H-how many?" Jonar asked, trying to sound calmer than he felt. He dared not look at Cisco and Delegar, who no doubt hoped he would still have all the answers.

"Twenty-five or thirty," Menila answered meekly, relieved that his responsibility in the matter had now shifted to the leaders.

"The Law..." Cisco whispered in reminder, his eyes wide. "Those who stand with an accused person will receive his sentence. Thirty people, Jonar!"

"I am well aware of the Law, Cisco!" Jonar shrieked, waving his hands through the air in a semblance of submission. The other leaders grew silent, no doubt awaiting his wisdom. Desperately, Jonar tried to think of a way around the Valley Law. Was he powerful enough to get away with a deviation? He needed time to think.

"Very well." Jonar nodded. "Let him go to them—the boy too. We will hold them all in the Listening Hall until tomorrow. I must..." Jonar's voice broke off, and he looked at Zuriel, hiding his terror with a hateful gaze. "I must hold a leader's Forum. This insurrection is getting out of hand."

♫♪

Zuriel blinked back the tears that blurred his vision when he heard that his friends would stand with him. Yet he was alarmed. Jonar meant business and did not appear to care what happened to anyone as long as he got his way. Zuriel had already faced death in the river, but he could not bear to think that he would cause more pain for his friends. How glad he was that Jonar had sent Johan outside the office before unleashing his violent attack! The brutality had shaken the adults; the children did not need to see it as well.

Menila helped Zuriel to his feet, leading him out the door to the holding area. As Zuriel's eyes met Delwyn's, they misted over and his throat caught. To think he had wanted to go die somewhere when he had friends willing to do this for his sake!

Evening approached in the community as Keepers and guards rounded up the twenty-eight people and locked them inside the Listening Hall, where guards with swords stood in the four corners of the room. Delwyn was able to talk to Zuriel in a small, enclosed closet. The two friends sat among shelves full of money boxes, music boxes, and sound stones. Both were grateful for the time alone, stuffy though it was in the small space.

Zuriel told Delwyn the story of his trip down the river, reporting the disintegration of the wall, the tree he saw through the cracks, and the window he knew was behind the Listening Hall to the north. If they could break through that wall, they would see northern parts.

"What could it mean?" asked Delwyn. "Why would the wall break up? And you say the cracks were wider today?"

"That was the most interesting part." Zuriel nodded, gingerly touching the tip of his finger to his torn cheek. "I could think of no deteriorating force that could do such a thing. There was no water, no rain, no earthquake, just a warm breeze...." Zuriel paused as he spoke the last few words, and his eyebrows rose.

"The Breeze—of course! The Breeze is tearing down the wall, letting the Music flow freely again.... Wait! Wait!" Zuriel jumped up, holding his hand in the air to keep Delwyn from speaking as he closed his own eyes in thought. *The inscription over the cave....*

"I remember!" Zuriel's eyes shot open as he recited:
Follow the death;
Come up from the Under;
Music flows free,
Breaking Silence asunder.

"I 'followed the death,' so to speak, when I followed Johan into the river where they bury the dead. We came *up from the under*—up the staircase from below. I broke through the wall and the Breeze helped me. I saw colors attacking the wall every time I hit it. And the Breeze rushed in through the hole in the wall, bringing in the Music.

"The wall is supposed to come down and allow the Breeze to come in! What were the other passages?" Zuriel searched through the sacred books that were kept on the shelves.

"Look at this, in Ornae," Zuriel declared. "*Feed the poor so that Music will flow.* We began feeding the poor years ago, and now Music is beginning to flow."

"I did not think of feeding poor as bringing Music," Delwyn said. "But this passage in Zemar says: *When the tyrea is played, the fortress of Silence will fall.* Also, *The keys of Music unlock the wall of Silence.* The wall of Silence and the fortress of Silence. This is referring to the wall around this valley! It is keeping the Music out because the Breeze will flow only if invited. As we have seen, the walls do not keep out the Breeze, but the Breeze has not been welcome here. This must be another of Gwenla's Secrets. Breaking down the wall is how we invite the Breeze back into the community."

"And now it is crumbling." Zuriel nodded, filled with joy. "Without the Breeze in the valley, I am certain the Lying Wind has been able to come and deceive the leaders and the people. Delwyn, we have become a part of this great change. You were called to play your instrument to gather the people, and my job was to sneak in the back door."

♪

The Valley Law released Julyiah that evening. They said she could not remain a prisoner because she had a nursing baby. Her mother and father waited outside and requested an explanation, but Julyiah would not speak. Both joy and sadness overwhelmed her due to the unfolding events.

As they headed home past the Listening Hall, loud crashing noises erupted from the music cells. The resident Keeper hurried over to investigate, peering inside the main door.

"I do not see anything," the Keeper remarked. "The music cells are empty. Everyone has gone home for the night." Continuous rumbling shook the buildings.

"Stay here, outside the door," the Keeper ordered, and the others obeyed. He disappeared into the halls of the music cells, and they heard him cry out.

"Stay here," echoed Harol and also vanished. Julyiah and Livi waited outside, but before long they heard voices. Harol and the Keeper reappeared.

"The Music cell of Zemar has collapsed," Harol panted, shaking his head. "There is no sign of vandalism. It must be deterioration of the stonework. The walls separating the other music cells are also crumbling."

"The Lying Wind has come in," the Keeper decided, rushing outside, out of danger's way. "I will have to close them." He shut and locked the music cell entry.

However, Julyiah had felt what blew out from the depths of the music cells before he shut the door, and she knew it was not the Lying Wind.

Chapter Thirty-One: The Council

♪ ♪

All five leaders, including a new one to replace Zuriel, attended Jonar in his office. Jonar had managed to compose himself after the announcement that a total of twenty-eight people had taken a stand together to await sentence, and he waited now as the extra chairs and leaders lined the room.

Surveying the group, Jonar caught each colleague's eyes, searching for the cooperation he needed and nodding in satisfaction when he felt he had it. The leaders, all terrified at what was happening, would no doubt follow his plan. He had heard no other ideas so far, and feedback had all been in his favor, ranging from absolute approval to genuine understanding over his actions with Zuriel. *I must not show fear again.*

Jonar called the Council to order and stood, allowing the hem of his spotless white robe to fall elegantly to the floor as he posed in silent confidence that he was the picture of ultimate authority.

"Friends," he began after clearing his throat, "we have a serious problem as you all know, but it will not be a permanent threat if handled with care." *The eager look in their eyes at the sound of his voice. The desperate hope that he had a solution. The ecstasy of supremacy!*

"Not a threat?" interrupted Jesero in a high-pitched voice. "There are cracks all over the North Wall—at the very foundation. The music cells are falling apart. Almost thirty people have stood with Zuriel. We can silence one for heresy. But thirty? That would not be looked upon as...."

"Jesero... Jesero..." Cisco pleaded in a fatherly tone, which suited his age. He eyed Jonar as he spoke to the youngest of their calling. "Jesero, we must remain calm. Panic will not help us."

Jonar was surprised at the calmness in Cisco's voice for he was surely as terrified as the rest of them.

"Indeed, yes," Jonar agreed, nodding to Cisco, who visibly rejoiced at the acknowledgement. Jesero sat back down in obvious frustration as he saw the others agreeing with Cisco's remark.

Jesero is always jealous, thought Jonar. *He will never be one of the Great Ones.*

"I have a plan," Jonar said, "which will take care of this entire problem for good. It comes from Gwenla's time and was used after her death. Confusion reigned, and it was thought that chaos would follow. Although a group of leaders had been chosen, the people still tended to follow the old ways. They banded together in groups in order to rebel. There were cracks in the wall then too." Jonar did not know if this was true, but it fit so well that he could not help saying it.

"Were there?" Delegar asked, eyebrows together in doubt.

"As you know," Jonar continued, ignoring Delegar's remark, "Jon tried to explain Gwenla's wishes, including obedience to the chosen leaders. But the people knew he had not been told Gwenla's Secrets, so they would not listen to him."

"He died after that," Cisco chimed in, "after writing *The Refuge.*"

Jonar did not acknowledge Cisco's contribution this time. *Do not let anyone steal your power,* his father had warned him. He stepped behind his desk and sat down, looking over the other leaders as a general sizes up his troops. *How they look up to me! They love the sound of my voice.*

"As you may remember, friends... it was a dark time." Jonar continued, picking up his pencil and twirling it absentmindedly. His father had taught him this as well:

"You could be one of the Great Ones," his father had told him. "You have the personality that attracts followers. Speak a little and pause for effect. Watch how the people's attention is poised on your every word. Pick up an object—something of value that none of the others have—something rare. Play with it as though it were nothing. You will be astonished at the effect this has on them. They not only gain respect for you but lose it for

themselves. They realize they have never risen to your position. In their eyes, you become like a god."

Elated, Jonar observed the other leaders. *How right my father was! This is my destiny. Look at them. They wait for my words with bated breath....*

After what he thought was the right length of time, Jonar continued, rising from his desk again, this time holding the pencil as he paced the room once again. "The leaders had to be heavy handed in those days, applying harsher sentences for minor infractions and the death penalty for rebellion. They even put some over the wall. But this is not all they used to steer the people in the right direction."

Jonar paused for effect again, phrasing the next few words in his mind with care before he spoke.

"They also found someone who could lead with complete authority, without having to deal with a consensus. The constant violations and issues required immediate decisions and action. A leader in complete charge like this had to be someone the people trusted and respected—somebody whom I have the privilege of being named after ... Jonaris Suntar, the greatest leader in the history of Victory Valley."

Jonar suspended his voice again, letting the memory of his great ancestor come back to everyone's mind so they could draw their own conclusions.

"I remember, of course," Delegar said, surprising Jonar that he was awake. "They gave him complete control because of the crisis. He was appointed as the One Leader, a position that no one has held since that time."

"There was a good reason for that, gentlemen," Jonar went on. "Jonaris knew the Secrets of Gwenla."

This incredible announcement threw the room into confusion. Many asked Jonar as well as each other what on earth he meant by this statement. Jonar allowed the noise level to rise to a certain point, enjoying knowledge that no one else had, even though he would make up a lot of it to suit himself. He called for quiet, so excited he could hardly contain himself.

Delegar spoke first. "Jonar, this is... amazing news. But how... how do you know this? Do you have another source than the books of recorded history?"

"I have, yes." Jonar nodded and beamed at the others. "I have another source. The Secrets of Gwenla have been passed down in our family by word of mouth for 400 years!"

Again the noise level in the room rose, and Jonar allowed it to continue for a few moments.

Cisco's suspicious voice rose higher than the others. "Why would your family hold the Secrets for so long? And how did they get them?" Cisco looked perturbed.

Jonar gave Cisco a patronizing smile. *He is concerned for his son*, Jonar thought as he observed Cisco's face.

"It is simple, my fellow leaders," Jonar continued. "When Jonaris was still young, he was standing near Gwenla while she slept. She began talking in her sleep and revealed some amazing things, including some of the Secrets. At first, Jonaris was surprised that the One had allowed him to hear this, but he began to feel the responsibility entrusted to him. As if this was not enough, Gwenla also said in her sleep, *These things must not be known for 400 years*. Jonaris realized that Gwenla's knowledge was meant to be kept secret, which is of course why no one has known them until now."

To Jonar's dismay, Jesero began chuckling. "Jonar, do you expect us to believe after all these years that you know something no one else...."

"Silence! It is the truth," Jonar said, displaying a wounded expression. "Friends, you know me. Why, I am not one to notice, but I have heard there are comments about my work as one of the High Leaders. These remarks have not been negative. Why do you question my good will?"

Silence followed. Cisco frowned. Delegar nodded gravely. Jonar was confident they would accept his plan. They had no choice. Everything was falling apart, and they had twenty-eight rebels on their hands. It was obvious they all needed a leader to follow—a great leader.

"Are you going to reveal the Secrets?" Cisco asked pointedly.

Jonar put on his most solemn countenance. "Friends, I must do as the Great Jonaris did—consider my position and the knowledge that has been handed down to me. As I watch what is taking place around us—the chaos and rebellion—the fortress and walls coming apart—I feel that the time has come.

"My fellow leaders, the first thing Gwenla revealed was that the time of many leaders would come to an end after 400 years. The need for one leader would come again—a single, strong figure for the people to follow in a time of crisis, whose word would not be questioned. Gwenla foresaw this time of rebellion and knew that one reliable leader was the only answer."

Jonar noticed that his voice had almost a hypnotic affect on them. "I submit this knowledge and plan to you this day to decide upon," he continued, timing all of his phrasing right. "I submit that we must choose this One Leader, according to the wishes and Secrets of Gwenla."

Each of the leaders began to nod, looking around to see whether the others agreed. They talked among themselves while Jonar listened to them: *Yes, it does make sense. No, we do not have any other choice, do we?* His plan was working; his time had come.

While the leaders were still conversing, Jonar happened to look down at his stone tile floor and spot a widening fissure. Alarmed at first, he pondered its significance. What was this destructive force that had struck the walls and buildings? Everyone believed it was the Lying Wind, which of course helped his cause. But what could it be? Earth movement? Then he had an idea.

Smiling to himself, Jonar put on his most distressed and alarmed expression. "Men—look what is happening to our sacred buildings!" He pointed to the crevice in his flooring. Panic followed.

Within ten minutes, Jonar was appointed the One Leader by the terrified Council of Leaders. He was in absolute control over the entire community and everyone in it.

After the room emptied, Jonar studied the fracture in the floor at close range. The thrill of complete power shot through him like a bolt of ecstasy, and he grinned in exultation, wishing he could shout his success.

It had worked! *Jonar, the One Leader,* he thought with blissful abandon.

Jonar, the One.

Chapter Thirty-Two: The Trial

♪

Julyiah was positive that every soul in Victory Valley was in town for Zuriel's trial. She stood with her parents at the intersection of Town Road and Main Street, unable to get any closer to the Listening Hall due to the hundreds of people who had already congregated outside. Unwilling to press in through the crowd while holding her tiny baby, she waited.

The raucous assembly discussed the reason for the multiple fissures appearing in the walls. Pieces of stone lay about on the ground in several places. The disintegration was the worst at the North Wall and close to the valley floor. Menila announced that the music cells had been closed due to the danger of further collapse, and rumors had spread that the leaders' quarters also indicated damage from the strange phenomenon.

"Relatives? Relatives of the accused?" A blue-uniformed Keeper walked through the crowd, checking for family members who had not reached the front due to the crowded conditions. The law required that all persons related to the accused should be present at the trial if possible. Julyiah raised her hand, and the Keeper pushed his way through the mass of agitated people to reach her.

"Do you need escort?" the Keeper asked.

"Yes. Oh yes!" Julyiah cried out in relief. She had been desperate for a way to see Delwyn. "But I have a nursing baby."

"We have attendants. He will be safe," the Keeper assured her. Julyiah was unsure of how long the trial might last and was torn between her concern for Delwyn and her newborn. She followed the man, her parents coming also, as Dawnli's guardians. Harol held Rashella up out of the multitude of bodies pressing in on every side. The Keeper used a stern voice of authority to clear a path for them.

The trial had been moved outdoors because the community had been notified, and the large numbers would not fit inside. Delegar and Jesero seemed pleased with the numbers that turned out, and Julyiah wondered why, having expected them to deal with the situation more quietly.

Delwyn's voice reached Julyiah before she saw him. Crying out, she hurried to reach his side, apologizing to a large woman who received Julyiah's wayward elbow in her ample stomach. But the guards turned Julyiah back and made her stand behind a dividing rope—one which separated the accused from the rest of the people. An attendant brought her a chair, and she sat with her parents.

An old metal platform used for major valley events held the accused and their judges near the music cells. Three chairs for the High Leaders dominated the dais. Julyiah was surprised to see that Jonar's chair had been raised higher than the others, as though he was more important. Julyiah knew the Law, that no single leader could have full power—a law laid down by the leaders themselves hundreds of years before, in order to lessen the possibility of corruption among those in authority. Her eyes narrowed when she saw Jonar. *What is he up to now?*

A Keeper rang a clanging bell to bring the congregation into proper order, and Delegar addressed the assembly.

"People of Victory Valley, before we start this trial, we, the leaders of this community, wish to make an announcement about which the entire Council is in agreement, and I am sure you will rejoice with us."

Julyiah marveled at the silence, where the noise level had been so high just moments before.

"As you all know, Jonar, the Most Respected One, has shown unequaled wisdom in his leadership. He leads as his ancestor, the Great Jonaris, did long ago...."

Delegar droned on, his aged voice quivering now and then. Julyiah recalled her parents saying that Delegar was the primary spokesperson for the leaders before Jonar was appointed. In retelling the story of how Jonaris was elected the One Leader in the time of crisis after Gwenla, she knew he was planning to say something unusual. It was not hard for her to guess what his announcement would be.

After describing the history of Jonaris, Delegar paused, allowing the crowd to take in the significance of his story. Some discussion broke out, but Julyiah observed how most of the people nodded and smiled in anticipation.

"I am pleased to announce to you today that, due to our current emergency and urgent need for so many immediate decisions, the entire Council of Leaders has unanimously elected Jonar as our Highest leader—our One Leader over Victory Valley!"

Our current emergency... Julyiah mused. So that was how Jonar did this. In a time of emergency, the leaders could declare almost anything, making old laws invalid or establishing new laws on the spot. Still, she had no doubt that Jonar had manipulated his own promotion.

♪ ♪

Feeling giddy with so much power, Jonar half expected to float. It was all he could do not to jump up and shout. A noisy acclamation followed Delegar's declaration, with the crowd cheering and clapping in approval. Jonar rose from his chair, grinning in acknowledgement. Delegar sat down again as Jonar assumed his position behind the podium. The noise did not subside for some time, and Jonar savored the applause and cheers.

Look at them, he thought. *They worship me.*

When Jonar held up his hand, the people ignored his desire to speak, but remained determined to show their approval. They did not stop the prolonged applause, and Jonar looked back at his fellow leaders with an expression of, *How do I stop them?*

At last, the ovation died down, and a hush told Jonar he could again address the crowd. "Friends of Victory Valley, we have a problem. This man…" Jonar indicated Zuriel with a disgusted flick of his wrist, "who I am ashamed to say was a leader with us, has committed an act of unspeakable..." Jonar's voice broke, and he pretended to be overcome with emotion. As he feigned a struggle to control himself, his sorrow-filled gaze ran over the crumbling wall, as though witnessing the death of a loved one. Calls for justice rang out among the people, along with other cries and murmurs.

"Forgive me, friends," Jonar said, his voice choked. The crowd quieted, and he took advantage of the silence to speak. "This problem is… is so important to … me …."

Jonar's face showed tremendous sadness and concern, while he allowed a visible tremble to show on his lips and chin. Many appeared as overcome as he was, some also looking at the beloved music cells with a tearful gaze. Jonar started to speak again, feigning a struggle, but he shook his head as though it was no use and sat down.

♪

Julyiah's deep disgust over Jonar's display of emotion caused her to take in a ragged breath. She knew he would not mourn the loss of anything, except maybe his own power.

As Julyiah considered Jonar's actions, she saw Jonar whisper to Delegar, who rose to address the gathering.

"Friends, Jonar is... unable to proceed at the moment. He has asked me to state the charges against Zuriel Destin, known as Zuriel the Truthful."

Delegar faced Zuriel. "Zuriel Destin, you are hereby charged with heresy as regards our Sacred Laws, written by the leaders of long ago."

Why does "long ago" always carry so much weight? Julyiah wondered. Many laws were given as much weight as the sacred books because they were of Suntarian heritage, as though this alone made them sacred for all time. Julyiah recalled how Gwenla spoke in her *Book of Secrets* against tradition, because ritual too often replaced true devotion to the One.

After the charges were spoken, Jonar stood up, appearing to have gained control of his emotions.

"Fellow leaders and citizens of Victory Valley, we have been lenient," Jonar's voice rang out across the area. "When certain problems arose several years ago, we were merciful, but in our desire for compassion, we ignored the consequences of too much kindness. We allowed one speck of rebellion to remain among us, and now..." Jonar's voice caught again, "now everything that we love is... is crumbling." Jonar waved his arm toward the music cells and the obvious fractures in the wall. Afterwards, he gazed over the community before him.

He is watching to see who supports him, Julyiah decided. She had seen him do this before.

"Most of you have noticed," Jonar went on, "that we are having trouble in the music cells and in the walls. First, small crevices began to appear. Then these grew larger. Now whole sections of music cells have fallen apart. We wonder—what will be next?

"You have heard, no doubt, what took place in our Sacred Listening Hall yesterday." Jonar paused, surveying the crowd. The mention of "what took place yesterday" caused the accused who sat with Zuriel to exchange joyful glances. But most of the people who attended showed fear and alarm. Jonar glanced around and acknowledged those who showed concern with a nod of understanding.

"There is no doubt among the Forum of Leaders and all of the faithful that this was a serious offense. The instigator of this unforgivable violation is Zuriel Destin. Alas, he used to be one who worked to lead the way to truth, but now Destin follows a lie and has used his position to encourage others to follow his evil plans."

That is not true! Julyiah shook her head with a grimace at Jonar's twisting of the facts.

"Fortunately," Jonar went on, "those involved have stood with Destin in this crime so that we may eliminate the entire problem at one time."

The group of relatives in front gasped at the word "eliminate" and discussed the fate of their friends and loved ones. Julyiah's mother cried out, "No!"

Mikela began to fuss, and grew louder, so an attendant came to care for him so that Julyiah could remain at the trial. Jonar saw the attendant take the baby and stared at Julyiah, his face darkening. Turning to Cisco, Jonar whispered in the other leader's ear. Cisco whispered something back and pointed straight at Julyiah, who wondered why Jonar was so interested in her. Jonar spoke and gestured angrily with Cisco, but Cisco shook his head and shrugged.

Wrath spread over Jonar's face when his eyes darted again toward Julyiah. Certain that he wished her to be included in the condemned group of people, Julyiah wondered what lengths he would go to in order to get rid of her. Jonar's expression remained ominous as he again addressed the crowd.

"Friends, the time of leniency is over. We tried to save our friends, but they would not listen. This crumbling that we are all witnessing is none other than the Lying Wind, which will stop at nothing to bring the Devastation back into Victory Valley!"

A stiff, chilly breeze rushed around the gathering as Jonar spoke these words, stirring up a whirlwind that wound its way around the perimeter of the crowd. People pushed their way toward the center of the attendees, shrieking in terror. It was as though what everyone feared had come upon them. Shouts of horror escaped some, along with angry calls for justice from others. The frightened community eyed the crumbling wall and the blowing breezes and huddled into small groups. To Jonar's great delight, a low, rumbling crash rose from deep within the music cells. A moment of complete silence ensued while the people stared at the music cells with dread.

The shaking of the ground is certainly well-timed, Jonar thought, putting on a horrified face. The mesmerized crowd continued to soak in his passionate concern for their safety. *Like Captain Jonaris Suntar of old,* he decided, having always believed he was at least as great as his renowned ancestor.

"We must act for the good of all, and we must act today," Jonar shouted above the din. "There is just one thing to do. We must purge Victory Valley of all who played a part in this massive undermining of our safety. In the old days, those who rebelled were cast over the wall in order to retain peace after Gwenla died. I assure you, friends, that if we send these out to the Lying Wind, the destruction will cease, for he will no longer have the cause or even the right to invade our peaceful world."

"Over the wall!" someone shouted. The frenzied mob took up the chant: "Over the wall! Over the wall!"

Chapter Thirty-Three: Separation

♪

Julyiah burst into convulsive sobbing, shoving her way toward Delwyn. She staggered back, pushed aside by several guards who stepped over to take charge of the prisoners. The guards tied the hands of each prisoner and shoved him or her into a line. Cisco turned pale and stared at his son Daleil, while ropes went around the young man's hands.

Delegar stood again and motioned for silence. The crowd grew quiet.

"By decree of Jonar, our One Great leader, any defense for these rebels has been waved," Delegar announced, followed by several murmurs of both approval and disapproval in the crowd. "The Council has decided, and it has been confirmed by the People, that the rebels should be let down to the Outside by way of the South Window. To avoid further anguish among the relatives, this sentence will be carried out today."

Loud cheers interrupted Delegar's voice. Julyiah doubted the motive for an immediate sentence was to "avoid further anguish among the relatives." When it grew quieter, a few howling cries of protest split the hush, but Delegar continued, "These rebels are considered outcasts with no hope of reconciliation, and since they are not expected to live, they will be given no provision. So be it."

The noise level of the crowd grew when Delegar stopped speaking. He nodded to a Keeper, who rang the bell to signal the end of the trial. The electrified crowd reverted to a raucous chanting of, "Over the wall! Over the wall!" The chant increased in volume, as though the people wanted to assist the guards in pressing the prisoners forward to their doom. Armed guards escorted the prisoners along Town Road toward the canal boats, with what looked like half the community population following.

Julyiah allowed the crowd to push past her. Recognizing that she was about to faint, she sat in an abandoned chair. Waves of sorrow rolled over her as she cried, struggling to remain conscious. Delwyn— sent to the Outside? *I must go with him!*

Willing herself to feel better so she could follow, Julyiah remembered her children. She would not leave them here, but she could not take them with her to the Outside either. With horror, Julyiah came to the conclusion that ripped at her soul—she must let her husband go without her.

The pit beckoned to her heart, and she wanted to give in to it. The darkness would be welcome, and the muck would numb her thoughts. A black haze swam before her eyes, and Julyiah reached up to grab someone to help her, but none turned to look. "Over the wall! Over the wall!"

"Julyiah!" Harol rushed to her side.

Julyiah returned to her painful reality and reached for her father, who knelt on the ground next to her chair, pulling her into his embrace. Livi reached for her daughter's hand to hold onto. Rashella fell into her mother's arms, trying to comfort her. Shep also recognized the distress of his mistress, and he nosed under her arm to indicate his share in her pain.

"I must go with them," Julyiah said in a weak protest.

The attendant returned with Mikela and handed him to Livi, explaining that as an attendant, she needed to follow the group that was headed to the South Window. Livi took her grandchild into her willing arms, but she fidgeted and humphed in apparent frustration.

"Julyiah cannot go, Harol," Livi insisted. "She is too weak, and it would cause her more pain to see Delwyn put over the wall."

In the presence of her children, Julyiah struggled to pull herself together. "No! I have to go," Julyiah sniffed, pulling away from her father and mother to show that she had strength. "I have to... say goodbye."

For a few minutes, Julyiah's parents hovered over her. People continued to push their way past, eager to see the enactment of this unusual punishment of Zuriel and his followers, oblivious to whoever was in the way. Although some looked on Julyiah with compassion, most did not stop to acknowledge the Hartbrook family plight.

Leaders boarding carriages to ride to the South Window attracted Harol's attention, and he rushed over to them. Julyiah cringed when she spotted her father seeking out Jonar.

"Jonar, please!" Harol called out. "Julyiah needs assistance. She is still weak from her hard delivery of the baby."

Jonar stopped, his eyes narrowing as Harol explained Julyiah's sad predicament. "Please! She needs a ride to the Window, to say goodbye to her husband."

♪ ♪

Ridiculous, Jonar thought. *She is the one who started all this.* If there was some way Julyiah could be put over the wall as well, Jonar would have seen to it. But when he had seen the attendant hand a small bundle back to his grandmother, Jonar knew that sending Julyiah out with the others was not possible. No one would look upon such an action with favor.

Jonar could not rest with Julyiah still in the valley. She had been the first to rebel, not Zuriel. Yet, as Cisco had pointed out to him earlier, there was this law—this minor, insignificant law that said no woman with a nursing baby could "stand with" an accused person. Perhaps he could abolish the silly law on the spot. *Yes, I could do that now….*

No, it would not work. The people held more power than they realized.

Jonar clenched his teeth in frustration. He had to find another way to get rid of this meddling woman. Julyiah Sarroll needed to disappear, somehow. She alone was left to threaten his… kingdom? Yes, it was a kingdom, was it not? He would not be called a *King*, but he was now a single ruler. How could anything still be in his way? Jonar stared at the young woman with the baby. He would have to arrange an accident as soon as possible.

"Guard!" Jonar said at last. "Provide transport for this woman. She is Delwyn's wife." Without another word or glance, Jonar set off with the other leaders.

♪

The crowd stopped their chanting after walking a ways with the procession, and Julyiah was relieved. It was a walk of several hours from one end of the fortress to the other, and those who stuck with the group had apparently grown wearier as the hours went by. Since the South Window was accessed by a dark, narrow staircase, it became obvious that just the guards and the leaders could witness the final ceremony. By the time the carriages arrived at the South Wall, most of those who were not family members had gone back to their homes or businesses.

After Jonar's antagonistic behavior toward Julyiah, Harol directed an appeal to Cisco to allow his daughter to be present at the actual letting down of her husband through the window. This idea was agreeable to the pain-softened Cisco, who nodded with a broken expression before turning his gaze back upon his son. Julyiah rushed into Delwyn's arms, and he was also allowed to embrace his two children before leaving them behind with Julyiah's parents.

The single file procession moved forward with Zuriel and those who had stood with him. Delwyn, with Julyiah now beside him, was walking near the back of the line. For Delwyn's sake, Julyiah tried to maintain her composure, but her tears continued to slide down her face.

"Delwyn, what will happen to you?" Julyiah asked, shoving aside the bleak pit that threatened to claim her heart.

Delwyn had a look of peace, his eyes dancing with excitement. "Do not worry, my darling," he said, stroking her hair. "It is the Outside, remember? We have been there on the wings of Music. There are wonderful places out there, and we will see each other again."

Pictures of flying boulders, swirling sand, and deep crevasses flooded Julyiah's mind. This was all they knew of the Outside—all they *really* knew. Could she believe the places they had encountered in their hearts actually existed? As they entered the stone structure and started up the depressing staircase inside the wall, Julyiah felt she was marching to her own death as well as Delwyn's. How could she bear to be separated from him forever?

"Delwyn, I am afraid you will not find those places. What if they are too far away?"

Delwyn gave her a brilliant smile. "Julyiah, I have this feeling. I feel like they are close—much closer than we think. Do not worry. Zuriel said the lower part of the North Wall is crumbling faster than the upper. When he was down there yesterday, he could see daylight through the cracks. There may be a way back inside from the north. If there is, we will come back shortly."

Julyiah's heart lightened. *Yes, it should be all right, soon, should it not?*

This hope held her together when they reached the little room where the guards had pulled out the stone in the South Window and had begun to lower some of the people down by rope. Time sped forward while Julyiah counted the number of people left until it would be Delwyn's turn. Emotion choked her chest when he was next.

When the awful moment arrived, Delwyn turned to smile and wave at her again, and they pushed her husband through the opening in the wall. He disappeared over the outside edge of the thick windowsill, hanging from the rope provided. Julyiah could no longer see him, just the movements of the guards who lowered him down.

Though her vision blurred through her tears, Julyiah looked anxiously through the open window, which provided a much wider opening than the small crack she and the children had peered through that fateful day over five years ago. Her hope wavered. She saw nothing but white sand. The outlying mountains looked barren—not the least bit inspiring as they had the day she and children had come. Julyiah remained to say goodbye to Dawnli and Daleil, noticing how torn Cisco was over losing his son. Julyiah's heart went out to him.

Zuriel was last, carrying Johan in his arms. He turned toward Julyiah with a glint in his eye. "At last," he said, "I am going to see what is out there!"

Julyiah gave him a weak smile. *I hope something is out there.* Before she could ponder the idea further, the guards pushed the huge stone back into place, and it was over.

♪

Outside, the small band of people huddled together, bracing themselves against the blinding sand. The hot southwest wind blasted its relentless breath against their faces, causing them to comprehend their fate with no water.

"We had better find the river right away," suggested Delwyn. His heart struggled as he looked around. Sand, sand—there was nothing but sand. What if they had only dreamed of wondrous places out here?

"But... the river must be at the northern end," Dawnli moaned. "It is half a day's walk from here."

"We had better get started," Zuriel said, pointing east, his enthusiasm undaunted. "We still have a lot of light."

The arduous journey to the southeastern corner of the wall took hours. Everyone was already so tired, and the wind blew sand into their faces. As they came closer to where the wall curved north, the group grew anxious to know if anything new would be visible. If there were anything at the northern end, the landscape would begin to change, Delwyn was certain. But nothing appeared to be changing. Everywhere he looked there was sand and faraway, gray mountains.

♪♪

Just before the final bend, Zuriel hurried forward to get a glimpse. His countenance fell. The view was blocked by the same barrier that ran through the midst of the valley from east to west—the Inner Wall—except out here it was a huge pile of rocks with no stairs.

The rocky layer was two thousand paces away, and they could not see beyond it. By the time they reached it, the East Wall was casting a nice cool shadow over the travelers' path. Exhausted and thirsty, the group rested in the shade before going on.

The climb up the rocky cliff was difficult and treacherous. They made slow progress. Bruised and exhausted, many wanted to wait until the next day to make the ascent.

Delwyn and Zuriel decided to go on alone, telling the others they would call out if the way ahead looked hopeful. The two continued the hike, braving the heat, wind, and sand that penetrated every crevice of their skin and clothes, in order to see what was ahead. As they neared the summit, the northern landscape came into view. Zuriel and Delwyn hurried to finish the climb and stood at the top with a clear view north. Breathless, they sank to the ground to consider all that was before them.

"I cannot believe it," said Zuriel.

"Neither can I," Delwyn agreed.

Chapter Thirty-Four: Silence

♪

Julyiah hung on to hope at the South Window while Delwyn's words still echoed in her thoughts, encouraging her, but at her parents' house that evening, the familiar surroundings without Delwyn amplified her anxiety. Would she ever see him again? She tried to picture the outcasts discovering lush greenery, water, and fruit trees in the north, but all she could see was hot, blowing sand and desolate countryside.

As Livi sat with her for comfort, frustration grew within Julyiah's heart. She knew her mother was happy that she had been spared, but the woman also mourned the loss of Dawnli and the others. As for Jonar—*how dare he? How dare Jonar assume absolute power?* Yes, they said it was decided by *all* the leaders, but Julyiah was well aware that Jonar could manipulate anybody into anything, including all of the other leaders if it suited his purpose. She had admired his leadership qualities before, but now… how dare he put Delwyn, father of two small children, over the wall just because he stood with a friend? Who would not have? And Dawnli, too? The girl had attended the Listening Hall and obeyed the leaders. Yet, because she stood with her good friend, Zuriel, they sent her to the Outside.

Julyiah heard Livi swallow down her tears. Dawnli had been like a daughter to her, and now she would never see her again. Julyiah knew she could not bear to think of the group on the Outside, suffering and dying. Livi glanced at the wedding talia in the corner—the one she had made for Julyiah, and then intended to let Dawnli wear. Julyiah's heart broke with the pain her mother must be feeling. Would that talia never be used?

♩ ... ♩♫

A dense mass floated over the community in a contented reverie, surveying his handiwork with satisfaction. A small gray puff blew up from the east, rolling over and over like a tumbleweed until it reached the shady mass who was his master.

"My lord, most of the rebels have been cast out. They are ignorant of the landscape and will die. Those who were sympathetic are broken and helpless. Jonar is in complete power and in his arrogance will continue to carry out your wishes. The wall has stopped crumbling...."

"Stopped?" The muddy mist halted its restful drifting and began to swirl a little. "Good. All will be well as long as Julyiah gives up. Without her help, they will never find out the truth— none of them will."

♩

Julyiah woke after a restless night with a glimmer of hope. After all, the walls were coming down. Delwyn and the others would survive on the Outside until then. The One would watch over them.

Anxious to know the progress of the wall collapse, Julyiah rose from bed with renewed incentive. After feeding and changing Mikela, she went out, taking the baby with her in a pack and leading Rashella by the hand.

At the music cells, Julyiah was surprised to see a crew of laborers bringing loads of rock and other building materials and piling them outside. Nearby a group of bystanders discussed the proceedings.

"What are they doing, Mama?" Rashella asked, pointing to the laborers.

"Excuse me," Julyiah interrupted the group of people, "do you know what they are doing?"

"Rebuilding the music cells, of course," said a man Julyiah did not recognize. "They have been falling apart for days, you know, because of the Lying Wind. But when the rebels were put outside the wall, the crumbling stopped, even as Jonar said it would."

Julyiah tried not to look as horrified as she felt. "The crumbling stopped? Completely?"

"Why yes, as Jonar told us," the man said with a smile. "He is a great man."

Julyiah gave the speaker an awkward smile, but her heart went into confusion. As tears filled her eyes, she turned away. *No… no…no…It cannot be!*

Despair tried to claim her heart, as detestable creatures in hideous muck jumped up, biting at her feet. At the moment, she was not sure whether she would rather get out of their way or let them devour her.

It cannot be true! Julyiah struggled to convince herself there was hope, but the conclusion became obvious. With the rebels ousted, the destruction of the wall stopped, even as Jonar said it would.

Could we have been wrong all along? Were all of our supposed encounters with Music the Lying Wind after all?

"Mama, when will Papa come back from the Outside?" Rashella's voice rang out, jolting Julyiah from her thoughts. She stared down at her daughter's questioning face.

"Outside?" the stranger near her asked, forming a frown on his face. Fear gripped Julyiah's heart as she realized she was not among friends. Many might not welcome the family of an ostracized man. Without responding, she turned and walked away as quickly as she could while pulling her three-year old along.

"Mama?"

"Please do not talk about it right now," Julyiah said, glancing at the nearby workers to see who might have overheard. "Mama is not feeling well."

Julyiah had no real answers, but at least she was not lying. She really did not feel well—she was upset. As she stumbled back to her parents' home, she worried over Delwyn. If the wall did not come down, he would die.

By the time Julyiah returned to the house, she knew what she had to do. Bringing out a sheepskin bag, she strapped Mikela on her back and asked a perplexed Livi to watch over Rashella. Heading out to Town Road, Julyiah resolved to find a way to get water over that wall—she had to. If Jonar did not like it, he could put her over the wall too. She would get water to her husband or die trying. Debating whether to take Shep with her, she decided against it. He had never been in a boat before, and she did not know for certain if he would be a problem.

It was not long before Julyiah's ride in a canal boat brought her to the south end of the valley. She strode up to the guardhouse at the South Window, attempting to look more confident than she felt. As she approached the door to knock, her hand shook, and she could not control it. Wondering what on earth made her think she could do this, Julyiah's determination and love for Delwyn urged her forward. She knocked on the door.

Greeted with the same rough, unfriendly manner that she had encountered on the window viewing day with the children, Julyiah stammered out a plea to the guard, but this time she had no pass. Within seconds, the door was shut in her face.

Mikela began fussing, and Julyiah brought him around in front of her to nurse him back to sleep, but he would not nurse and began to cry. After the baby settled down, Julyiah allowed herself to cry too, hoping it would soften the guards. But when it grew quiet, the brisk clip of other guards descending the inside staircase reached her ears. She feared they might arrest her. Sensing great danger, she turned and ran along the path to the nearby orchard, knowing she must escape and hide before they began looking for her. Turning, she saw the guards outside talking and glancing in her direction, but when she reached the orchard gate, she saw them re-enter the guard station.

Julyiah stopped to catch her breath and put the sleeping Mikela back into his sling. Through the trees she saw the small cabin of the old Orchard Keeper, Draya. Although she did not know him, desperation drove her to the cabin.

♫ ♪ ♫

Bright sprays of color shot into the air and burst into thousands of bright sparks, surrounded by beautiful Music. Another, smaller swirl of blue watched the carefree dance of hues in astonishment.

"I cannot help wondering... how can you be so lighthearted? All looks so bleak—as though our enemy has won. The wall is no longer disintegrating, and Julyiah is in peril. You know that the timing must be perfect, or all is lost. You cannot be sure she will do it."

"She will keep searching. She will not give up," the Voice said.

"But... what about the others? They have no food or water, and they are lost."

"Yes, I know."

Chapter Thirty-Five: The Cabin

♫

Delwyn shook his head over what they had seen to the north, as he helped Zuriel keep everyone's spirits up on the morning of the second day. The exhausted group trudged southward, the relentless wind and blinding sand continuing to beat against their worn out bodies.

"What if there is no passage on the western side either?" one from the Underground complained. "We should have kept going north."

"We told you," Delwyn said in a cracked voice, throat parched from lack of water. His tongue felt like a dry cotton ball. "There was no way across the chasm. It was extremely deep and too long—we could not see the end of it."

"We should have found a way," someone else mumbled, wiping a weak hand across her brow, and tasting the sweat. *She is looking for some kind of moisture,* thought Delwyn. "There was no way across on that side," Delwyn assured them, wishing he had drank something before they left. All he could think about was water. "We would have had to walk for days into the desert in order to go around the canyon. We do not have the provisions for such a trek."

"And what you saw in the north?"

Delwyn looked at Zuriel, wondering how to respond, but when Zuriel opened his mouth to speak, he choked. Zuriel waved his hand forward and in an arc, indicating they should continue on around the southwestern corner of the wall. Delwyn hoped that a way to the north would open up for them on the other side of the old fortress. If not, they would die.

♪

An elderly man with a long white beard and a grumpy face opened the cabin door. Julyiah stepped back, unsure, but she saw a slight glint in his eyes at the sight of a visitor, as though she might be welcome. His demeanor softened at once.

"Come in, young woman. I do not get much company. Would you like a drink? Some fruit?" The wrinkled face grinned at Mikela. "That is a beautiful child you have there."

♫♪

The thirsty people on the Outside made their way with dragging feet along the South Wall, heading west. As they passed under the South Window, they looked up but realized they could not reach that window any more than they could get across the chasm on the east side. Their final hope lay beyond the southwestern corner. It was just a couple of hours away now but felt impossible to reach.

Pressing forward, step by step, they encouraged each other along. They no longer spoke unless it was necessary, because sand blew into their mouths each time they opened them. Zuriel was concerned about the older ones, as well as Johan. He had to pull the boy along, marveling at the irony that he and Johan had once almost drowned. Now they were about to die from lack of water.

The wind would not stop its relentless assault. The fortress corner grew closer, but the wind would be worse on the west side. The hot, swirling sand tried to rob them of any hope for deliverance existing around that corner. But they did hope, because that corner held the only possible reprieve short of the entire wall falling down. If they could not reach the river that flowed out from the north, they would die.

As they came around the long curve at the southwestern corner, hopes dimmed. The wind grew stronger as expected, and when they faced full north, a dismal sight met their eyes—the same pile of rocks that continued from the fortress wall far off to the west, plus another barrier they had not counted on.

"The Durnee Break...." croaked Delwyn.

Between the rocky cliff and the group, the Durnee Break gaped before them as another impassable obstruction that extended west into the desert. Lined by a few pointed boulders, the giant hole opened into the earth, sand swirling above it before striking the rocks and falling in. They could go around it, but the rocky barrier beyond squelched any hopes of reaching the north.

Many sagged to their knees, giving up the struggle. "There is shade on the other side of these boulders," one man rasped, his voice barely audible. "They will block the wind a little, too. We can rest here." He headed for the space between the boulders and the wall, before collapsing on a cool pile of sand, turning his face away from the wind. Others followed.

You mean we can die here, thought Delwyn.

"We should have stayed on the east side of the fortress," another man added before lying down with the others. Zuriel gazed at the rocky cliff.

"Zuriel?" Delwyn questioned through lips that felt like chalk. "There is no way across this."

"We could cross the top of these boulders to the cliff," Zuriel mumbled. "I have faced death three times now in five days. I have to keep going."

Delwyn nodded, staring at the huge stones, wishing they went high enough to scale the wall itself. But neither the boulders nor the cliff beyond them rose more than half way up the side of the sheer structure. The pile of rocks that made the chasm cliff could be accessed by scaling the boulders and walking precariously across the top of them. If they had all their strength and some water, they might be able to do it. But exhausted? In a sand storm?

"You are right," Delwyn said, in support of his friend even though the task was impossible. He forced himself to stand, wincing at the blisters that had formed in his sand-filled shoes, and stumbled over to climb the boulders with Zuriel. Julyiah was inside, so he would go on for her and for his children.

♪

"Where did you get all these books?" Julyiah asked in astonishment as she entered a small back room in the cabin with Draya.

"Had 'em most of my life. I collected them. Do not spend sokens on much else, except food, of course." Draya mumbled through mostly toothless gums as he shuffled over to the bookcase.

"I see you have a copy of *Captain Suntar*," Julyiah said. "I used to read that to the schoolchildren. Oh, and here is the *History of Durnee: An Interview with the Founder*. I have never heard of that."

"There is no other copy," Draya told her.

Julyiah continued looking over the books in delight until she came across one called, *The Geography of Victory Valley and Surrounding Area.* The words "Surrounding area" caught her attention. Did this show the terrain on the Outside?

"May I look at this?" Julyiah asked.

"Certainly," Draya said, obviously happy that she cared. "Look at any you wish to." He smiled as though with great relief and shuffled toward the door of the room.

♪♪♪

Draya turned in the doorway and looked back at Julyiah. *Hmmm... a schoolteacher.* As Julyiah eagerly searched through the books, he nodded and headed out of the room.

♪

Julyiah found several maps inside the geography book. There was one of the fortress area, a close up of their little town, and even a map of the Underground. At last, she found what she was looking for—a map of the area around the old fortress. Julyiah's eyes grew wide, and she almost dropped the book. On either side of the fortress, a deep chasm extended for a great distance—to the east and to the west. Delwyn and the others would never be able to make it north. They would die!

Tears of anguish sprang to her eyes, and Julyiah squelched them as she focused on what to do. One of the songs she had heard in her heart when Delwyn played the tyrea came to her, and she began to hum it, hoping for direction.

When the tyrea is played, the fortress of Silence will fall.

Yes! Was it not when Delwyn played the tyrea that the wall had started to deteriorate? And when Delwyn and the others were arrested, the wall had stopped its collapse. Jonar had taken the tyrea, but what if she could get it and play it herself? Would the wall begin to crumble again?

Julyiah put the geography book back and rushed out of the room.

"I... I... I am sorry, Mr. uh... I mean, I have to leave right away. I read something... important, and I have to leave." Julyiah turned in order to rush to the door.

"Wait, please! Young woman, I want to give you something." Draya rose to his feet, while Julyiah eyed the door.

"No, I... I am sorry, but I do not have any time to lose!" Julyiah did not look back at him as she jerked the door open.

"But I want to give you a book."

Julyiah stopped before stepping out of the doorway when she heard Draya's last statement. His voice faded out as he wandered into the back room. He could have offered her food or money, and she would not have cared. But a book of her own? She could not turn that down! Even the most unwanted, poorly written book would be a treasure. She hurried back into the room, watching the old man with increasing excitement.

When Draya handed her a copy of *The Refuge*, Julyiah began shaking.

"Oh, you must not... this is a mistake," she insisted. "This is a copy of *The Refuge*. There are only two copies in existence—I mean *three* copies, obviously, but it is one of the Sacred Books. You must not give it to me."

"You take it," Draya insisted. "I know the value of this book. That is why I have searched all these years for someone worthy of it. My son hates books—an endless disappointment to me. This book has been passed down in our family for many years. No one lives that knows I had it, and now, it will be yours. I will leave the others to my son, whether he reads them or not. Who knows, maybe someday he will."

"Thank you, so much!" Julyiah hugged the startled old man. "I will be back again, but right now I must go." And before either of them could say more, Julyiah was gone.

Chapter Thirty-Six: The Refuge

♪

Julyiah would rather have run north up Sylar Ridge straight into town by the road, but she feared she would not have the strength to make it if she went from one end of the community to the other on foot. She needed energy to carry out her plan, and Mikela needed changing and feeding. So Julyiah pulled the baby around to her front and sat herself in a canal boat, hoping the guards at the South Window would not bother her when she floated by.

Normally, the ride in a canal boat would have been enjoyable, but Julyiah's thoughts were far from pleasure. A single-minded purpose engulfed her—breaking down those walls so Delwyn and the others could get to the water they so desperately needed.

Mikela awoke soon after she pushed off from the shore, so Julyiah changed his diaper and fed him while she waited for the boat to carry them around to the Inner Wall and the staircase. In her desire to do something besides sit and wait for the drifting boat to reach her destination, Julyiah picked up her new book. Though she had heard the story before, Julyiah started from the beginning, awed that this magnificent object belonged to her.

The Refuge, written by Jon, successor to Gwenla, Keeper of the Books. This is the record of our beginning years within the wall which sheltered our people from the Devastation.

Julyiah read farther, and began to skip sections, turning the pages to find her favorite ones. *Aha!* She found the exciting story of Gwenla's death. How mysterious that had been.... But what Julyiah saw on the page before her was not what she had previously heard or read. Was this not an authentic copy? Why was Jonaris's name on this page? It was at the place where Jon went in to see Gwenla.

"What is happening here?"

Leader Jonaris looked toward Jon from the side of Gwenla's bed.

"I am sorry. She is dead."

Jon's gaze moved toward the books on the table. He was glad that Gwenla had given him her secret writings before she died, but although she told him to hide them, she had never explained them to him. Sorrow filled his heart as he sank into a chair.

Jon wondered why Jonaris was there with a small bottle in his hand. What did the bottle contain? A doctor came in and took charge, making Jon leave.

Julyiah stared at this passage in dismay. Why, this made it look as though there was suspicion surrounding Jonaris's presence by Gwenla's side. Why was his name eliminated in other copies of this book? They said just, "A familiar face." There was no mention of a bottle in the other copies—the sentence ended after "Gwenla's bed." And she had never seen most of the last paragraph at all. It was a short section of text on the next page—a page she knew did not exist in the other copies of the book.

The awful truth struck Julyiah full force—*Jonaris murdered Gwenla! He changed Jon's book before anyone could see the truth.* Julyiah gasped, and all the tiny hairs on her arms stood on end as she recalled Jon's death. There had been a rumor that he was poisoned—a speculation that was never confirmed. With alarm, Julyiah recalled hearing of a fire in Jonar's office that damaged his personal copy of *The Refuge* a few years ago. Could he have damaged it on purpose?

The shocking reality of what Julyiah knew sent shivers of horror through her. Yet, it added further resolve to her plan. Her mind could no longer focus on the words in front of her, so she closed the book. She must get that tyrea! Jonar's corruption of authority had been passed down through his family to him. As Julyiah's boat reached the Inner Wall, she grabbed Mikela and the provisions and jumped out with new vigor, clutching the book under her arm. Its value had now increased a thousand fold.

♪…♪♫

"She knows." A squishy gray mass like quickly rising bread dough slopped over the ground. It stopped, huge bubbles growing and going slack, like something breathing. "She knows."

"We tried fear. It inspired her with more resolve."

"Fool!" the giant roared, spewing goo in all directions, leaving "breathing" blobs strewn about. "Do not you see? It will not work. The other has taken them through despair. Their perseverance has been tested, and they will not easily be defeated. They will not give up. *She* will not give up."

For a few moments, quiet reigned in the unseen world, except for the slurping sounds of the huge gray monster.

"You are looking a little pale, my lord."

"Quiet!" his master returned. "Go and stir up Jonar against her. Perhaps he will have the sense to kill her before she can succeed."

♪ ♪

Jonar sat at his exquisitely carved desk, looking around his office full of antiques and other valuable artifacts. The walls were no longer breaking up, as he had predicted. He could not have timed the few breaks in the wall better if he had planned them.

Maybe somehow he had control. Either way, Jonar's small deceptions would be overlooked since they were valuable to the community. Order was restored, and he was receiving all the praise.

"And I have not used this," Jonar held up a tiny music box. The box was plain, not decorated in silver or gold as the other music boxes were. It was made out of wood, and the latch was in the shape of a key. Where the latch connected, a tiny dot of red wax sealed the container. No one could open the box without breaking the seal.

Everyone feared the box, because it was known to have music of great power. It was called *Gwenla's* secret music box. She had opened it long ago to calm the people and restore order. But before she died she sealed it, and nobody knew why. Since then, it had been in the hands of the leaders. A mysterious inscription that no one understood adorned the box. *But I will understand it*, thought Jonar. *I am as the voice of the One for the people now—they are too afraid to seek for themselves. I will have the wisdom and knowledge needed.* Jonar read the inscription:

Music in this box will make
Order come and Silence break.
Opened by a worthy one,
Chaos will be stopped, undone;
Opened by unworthy rabble,
Walls will fall, a man will babble.

No one had opened the box since Gwenla had sealed it. Someone worthy of the honor could open it, and no one had yet dared to claim such worth. Also, there had been no great disorder to justify opening it.

Jonar stared at it, fingering the latch with longing. The power of Gwenla—that was what he wanted. No one had been as powerful as Gwenla, not in the entire history of his people. As long as things went Jonar's way, he need not risk opening the box. He was certain, though, that if anyone was considered worthy, it would be himself.

Voices outside his office door interrupted Jonar's thoughts, and he hurried to put the box away in his desk drawer and lock it. He recognized Julyiah's voice, and it grew louder.

"But this is not one of the known copies of *The Refuge*. It has been handed down in the Orchard Keepers' family for generations!"

The Orchard Keeper! A dreadful foreboding invaded Jonar's peaceful thoughts. *Another copy of The Refuge? In Julyiah's hands...* Jonar had no time to lose. He bolted through his office door, strode up to Julyiah, and snatched the incriminating book from her hand.

"So that is where my copy of *The Refuge* has been," he roared, looking with anger at Julyiah as though she had taken his most prized possession. "Menila, arrest her. She will not get away this time."

Keeper Menila's mouth dropped in surprise, and he eyed Jonar with suspicion before reaching his hand out to take Julyiah into his charge.

"Well? What is the matter?" Jonar demanded, glaring at Menila before walking around the room, looking through the book in apparent concern. He found the sought-for passage, and his eye caught the name, "Jonaris." *How could it be? After all this time, how could another copy suddenly turn up?*

Jonar's mind whirled to develop a plan. He must get rid of this book.

♪

Menila took Julyiah to the small holding room for prisoners, and her heart sank as she stepped inside. Mikela began to cry, so Julyiah sat in a chair, pulling the sling around to her front to tend to him. He quieted when she held him in front of her face and cooed. Glancing up, she noticed Menila standing in the doorway, watching her.

"That was indeed a different copy of *The Refuge*," he whispered, appearing awestruck by his own words.

Hope shot through her, but when Julyiah tried to respond, her sudden intake of air at his comment caused her to choke. Mikela began to cry again as his mother's body jerked with the coughing.

Menila hurried out to get her a drink of water, closing the door to the holding room when he returned.

"Yes, the Orchard Keeper, Draya, gave the book to me today," Julyiah stammered out a response, her throat still irritated as she sipped the water. "How did you know it was not the same copy?"

"Because," Menila said, "Jonar's copy has a different cover. It is in his office, and I have dusted it many times. It is blue like the one you brought, but the gold lettering on the spine is not the same."

Julyiah changed the baby's diaper while talking to Menila. "Please... this is important. Can you help me?"

Menila gaped at her, looking with alarm at the closed door. Everyone feared Jonar, and Menila was no exception.

"Please... please tell me where the tyrea is that Delwyn had before he was arrested."

"Tyrea?"

"Yes, the musical instrument."

Menila paused in thought. "Does it look like a short metal stick with several holes on each side?"

"Yes!" Julyiah tried to keep her agitated voice low.

"It is in the chamber where they keep the extra books and music boxes, in the Listening Hall."

"Can you bring it to me?"

Menila's eyes widened. "But, Jonar...."

Julyiah smiled, trying to remain calm, even though she had little time to be patient. "I know how you must feel. But Jonar lied just now. You heard him. He is trying to protect himself from what is in that book. His family altered the other copies but did not know about this one. He has been too clever for anyone to catch him yet. Now he has a position of complete power, and the only way to stop him is to give me that tyrea."

Menila frowned in thought. "I...need more time to think about this. How can the tyrea help?"

"There is no time to explain," Julyiah shook her head. "I am sorry. Jonar is going to destroy that book if we do not do something *now*. You will have to trust me. It is imperative that I play that tyrea."

Menila looked perplexed and left the room, returning with the instrument. "I do not know how this object will help," he told Julyiah as he handed it to her. "But I do know I am going to do something about that book."

Julyiah prepared to nurse Mikela, so Menila turned toward the door to give her more privacy. "Cisco might listen to me," Menila said. "He mourns his son, and if he will listen, maybe the other leaders will also."

When Julyiah had finished taking care of Mikela, she wrapped the sleeping child in the sling and swung him around to her back.

After checking outside the door for Jonar, Menila let Julyiah back out of the holding room. He went outside, headed for Cisco's home, and Julyiah turned to the right and faced the patched-up hole in the Listening Hall. No one was around as she began to play the tyrea.

Chapter Thirty-Seven: Desolation

♫

Delwyn was positive that he and Zuriel could not climb the vertical boulders in the afternoon heat, in the midst of a sand storm, after two full days without food or water. Yet, he knew they had to try. Unwilling to abandon hope, he lifted shaky hands and blistered feet to the jagged stones along with Zuriel. But their strength was limited and their footing questionable. Zuriel fell from the second ledge he stepped up to and lay panting for breath in the sand. Delwyn did not even have the strength to pull himself above the first ledge he managed to reach.

Knowing this meant defeat, he did not look at Zuriel but remained on the sand.

"Maybe..." Zuriel began, but choked on a dry mouthful of fine dirt and spent some time clearing his throat. "Maybe after we have rested," he croaked, "when it is cooler."

Delwyn nodded when Zuriel looked his way. They both turned their attention to avoiding the hot afternoon sun and endless waves of blowing sand, pulling their clothing up over their heads for protection.

"It does not matter," a voice said nearby. Delwyn turned to see that Tomli had followed them. He collapsed next to Delwyn.

♫ ♫

"Stop, Jonar!"

Cisco's voice echoed in Menila's ears as he and two guards followed Cisco into Jonar's office unannounced.

Jonar looked up with an innocent smile as they entered. "Stop? Stop what?" He waved his hand toward *The Refuge* to indicate he had been reading; it lay open in front of him. "Julyiah stole this book from me, and I am relieved to have it back where it belongs."

"That is not your copy," Menila said as he flipped the book shut to expose the cover. But the sight of the cover caused his heart to jolt in dismay.

"What are you doing?" snapped Jonar in apparent offense. He rose to his feet as though awakened to a nasty reality from a peaceful dream. "Have you gone mad?"

Menila frantically searched the room for Julyiah's copy of *The Refuge*, a sick feeling rising inside him. His eyes sought the dyed, blue leather cover in another place, but he realized Jonar would have hidden it by now.

Cisco's countenance blanched, and he viewed the irate Jonar in terror. "He... he told me that you..." Cisco waved a shaky finger at the distraught Keeper.

Jonar shifted to an expression of hurt and sat down again, his brow furrowed as though with pain. "What have I done to warrant such treatment?" He shook his head and covered his face with his hands.

The deflated Keeper stopped searching the room and stared hard at Jonar, trying to somehow extract the truth. When Jonar looked up, Menila regarded the intense hatred he had seen Jonar fix upon others. For some reason Menila did not quite understand, his fear turned into equal hatred—a look which brought confusion to Jonar's face.

But something happened to divert the attention of all in the room. A low, rumbling noise beneath their feet grew louder until the office floor began to shake. The stone tiles split right up the middle and spread. The entire room creaked and heaved, cracking rock and splintering wood. Those inside had trouble standing and worked their way to the door, lurching across the rolling floor.

In the commotion, Menila saw Jonar dart a worried glance at a stone cupboard—a hidden storage area that Menila discovered a few months before. Jonar acted as if he was merely surveying the destruction of his office, and Menila pretended not to notice the revealing look. Now he knew where Jonar had hidden the incriminating copy of *The Refuge*. He caught Cisco's eyes and smiled as they all left the room.

♪ ♪

As Jonar watched the people outside running about in the dusk of evening, screaming in panic, he again considered using Gwenla's secret music box. Having slipped it into his pocket before coming outside, he pulled it out now and read the inscription again as he stood near the light rock over the Listening Hall.

Music in this box will make Order come... Jonar read.

Jonar mused over this. *I am the one holding it, and I am the one in a position to restore order as well as the one who wants order. Who else could bring order?*

Jonar read more: *Opened by a worthy one, chaos will be stopped, undone.*

Who could be more worthy than I? Jonar thought. *Surely I am destined to open this box and fix this chaos.*

Opened by unworthy rabble, walls will fall; a man will babble.

Jonar considered the consequences. If I am wrong, some walls will fall down, and some lower class idiot will be reduced to a babbling baby. That did not sound too terrible.

Yet, Jonar hesitated. This moment was not meant to occur without an audience. A major part of having order was having a strong leader to restore it. And you cannot have a strong leader who hides his power from the people.

Jonar fingered the latch on the little box. Yes, he would gather a crowd first. It had to be that way. But first, he must arrange an accident with a certain meddling young woman.

"Find her and stop her," Jonar said to the two guards outside his office. "Use whatever force necessary. We must stop her before she calls upon the Lying Wind again to break down the walls."

At the mention of the Lying Wind, the two guards' eyes grew larger. Bowing, they hurried out to obey.

Jonar raised his chin as he watched them rush off. He was the One Leader now, and everyone had better realize it.

♪

When Julyiah played the tyrea in the Listening Hall, the repaired area on the North Wall disintegrated before her eyes. The outer wall still blocked her view as it had Zuriel's, but Music on the Breeze flowed through the hole and caught her up and away.

The Breeze took Julyiah to a different kind of place than before. She floated unseen above the West Wall on the Outside, where Zuriel, Delwyn, and the others sprawled on the sand near the boulders in the dimming light of day. She could tell they were at the end of their strength and needed water.

The minute she came back to the Listening Hall, Julyiah raced out the door, tyrea in hand. Inside the wall opposite to where Delwyn was, a marsh had formed due to a leak in the canal. Julyiah hurried along Valley Road to reach the marsh, a sheepskin bag flapping at her side and little Mikela a bouncing bundle on her back. Shep spotted her from her parents' house and bounded after her.

"Shep! Okay, you can come," Julyiah said, stopping to catch her breath and pet the dog, whose wagging tail and friendly bark told her he wanted to join in her adventure. "You might not be so happy you came along when the walls fall down around us," she whispered.

At the stairs going down from the Inner Wall, Julyiah and Shep had to wait for several panicky people to descend ahead of her. A troop of Valley Law guards gathered at the Listening Hall with their gaze riveted in her direction. Heart fluttering, Julyiah scurried down the stairs, pushing past the others. The height of the cliff did not enter her mind.

At the canal, Julyiah refilled the sheepskin with water while Shep took the opportunity to lap a drink as well. Julyiah turned toward the West Wall. Blocking out the screams and shouts of those around her, she focused on reaching the wetlands. The ground shook again, and everyone hurried to find family members and shelter. *The Music must have shaken the entire valley.*

Standing breathless at the marsh, Julyiah raised the tyrea to her lips, her fingers fumbling over the holes, which resulted in several strange notes. Gulping air in an attempt to regain her ability to blow through the instrument better, she managed to make some music with the device. Her objective was to bring more Music to the West Wall, to topple it sooner. She feared it might fall on someone, but time was short, so she took the risk.

Mikela had started crying as soon as Julyiah stopped running, but she continued to play the instrument. Only when she heard the *Crack!* of splitting stones did she stop. Shep whined his disapproval of their close proximity. Putting the tyrea in her pocket and the skin of water on the ground, Julyiah sat on a rock. She gave her dog a pat on the head so he would stay calm.

Glancing up, Julyiah saw guards at the top of the Inner Wall looking straight down at her, and fear gripped her heart. The tall stairs jammed with terrified people blocked the way for the guards, who tried to push their way down the stairs. Julyiah had some time before they could reach her. As the sunrays dimmed in the west, she jumped up, flung the baby sling to her back, grabbed the water, and headed closer to the wall. Delighted to keep moving, Shep leaped after her, barking at her that she was surely going in the wrong direction.

Chapter Thirty-Eight: Jonar

♪ ♪

Light rocks glowed with more noticeable brightness as the sun set. Jonar surveyed the community, which was shaking again under the influence of some unknown power. Huge fissures running from top to bottom became visible in the walls where light rocks shone near them. One huge light rock at the southern end fell out and lay shining forlornly on the ground. Gaping holes had opened in the top of the North Wall, where large stones had come loose and dropped out, somehow avoiding any demolition below them. The huge wooden doors to the Hall had fallen flat, however, and strong breezes swept through the Hall, continuing the length of the valley.

The Keepers and Valley Law guards ran about in chaotic patterns, trying to save the books and other important artifacts from the rubble. With no safe place to put them down, they held the precious books in their arms. People shouted to be heard above the din.

As the hectic evening wore on and more people lacked direction, they gathered in small groups outside the Listening Hall. Those who trusted Jonar headed toward him.

To Jonar's delight, the community formed a circle around him near the amphitheatre, calling to him, asking for answers. When Jonar stepped onto the metal platform, the crowd's noises diminished, revealing the eerie groaning and cracking sounds in the wall and the loud whistle of the breeze rushing through the dark, North Window.

Jonar's powerful voice rose above the tumult. "Friends, the time has come to restore order." Observing how each person in the audience hung on his every word, he paused to savor his moment of glory.

As the breezes whipped his robe about his feet, his fingers caressed the little music box. Jonar shivered with the thrill of the power he held in his hand. Raising his voice with confidence, he looked over the heads of his audience at the distant horizon.

"When every mercy has been tried, but our enemy continues to torment us and destroy all that we love—

"When we have done all that is good yet those that are evil still cause suffering—

"When chaos reigns, we must resort to the ultimate remedy."

How well that sounded! Jonar admired his own ability to speak the poetic words, as he held up Gwenla's music box with both arms extended. The spectators who recognized the object gasped.

"Herein it is written," Jonar read the inscription:

Music in this box will make
Order come and Silence break.
Opened by a worthy one,
Chaos will be stopped, undone.

Jonar left off the end of the inscription—he felt it did not pertain. "Yes," he continued in a solemn, dramatic voice, "the time has come for order. The time has come to stop this chaos that has entered our peaceful community from the Lying Wind. The time has come for a 'Worthy One' to open the box and send true music out to break the evil Silence. My Friends, I AM THE ONE!" With the sleeves of his dekat flowing majestically in the breeze from outstretched arms, Jonar broke the seal and opened Gwenla's music box.

♫ ♪ ♫

In the unseen world, a myriad of colors danced around their master impatiently and sang in protest of Jonar's statement.

Only the Voice is worthy to break the Silence!

♪ ♪

The wind and upheaval in Victory Valley ceased when Jonar opened the box, and a deathly stillness prevailed. The crowd held a collective breath. Jonar's heart jumped in triumph, and he was fairly giddy with joy. *It worked! Order has come, and I am the "worthy one" who brought it!*

While a reverent silence remained over the community and the people, a barely perceptible wisp of glittering blue stole out of the box and flitted through the air like a graceful butterfly, trailing up and down and around Jonar. He dropped the box, staring at the stunning cerulean entity in terror. Making a feeble attempt to recover his dignity, Jonar took a step toward the box to pick it up, but a golden streak emerged, flowing away in a different direction. As he backed away, a crimson streak followed and a green one and a violet hue. Before Jonar could figure out what to do next, combinations of rainbows started pouring out of the box and fluttering about.

Jonar's eyes followed the colors flying through the air. Both fear and delight coursed through him, as he tried to grasp his share in the moment. The people called out *Ohhh!* and *Ahhh!*, obviously delighted with the magnificent display that Jonar had not expected and did not understand.

The brilliant hues curled away from the area, toward the surrounding walls. The blue one grew larger and flowed toward the Listening Hall. Music poured into the valley from the north, and joined the colors. A mysterious, haunting melody built in a matter of seconds to an overwhelming crescendo that permeated not just the ears but the soul.

Many people burst into tears or shouted in joy. Jonar hesitated to say anything, yet he was determined to hold onto the glory even if he had no idea what was happening.

"Friends, order has come..."

Jonar's planned victory speech was interrupted by a tremendous *BOOM!* sounding from the direction of the Listening Hall. Again, a loud *BOOM!* rent the air. With the second explosion, the entire front wall of the Listening Hall collapsed, as though all connecting mortar had been removed. The ground shook. People screamed and ran away as more of the North Wall broke apart and started to fall.

When the dust cleared, a huge pile of rocks lay where most of the North Wall had been. The leaders' apartments above the Hall had disintegrated, leaving only the bottom buildings standing. The sides and ceiling of the Listening Hall remained in place like an archway, but the front and back had fallen, exposing the north.

♪ ... ♪♫

Another clamor arose but in a different place, unseen. Ugly gray clouds whirled in agitation around a windy mass that spewed darkness in every direction. The sinister giant moved closer to Jonar. The gray clouds twirled about with glee, watching with morbid fascination as the huge darkness engulfed the man standing on the platform.

When the walls came down, Jonar felt a little odd, but he could not tell what was wrong. Perhaps he was overcome with the intensity of the moment? Everyone else looked all right. Why could he no longer stand? He felt himself sag, lean to one side, and then collapse on top of the dais, unable to rise.

Jonar's confused mind frantically sought for clarity. What had he just been doing? He could not remember. Had his mind drained out of his body? Moments later he could not remember how to speak. Trying to explain to those who rushed to his side, he felt that his mouth was not working properly. Noises came out instead of words.

As he tried with more determination to speak intelligible words, Jonar created only sounds that he did not intend. He tried to sort through his jumbled thoughts, but nothing made sense. At last, he gave up and lay on the platform, staring at the people who spoke to him. As all the energy left his body, Jonar could no longer move any of his limbs, his head, or even his eyes. Within minutes, he could do nothing but moan and drool.

♪

Julyiah had run to the other side of the marsh, closer to the West Wall, the heavy boots of the guards thudding on the ground close behind her. Trying not to panic, she approached the wall, afraid she might be captured. The meaning of the curious noises at the northern end of the valley was hidden for her, since she was unable to see above the Inner Wall. Focused on the West Wall, which was breaking up as planned, she hoped it would not fall on top of her and her companions. Julyiah attempted to get as close to the wall as possible to continue, while Shep jumped about and barked to notify her of his continued concern.

Boom! A huge fissure appeared at the top of the wall in front of her. Shep's barking stepped up a notch, and Julyiah stopped running as a thunderous noise announced the widening of the crack. Julyiah turned around to see the retreating forms of the guards. Relieved, she turned and ran after them, Shep yipping his agreement with her new choice of direction. The huge stones rumbled and fell behind her, and a few small ones rolled out past her and Shep as they ran away from the destruction.

♫ ♫

The Music and colors had so captivated most of the people's attention that few noticed their One Leader had fallen. Holding tightly to a few of the books he had rescued from destruction, Menila gaped at the shadowy expanse to the north, trying in vain to see through the darkness to what lay on the Outside. There was little time to speculate, however, for the area began to explode with spectacular sights and sounds, the Music surging in on the Breeze with gathering intensity. Streams of color flitted around the people, flowing with the Music and streaking skyward, lighting up a few clouds overhead in a beautiful display similar to a multicolored sunrise.

Menila felt entranced with the spectacle, but some were terrified. A man screamed, "The Wind!" and ran to hide somewhere, causing others to follow suit. But with all the crumbling of rock, there was no safe place to hide, so the people ran back and forth, or in circles, fleeing in one direction or another, huddling in terrified groups.

Next, the ground shook, not with a destructive force, but with the thundering of hooves. A herd of horses charged through from the northeast corner, leaping over stones and inside the fortress, running about as though dancing with the Music. Snorting, eyes flashing, and hooves pounding the ground, they flooded the community with an awesome presence that none could ignore.

More loud booms and cracks continued all up and down the valley, tearing Menila's attention away from the horses, as several sections of the great fortress broke into rubble and disintegrated into heaps of gravel.

♪

When the noise subsided to the west, Julyiah ventured to slow down enough to look behind her at the wall where she had been playing the tyrea. It was over. A huge opening now gaped in the West Wall, the stones having turned into debris. She called to Shep and headed straight for it. Thankful that her legs still functioned, Julyiah spotted Delwyn beyond the rubble and climbed over it to reach him. Shep followed, whining at the rocks that moved under his feet.

Though they could barely move and were choking from the dust of the collapsed stones, Delwyn and Zuriel were alive. Huddled with the other people next to the tall boulders outside, their eyes met Julyiah's with hope in the midst of dried out faces and scraggly hair. Julyiah hurried to Delwyn's side and threw herself down next to him.

"Delwyn, you are safe! Are you all right?" Julyiah threw her arms around her husband and held him, crying for joy. She touched his parched, sunburned face, pushing aside his dark hair to kiss him, noticing how weak he looked and that he was reluctant to speak.

Shep whimpered as he shoved under Julyiah's arm to get to Delwyn. The dog howled at his master as though scolding him for being gone so long and greeted him, with a slobbery tongue that Julyiah figured must feel good after the lack of moisture.

Removing the cap on the skin of water, she handed it to Delwyn, who clutched it with unusual eagerness. Unable to do more for him at the moment, Julyiah turned to sooth Mikela, who had begun to voice his disapproval of being ignored.

After Delwyn took a drink, he handed it to Zuriel, who gulped down a few swallows before passing it on. "Water!" Those whose could speak begged to receive some of the precious substance. A few who could move scrambled over the rubble to reach the nearby canal.

Soon all had regained enough strength to make their way to the canal. The happy travelers drank their fill and soaked their exhausted bodies in the abundant liquid. Shep joined them, and Delwyn encouraged the dog to shake off the water well away from those who sat near the canal bank. Refreshed, they reclined on the cool grass near the canal, chatting among themselves about their great adventure and the events taking place around them.

Julyiah's father walked up, with a pack on his back.

"Father!" Julyiah cried out. She prepared to rise and greet him, but sank back when she realized how exhausted she felt.

"Stay where you are, daughter," he said as he knelt next to her for an embrace. "I brought some bread and cheese." He reached up to lift the pack off his shoulders. "When the walls began to come down, I looked around and saw you on the west side before it got dark. You were much too close to that wall when it collapsed, my girl!"

Harol's voice sounded shaky, and Julyiah's heart was touched by the love and care in his tone.

"I had to get close to the wall when I found out that Delwyn was on the other side," Julyiah told him.

Harol's brow wrinkled. "But how could you possibly know where he was on the outside?"

Julyiah tilted her head, with a knowing grin. "The Music came on the Breeze and showed me."

Delwyn sat on the grass next to the water and continued to lean over the canal to splash water on his face now and then, as though he could not be revived enough times. Julyiah shook her head in the solemn realization of how close to death he must have been.

"Did other walls come down?" Delwyn asked Julyiah in a raspy voice, between bites of bread. "I could see an opening over there," he indicated the east side with his hand. "What about the north?"

Julyiah saw Delwyn's eyes light up when he mentioned the north. "I did not see what parts fell," she said. "I was too busy. We will be able to see it in the morning."

"Yes!" Harol answered Delwyn's question with enthusiasm. "The entire second floor of the North Wall fell, and walls in back of the Listening Hall. There is also a large opening on the other side of Suntar Hill."

"Good," Delwyn said, grinning.

Rikial Keenar brought a loaded wagon from his ranch, bearing food, blankets, and light rocks, which were received with gratefulness. The cacophony of sounds in the valley had died down, but with so many light rocks gone from the walls, it was difficult to see anything far away. For now, the travelers were content to rest.

"I need to get back and report to your mother," Harol told them as he rose to leave. "She has been so worried. I do not suppose you want to walk home tonight, so I will let you rest here. Goodbye!"

Julyiah hugged her father again before he stood and walked back up Valley Road. She found places for them to sleep for the night among the rocks scattered about on the West Ridge. Julyiah spread out a blanket and finally convinced Delwyn to come away from the water to rest. She nestled into Delwyn's arms, and little Mikela slept next to Shep, who had pulled up a corner of the blanket as soon as it was available. The dog announced his opinion that it was time to sleep by heaving a great sigh.

The friendly Breeze and quiet Music caressed all hearts as all drifted off into a peaceful sleep.

Chapter Thirty-Nine: The North

♪

Julyiah woke to Mikela's fussing, and she found herself lying next to a mound of rocks at the southwestern corner of Victory Valley. The other outcasts still dozed among the piles of stones and gravel. Near the Suntar Canal, they had rested well on the soft grass. The surrounding area remained quiet in the dim light of dawn, except for the gentle sound of Music.

The strange angle of sunlight that morning caught Julyiah's attention. She turned her face east and saw the sun rising—not over the wall as she had always seen it, but from the top of the far off mountains. An opening in the East Wall revealed snow-capped peaks that she had never seen. These mountains stood much closer than the ones viewed from the South Window. The tinges of red and orange in the eastern sky lit up the snowy peaks in a brilliant sunrise. The mountains continued in a chain of peaks that came closer as it ran north.

Turning to the north, Julyiah took in a sudden gulp of air. A large group of healthy-looking horses grazed in serene groups along the east side of the Inner Wall. Julyiah nudged Delwyn, hating to wake him but knowing he would not want to miss this sight.

Shep jerked his head up when he saw Julyiah moving around. He stretched his front and back leg muscles with more vigor than usual. "Yesterday was busy, was it not?" she said to the dog with a grin, as Shep rose and sauntered over to greet his mistress.

♫

Delwyn moaned when his stiff muscles protested. He stretched a few times and rolled over before opening his eyes, but the increasing sunlight lured him to wakefulness. When he gave in at last to the world of sight, he gaped in awe at the changes around him.

In between sections of wall that still stood, heaps of rock marked a stark contrast between the watered area inside and barrenness outside. The farms and ranches remained surrounded by a protective wall, the west wind still blocked by the huge boulders near the new opening. The east side was calm, and Delwyn admired the peaks beyond the desert area.

Julyiah pulled on Delwyn's shoulder, pointing and waving his gaze to the north, but her hand went to her mouth along with a sharp intake of breath.

"What? What is it?" Delwyn asked, yawning. Julyiah did not speak as she continued staring north, eyes alight with wonder. Delwyn had seen parts of the north from the rocky cliffs on the outside, so he nodded, knowing the beautiful scenery she must be viewing. Wishing to share in her joy and anxious to see it again himself, he rose to his feet, wincing at the terrible soreness he had acquired from the journey of the past two days.

Delwyn's heart swelled, for his gaze riveted on the horses at the top of the Inner Wall. He had not expected this! When he and Zuriel had seen the north from the outside, they had not seen any horses. He feared his heart might burst with joy. The possibilities piled up in his heart faster than he could imagine, but one idea rose higher than the others— *Maybe I could have my own horse!*

As Delwyn stood on the West Ridge admiring the animals, he could see well beyond the Inner Wall in the increasing daylight. The lush green tops of many trees rose beyond the North Wall, now half the height it was before. Emerald, mossy cliffs stood between the trees, and a multitude of pine and oak trees thrived on high foothills to the northeast, where the eastern range met the northern range. Much closer than the mountains to the east, tall snow-capped peaks ascended farther north—the same mountains Delwyn had seen in his heart journeys with the Music. He longed to explore the woods.

Sunlight glinted on the mountain glaciers in the peaks and lit up the grassy meadows in the hills below. Delwyn realized this view had been obstructed on purpose by the upper story of the

North Wall, for 400 years. Why was this breathtaking view blocked? No doubt the builders were afraid the people would want to leave the fortress. *And they were right... I want to leave it!*

The openings in the fortress walls looked like old gateways. One gateway opened directly east, just below the Inner Wall, opposite the one that opened out to the west. The boulders that rose next to the outer Durnee Break blocked the view west as well as the desert wind. The gateway to the east revealed sandy desert with mountains beyond it.

"Zuriel!" Delwyn woke his friend, who moaned at first, but gazed around with joy after opening his eyes.

"We made it," Zuriel grinned. "Thanks to the One!"

They roused the others that had spent the night on the ground around them, wanting to head north but hoping to stay together until they knew what stance the leaders would take regarding the state of the community.

When everyone was awake and ready to move again, the weary but excited group headed north, all eyes studying the changes around them. They headed down the hill on Valley Road, where the view of northern parts diminished behind the obstruction of the Inner Wall. Delwyn turned his attention to the new sights around them. Children played among the rocks and adults peered with anxious faces over their stone houses, no doubt looking for damage. Some pointed at the new openings in the Wall to the outside, discussing them.

Shep darted among the houses they walked by, searching for any stray food but also finding fellow members of his species. Greeting Shep with caution at first, the other dogs jumped, put their front legs down, and yipped, inviting him to play.

As the group climbed the stairs to the top of the Inner Wall, the mountains rose into view above what remained of the North Wall. To the northeast, a large gap had formed in the wall near Suntar Hill. Outside, abundant water cascaded from a mossy cliff, over rocks and down a hill, the water flowing under the fortress wall and below the ground. Part of this river emerged again to form the pool just below Suntar Hill. Feathery ferns and colorful wildflowers grew in abundance beside the wet area at the waterfall. The morning breeze blew down the foothills from the mountains, lifting the water into a fine spray.

Overcome with the magical quality of the air around him, Delwyn touched Julyiah's shoulder to indicate they should stop walking a moment. An unusual mist pervaded the area, swirling quietly about, tinted with pastel colors and the slightest hint of Music. Numerous hues hovered and floated about the Listening Hall in particular.

Zuriel headed straight for the Hall, not waiting for the others.

The gap in the wall behind Suntar Hill revealed a huge meadow above a chasm—the same chasm that had blocked Delwyn and Zuriel's way north when they were stuck on the outside. Dotted with fruit trees and flowering bushes, the meadow ran to the north, where a cliff dropped off along with more of the river below the back of the Listening Hall.

This meadow was where the horses must have been, before stampeding into the valley the night before. A narrow opening in the fallen rock revealed how they had come through the debris on the ground, but why they had come through remained a mystery. Some men had rolled a large boulder across the gap in the fallen rock, which prevented the horses from finding their way back out.

The frisky foals cavorting about on the grass brought tears to his eyes, as Delwyn remembered what he had envisioned the day all their adventures began. The foals rushed to their mothers when the group of people approached, and the youngsters eyed the strangers with caution. A magnificent chestnut stallion with a flaxen mane and tail snorted and charged around the herd, stirring the other horses to follow him to safety. As one body, the herd stayed with their leader. Making a wide turn before they came to the cliff of the Inner Wall, they curved to the east, heading for the river. Delwyn had never imagined such a beautiful horse as the stallion, and his heart was drawn to ride him.

Julyiah and Delwyn continued to walk down Main Street where they joyfully reunited with Julyiah's mother and Rashella. Livi hugged Dawnli with tears in her eyes. Some of the outcasts had gone back to their homes, but those from the Underground sat about in the grass, unwilling to return to the darkness below. The kindhearted Livi brought food out to the hungry people and spoke welcoming words to them.

♪

Anxious to see all that was new, Julyiah walked with Delwyn toward the north, gaping at the Listening Hall which was indeed a "hall" now. The inside was an empty shell except for the one ancient music box—the one about how the Voice died to save the people from Silence. All else had disappeared except for the books that the Keepers had rescued and still held in their arms. Surprised at what had been spared, Julyiah wondered what it meant.

Deer grazed in the northeast meadow, stopping to stare in wonder at the people. Touched by the graceful beauty of these animals, Julyiah could only imagine what other creatures dwelt on the Outside, and she hoped to travel and find them. With a rush of joy, she realized they could tame and ride the numerous horses that had entered the community.

Zuriel knelt in the center of the Hall, looking northward toward the mountains with rapt attention. Colorful swirls curled around him and fluttered with musical notes. Moments later, Zuriel jumped to his feet, walking toward the flight of stairs that went down to the left of the Hall—the same stairs he and Johan had used to come up from the ruins. He disappeared among the piles of rubble that had been the North Wall and music cells. The ground dropped off north of the Hall, which was why the stairs were needed in the old fortress. The upper and lower parts of the river ran out from underneath the ruins to meet up in a northern meadow and make a wide circle, before dropping into the gorge on the west side of the fortress.

"Where is Zuriel going?" Delwyn asked.

Julyiah shrugged, but Tomli spoke from behind them: "Something important is down there," he said. "I am certain of it. And look, I found these." Tomli held an armload of stringed musical instruments, which had fallen out of their clear cases in Jonar's office in all the shaking. "We can play musical instruments again!"

The excited young man carried the instruments over to a flat rock and set them down, calling to his friends. Other young people gathered around him, and some began to try out one of the implements of music. Those who followed Delwyn from the Underground joined the group and helped the others understand how to bring forth the desired sounds.

A pathetic assemblage formed in the amphitheatre, where two guards picked up the disabled Jonar from the platform and headed toward his carriage. Surrounded by Menila, Delegar, and Cisco, the procession passed Julyiah as though they were on a funeral march. She heard Jonar mumbling to himself, but no one paid any attention to whatever he tried to say, since his eyes appeared vacant of any remaining intelligence. Delegar carried a book with a blue-tinted cover, which Julyiah assumed was her copy of *The Refuge*. She wondered if she would ever get it back.

Cisco read the key passage aloud from the book about Jonaris murdering Gwenla, while Jonar's head was down. The others nodded, murmuring and shaking their heads. Apparently convinced of Jonar's deceit, they looked upon him with pity. The guards put the broken man in chains, packed him into the carriage, and drove him away.

When Daleil arrived, he ran to Cisco, who received the young man with tears of joy. Touched by the scene, Julyiah hoped that Cisco would soon believe as his son did, and join them in listening for the Music on the Breeze.

Not all were able to see the colors or hear the Music, including Jonar's brothers— Bothleil and Jadleil Suntar. As Julyiah walked by them, she overheard their intent discussion of plans to build gates in the new openings in the walls, to keep the horses in and any invaders out.

"There are differences in the formation of the wall structure that indicate these openings were there before, probably with wooden gates," Jadleil said.

"But how could we possibly find so much wood to rebuild the gates?" Bothleil asked his brother.

"You forget," Jadleil said, and Julyiah thought he seemed disgusted with his brother's slowness. "There are plenty of trees now." He motioned for his brother to look at the huge forest in the hills. "We can even build houses out of wood if we wish, and new boats and wagons. There are more horses to pull them. We can round up the horses and... What?"

Jadleil had turned to look toward where the horses grazed, but they were gone. "Who took the horses," he demanded in an outraged voice, though no one but Bothleil was listening.

That is interesting! Julyiah thought, unable to find a horse in sight. Where did the horses go? She heard a whinny and knew they were still there, but... *they are invisible?* No wonder Delwyn and Zuriel had not seen them when they looked across the chasm toward the north! Those horses could disappear!

Julyiah observed Ruti, sitting on a rock and crying over the loss of her brother's mind. Julyiah shook her head over Jonar's brothers, who did not appear to care about Jonar or anything else, unless it might bring them profit.

There will always be men like this, she decided. *Selfish men, like Jonar.*

At the moment, Julyiah preferred to think about the unique horses. What kind of land and creatures would they discover beyond these walls?

Chapter Forty: The Revelation

♪

The leaders consulted together near the Listening Hall. Cisco pointed to the remains of the music cells and shrugged. The leaders' homes that had been in the upper level of the North Wall were destroyed. *They must be wondering what to do,* Julyiah decided.

Zuriel charged back up the stairs, breathing hard as he stood grinning and holding an old roll of parchment, calling for everyone to come closer. Most complied and seemed willing to listen, including the leaders.

When the people gathered around him and grew quiet, Zuriel held up the parchment. "I was kneeling here, singing with the Music, when I perceived a secret hiding place in the ruins below. I found something Gwenla wrote, with her seal on it—the same seal that was on the *Book of Secrets* and her music box."

Zuriel held out the parchment to Delegar. "I submit this to you, Delegar, as our senior leader, and I ask before all these people that you read it aloud."

Julyiah watched in alarm as Zuriel handed over the scroll. What if he took it away and did not read it? What if he destroyed it? But Zuriel had made a wise choice, for Delegar was not a power-hungry leader like Jonar, just a misled one.

Delegar took the scroll with trembling hands and a wistful gaze into his former colleague's eyes. The animosity was gone, and Zuriel felt only forgiveness of any wrongs Delegar may have done to them, since he was ignorant of Jonar's deceit.

The suspense increased as Delegar broke the seal and opened the scroll, his slow, deliberate actions intensifying the unique moment in time that suspended the people between mystery and revealed truth. At last, he coughed, cleared his throat, and began to read:

I, Gwenla, am about to die. I will be murdered by someone who intends to take my place of authority, solely for the power. He is shrewd—a man like his fathers before him, but of a type I have had to deal with as the Voice has directed me. It seems there are times in our history when we must be ruled by such people.

The man is Jonaris Suntar. I foresee a whole line of dishonest leaders from the Suntar Clan who will deceive the people with clever lies and disguises. They will try to hide my secrets, some of which they will know but will not want known. Jonaris will kill me because of the secrets, for he understands that the people's knowledge of the truth destroys his power.

Despite their deceit, these corrupt men will be this people's finest leaders, directing them through crises, organizing them, pulling them together, and restoring order. Yet their unique ability to lead will feed their thirst for power and their insatiable pride. They will go beyond what has been directed them to do and to teach, adding their own ideas for evil purposes.

Someday one of the Suntar men, in a bid for complete authority, will make an irreversible mistake, underestimating those he sees as weak. This error will lead to another and another. All the while he will continue to believe he is gaining the control that he is, in fact, losing. His arrogance will cause his final destruction. When he least expects it, his whole world will tumble down around him and he, as well as his ancestors before him, will be exposed for their corruption. In the end, he will be consumed in Silence.

When that day comes, the community will be in jeopardy, lacking the strength of leadership they have always had in the Suntar Clan. The people will have help from those who understand, but all must begin to hear the Music for themselves, or die. No single leader will be allowed to have complete control again, although some will attempt to do so.

The fortress was intended to protect us from the desert wind, but make no mistake—nothing physical can protect the heart! It is a deception of the Lying Wind that a wall can keep him out.

Indeed, it is a walled-up heart that lets in the Wind, but keeps out the Breeze.

How then can our hearts be guarded? Nothing protects the heart more than a complete trust in the One and His Voice, especially as you listen to the Music on the Breeze. The sacred books contain His truth for all to know. Those who understand these things do well.

When the walls fall, many will wonder why anything stands. Let them be assured—only that which CAN stand, WILL stand, and only that which was meant to stand will stand.

I now know that this information and explanation of my riddles, which I intended to tell Jon, will not be known for hundreds of years. The truth must be hidden from those who would use it for evil. But the secrets will be revealed to those who hear the Music in those days, after much suffering, and these pioneers of truth will continue to help the people in the days that follow.

So be it.

—Gwenla

♫♪

Delegar's shaky voice cracked by the time he reached the end of the scroll, and the swirling colors around the entire gathering glowed brighter.

Zuriel sank to his knees on the floor of the empty Listening Hall, weeping, overcome by the words. When he regained his composure, Zuriel looked up to see that the people had knelt or sat on the ground with tears in their eyes also, and he sensed a strong unity with them. All was quiet.

Zuriel reflected on the words just read as he looked over what had fallen. Apparently, the sides and top of the Hall were to remain as a place of worship. The music box with the song about the One sending His Voice to save the people from the Silence had not been damaged either. The books lay untouched. But all the rest— the music cells, the other music boxes with recorded music in them, and the various structures that had been considered sacred were gone.

Deceived! All the beauty and freedom on the Outside would have been theirs, if not for the lies. The Music on the Breeze had been waiting for centuries to be heard, but they had continued to regard the walls as more important, thinking they were vital protection. *But the walls did not block the Lying Wind—the Wind has had access to the valley all along.*

Several people, including Cisco and Delegar, came and sat beside Zuriel, looking into his face with apologetic, pleading eyes. "Please," they said, "tell us what you know about the Music."

An indescribable joy flooded Zuriel as he looked into the hungry, expectant faces, ready for his words of truth. Reaching out to help the people in this way fulfilled his deepest desire. At last, he could lead! As long as he did not try to dominate and control as Jonar did, he felt free to help.

"I am sure that what Gwenla said in that letter is the most important thing I could tell you," Zuriel said. "Anyone can listen and hear the Music. I do not mean just *hear* the Music but *experience* the Music. We can listen for the Voice to sing to us and we sing to Him. And as the books say, *Music will come to those who seek.* The Breeze does not flow for a heart that is walled, or a community that is walled. When hearts open, the Music will flow."

"Tell us what the Voice has spoken to you, or your people," Cisco pleaded, glancing around at the other outcasts, resting his gaze on Daleil with hopeful eyes.

"We do not know everything," Zuriel said, "but we found the meaning of several of Gwenla's riddles in the *Book of Secrets*, and we understand some of the other books better. There is still more truth to be discovered, perhaps as the Music flows."

Zuriel's heart soared as he went on to describe the meaning they had found for some of the riddles. He told of his own experiences with the Breeze—the places he had seen and the keys they had found. Understanding more even as he spoke, Zuriel delighted in helping others to understand.

♪

Delwyn clasped Julyiah's hand as she soaked in the contentment of being at peace in the morning sunlight. She gazed at the mountains, knowing they would explore them, as well as the places beyond. Dreaming of having their own horses, she pictured herself riding over the meadows and through forests to see what lay in the beautiful lands beyond the walls.

Listening to Zuriel answer questions, Julyiah remembered what started all of this change—a child's question: "What does it look like outside the wall?" Julyiah searched the crowd and found Tomli taking in the scenery. She wondered what Tomli's role would be in this new era.

Julyiah pondered all that they had gone through the last few years—all the pain and hardship—all for this. As she listened, she marveled that she could hear the Music all the time now. The Breeze blew around them without ceasing, whispering Music.

Yes, it was worth the pain, but those difficult years were now behind them. The unknown no longer filled her with fear, and she had great hope for the future. The adventure had not ended, for there was more truth to find within the *Book of Secrets*. Her heart leaped at the thought that there was so much more to discover.

Julyiah's eyes filled with tears. She took a deep breath and let it out slowly as she gazed at the sleeping baby in her arms and reached out to tidy Rashella's hair. For Julyiah's children, being enclosed within the walls of Victory Valley would be something of the past—something that Rashella barely remembered and Mikela never knew. Instead, they would listen to the Voice sing freely with the Music on the Breeze, and they would travel to faraway places, searching for more of the Secrets of Gwenla.

The End

The Sequel

What will Delwyn and Julyiah find in the forests and mountains beyond the walls? Will everyone begin hearing the Music on the Breeze, or will some still resist? Will the Suntar Clan try to take over control of the valley again? Why did the herd of horses disappear?

Watch for the answers in the next book, *Secrets in the Underground,* as the residents of Victory Valley move beyond the fortress walls and uncover more of Gwenla's riddles. Join Zuriel as he faces the challenges of his new position in leadership. Find out what roles Dawnli, her brother, and Tomli take on and how the poor find a surprise of great value right under their noses!

Most of all, you will enjoy Julyiah's ongoing adventures, as she and Delwyn travel with their children to discover more of the Secrets of Gwenla.

About the Book

This book is partly an allegory, which means some of the words, situations, and terms are symbolic of something else. As the seeker of truth, you can find the hidden meanings for yourself.

There is a Bible study about the symbolism I used in *Secrets of Gwenla*, with scriptures concerning the understanding of our hearts, called, *Hearts of Understanding*. The ideas and symbolism in *Secrets of Gwenla* were born out of my own imagination, most of them arising between 1979 and 1993, so I trust they do not resemble anyone else's ideas. If for some reason they do, I apologize.

I'd like to say that none of the characters in this book are intended to represent anyone, but that isn't entirely true. The characters are intended to represent a lot of people—people who have lived throughout history, people who live now, and people who will live in the future. But I made up the situations and names, and nothing in this book is intended to represent any single individual or organization.

About the Author

Laurie Penner has been writing fiction for fifty years and has published books in many genres on Amazon. Living with her musician husband of forty years in the mountains at the top of California, right next to Oregon, she also enjoys gardening and quilting.